AWASH IN MYSTERY

Isla de la Tortuga Grande

By
Ken Filing

Order this book online at www.trafford.com
or email orders@trafford.com

Most Trafford titles are also available at major online book retailers.

© Copyright 2009 Ken Filing.
All rights reserved. No part of this publication may be reproduced, stored in a retrieval system, or
transmitted, in any form or by any means, electronic, mechanical, photocopying, recording, or
otherwise, without the written prior permission of the author.

Note for Librarians: A cataloguing record for this book is available from Library
and Archives Canada at www.collectionscanada.ca/amicus/index-e.html

Printed in Victoria, BC, Canada.

ISBN: 978-1-4269-1625-0 (sc)

ISBN: 978-1-4269-1626-7 (dj)

Library of Congress Control Number: 2009936086

*Our mission is to efficiently provide the world's finest, most comprehensive book publishing
service, enabling every author to experience success. To find out how to publish your book, your
way, and have it available worldwide, visit us online at www.trafford.com*

Trafford rev. 8/31/2009

 www.trafford.com

North America & international
toll-free: 1 888 232 4444 (USA & Canada)
phone: 250 383 6864 ♦ fax: 812 355 4082

To my wife, the real Teddy, who encouraged me and gave me inspiration to give it a try.

PREFACE

Writing AWASH IN MYSTERY started as all my other attempts at writing, a fun project for my family and friends to read. As it grew, as family and friends read it and at the urging of TEDDY, I made the decision to take a flyer and publish it. Then I started the chore of making it "publisher ready". Several of the adventures, not the hijacking nor the kidnapping, were experienced by TEDDY and me on our sailboat, the ROSIE II. It was a fun project and brought back fond memories of my years in the U.S. Navy and sailing on the ROSIE II, as well as on my trawlers the SEA ROSE and the SEA ROSE II. The descriptive nautical terms, seamanship and other mariner situations were a collection of my experiences on all the above. I sailed on two different Navy ships in the Pacific Ocean, Indian Ocean, Yellow Sea, Sea of Japan, Atlantic Ocean, Caribbean Sea, the Panama Canal and possibly others that I may have forgotten. On my sailboats and trawlers we sailed Lake Erie, Lake Ontario, the Welland Canal, Lake St. Clair, the Erie Canal, Hudson River, Atlantic Ocean, Delaware Bay, Chesapeake Bay, Intra Coastal Waterway, Caribbean Sea as well as many rivers, sounds and bays. All the research on the HMS Bounty, its survivors and descendants, the Polynesian History, the Panama Canal as well as the geographical descriptions of many locations were derived from the internet by using the Google Search Engine. I hope that it is as enjoyable for you to read as it was for me to write.

PROLOGUE

In the midst of the Indian Ocean, sometime in the early winter of 1993, as the sun's rays bounced off of the waves, something mysterious happened aboard the 127 foot trawler, long line fishing boat, the Sea Rose.

The boat was first spotted by the crew of a twin-engine Bombardier de Havilland Coastwatch surveillance plane. She was far from the Marshall Islands, where passing ships had reported spotting her, and now she was near the Rowley Shoals, some 150 miles off the coast of Australia.

A photo was taken by the custom agents showing the deck of the Sea Rose to be devoid of human activity and the agents did not see anyone aboard the boat. This was not a cause of suspicion because it was a foreign ship inside the Australian fishing zone, which extends 200 miles out to sea. Often times foreign fishing crews will stow their gear and go below while in Australian waters. But the customs agents radioed a report to authorities in Canberra, the capital, describing the drifting ship.

The Australian Navy responded and came upon the Sea Rose. She was drifting in Australian waters with no crew or evidence of what could have happened. They hailed her and when they received no response, they boarded her.

The main fuel tank was dry but the auxiliary tanks were full and not switched on. There was evidence of storm damage but not enough to cause any danger of sinking. The engines were operative and on full throttle, the valuable navigation instrumentation and high-frequency radio was all intact.

Crew member's clothing and documents were neatly stowed where they should be and provisions were still in good supply. The refrigerated hold was empty of fish but there was evidence that a large quantity of bonito tuna had been stored there recently. The personal gear of Captain Kent Allison, and of his wife Teddi Allison, was still on board along with their documents.

Was it piracy? Were they boarded under some ruse? But there was little evidence of foul play. A small splatter of blood was found next to a damaged life line but not enough to indicate a mutiny. Maybe an accident? Did they all abandon ship? The life raft was missing, if there even was a life raft in the first place. The dinghy storage rack was empty. Every theory is quickly dashed on the shoals of contradicting facts.

The vessel was taken in tow to the nearest Australian port which was Willie Creek and was stored with a collection of other derelict vessels, a place that also housed derelict men. Most had found their way there for a variety of reasons, and many for something done illegally in Australian waters. There the Sea Rose sat for the next several months with no further explanation.

Willie Creek is nothing more than a ramshackle collection of structures at the end of a red dirt road that runs through a wilderness of acacia trees and shrubs, and populated by gray kangaroos and dingos. A good place to get lost.

Robert Craig, who lives there in a collection of structures, had towed her in and intended to apply for salvage rights or profit in some less than legal way. The insurer of the boat may make him an offer. But he must wait for the proper authorization before he can do anything legally about the ship that was "AWASH IN MYSTERY." And this may take longer than he'd like to wait. He would act now.

CHAPTER ONE

Early in 1992, Kent and Teddi Allison flew to Taiwan to pick up their 127 foot trawler to be used as a long line fishing boat. They dreamed of this day and had saved for years, to own their own fishing boat, after crewing for others for the last 10 years. It had been a real struggle and many times they just wanted to call it quits, but the thought of being able to hit it hard for another 10 years and then buy a fully equipped Cabo Rico cutter and cruise the world kept them going.

Kent and Teddi had met after his tour in the U.S. Navy. He had signed on as a crew member on a long line fishing boat and had a lay over in Honolulu, where he now lived. He had just returned from a long fishing cruise and met Teddi through a mutual friend. The sparks flew immediately. The Hawaiian ambiance was made for Teddi. She wore it like it had been designed especially for her. It seemed to make her hair sparkle like jewelry. Her face was painted in lustrous shades of honey from her glow. She was very young, 19 or 20, slim of body and with an elegance reserved for the young. She was first class all the way and Kent knew this from the start. He was smitten.

It wasn't long before wedding bells rang and they both were blissfully happy. Then it came time for Kent to ship out and Teddi was beside herself and lonesome all the while he was gone. She made a decision to learn how to be a ships cook and she hired on with the same company that Kent worked for. It was a complete surprise to him but he jumped for joy when he found out that she could be assigned to the same ship on which he crewed. Now he could remain doing what he loved to do and still be with the love of his life. The captain was only too pleased to make special living arrangements for them and made Kent 2nd Mate.

He was about average in height, but gave the impression of being bigger and his shoulders were wide and powerful. His hair was very dark, very thick and brushed back from an unlined forehead. He carried himself with self assurance and gave an impression of authority. The promotion meant he would now get a percentage of the catch.

They progressed with the company and Kent was made skipper of one of the ships. They worked hard and saved until one day they had enough to buy their own boat. They were able to pick up a used 127 ft. trawler built in Taiwan and now being refitted there. They, along with Jacques Chenier, flew to Taiwan to take possession.

The plan was for the 3 of them to take a shake down cruise to Padang Bai on the island of Bali where they would hire a crew of Indonesian sailors and embark on their first trip to catch bonito tuna. They reached Bali, one of the larger islands of Indonesia, with only minimal problems, which they easily solved. Jacques was an excellent diesel mechanic. His heritage was a mystery. Some French, but a mixture of some Polynesian also.

Finding good crew members proved to be a little more difficult than Kent expected. After cruising the docks all day, he happened on two sailors standing outside of the local pub.

"Hey, do you guys speak English?" yelled Kent.

The tall one answered "Yessir! We speak very good."

"Are you for hire to crew on a tuna boat?"

"We're very good sailors. Much good experience and we'll work very hard."

"Can you be ready to leave next week?"

"Yes, we'll go any time."

After Kent negotiated a percentage of the catch for payment he asked their names. The larger one said "My name is Adam Mauatua and my friend is Arlis Teraura. The last ship we were on, I was 1st mate and Arlis 2nd mate. We can scout around for you to round up more men."

They still needed more crew so Kent asked Adam to check around and meet him at the Sea Rose in the morning. Kent and Jacques returned to the boat and Teddi was there to greet them with a bottle of Dewars. She said "I just thought both of you would be ready for a little attitude adjustment right about now, and the timing is perfect since the sun just went behind the yard arm." Kent told her of their day, while he was sipping on Dewars, and of hiring Adam and Arlis.

"Tell me about the men you hired." asked Teddi.

"Well, they are both Polynesian. They look a cut above anyone else that we ran into today and they seem to have good experience. I guess it's a crap shoot as to how good they turn out to be."

"What do they look like?" she said.

"They have Polynesian names but call themselves Adam and Arlis, I guess to make it simple. Adam is the tall one. He's always smiling and seems to be very happy go lucky. Arlis is a little shorter but still a pretty big guy and with an athletes stature. Both have the Polynesian good looks. They offered to look for some more men.

She continued "I was able to start provisioning and I'm going to serve a gourmet meal tonight as a celebration in honor of the success of our maiden voyage. We'll start with Lobster bisque, a Caesar salad, Duckling ala orange and wild rice. I found some fresh limes, so for desert we'll have Key Lime pie. And I also have two bottles of Pinot Grigio on ice. And if that doesn't suit you, you can both take a hike and I'll serve it to Adam and Arlis." They all had a good laugh and the tension was gone.

After the delicious meal, they all pitched in and cleaned up the mess and then sat topside watching a beautiful sunset and sipped on Tia Maria. Talking and planning the trip soon came to the point of repeating themselves and all were completely relaxed. Kent said, "O.K. Teddi, time to call it a day." So they retired to the captain's cabin in the stern of the boat. Jacques decided to stay topside a while longer in respect for their privacy.

About a half hour later, Kent breathlessly whispered to Teddi, "Honey, you sure know how to end a perfect day."

The next day dawned bright and beautiful. After breakfast, Kent and Jacques started the final preparations for a long fishing voyage and Teddi set out to finish the provisioning. They planned on being out to sea for a few months. Maybe less if the catch was good.

"Hey boss, I found you a good crew" someone called from the dock. Kent saw Adam, along side with Arlis, and three scruffy looking sailors.

"They work cheap, no percentage, just money for family."

"Do they speak English?"

"No, boss, but don't worry, I'll tell them what to do. They'll work very hard."

"Okay Adam. Tell them to get their gear and be ready to sail the day after tomorrow."

"They're all ready now boss. We've come to help you get the boat ready." said Adam as he and the rest of the crew climbed aboard.

They were Chinese and he listed them as Ling How, Wu Chow and Ming Low on his roster. Our crew was French/Polynesian, Polynesian and now Chinese.

Five crew members along with Jacques and Kent would be the minimum needed to make the trip. So, all efforts were guided with the intent to leave in two days.

They got underway at first light and set a course to where Kent was sure they could catch a hold full of bonito tuna. All went well, the seas were flat and they made good time going to a spot that Kent had been to before. On the way they spotted several other fishing boats and got information on where the fish were hitting. Kent took their advice and changed course to the south. Sure enough, after a few days, the fish finder showed a lot of activity and they set their long lines. After a week of hard fishing they had at least 30 tons of bonito tuna in the refrigerated hold. They all were spent, since they were short handed anyway, and none of them had ever seen the tuna so thick. What great luck for their first commercial fishing trip.

The next day saw the weather deteriorating, a pretty good chop developed and got worse as the day progressed. Weather radio said that a storm was brewing, so Kent made the decision not to test Mother Nature and to head for port. But Mother Nature had other plans for them.

Kent and Ling How went forward to secure loose gear before the storm hit and as they hurried along the open foredeck, struggling to get to the bridge, the wind caught them, a single shrieking gust that had them reeling and staggering. They grabbed onto anything for support, to keep from being slammed about. Then the gust was past and it subsided to a steady gale force wind which again was formidable but manageable. Suddenly a rogue wave lifted the bow so that it seemed as if they were climbing a mountain, the ship reached the crest of the wave and just hung there for an instant and then plunged downward, with green water pouring over the bow. The terrific force of the water swept Kent off of his feet and sent him tumbling head over heels. He lost sight of Ling How and went crashing headfirst onto the anchor windlass. He landed on his left shoulder and felt a numbing pain which traveled the length of his arm but was able the grab hold of an anchor link with his right hand to keep from being washed overboard. When the surf receded he looked for Ling How and saw him clinging to the lifeline with a look of panic on his oriental face. His eyes were as big as saucers and Kent could see that he had a death grip on the lifeline. He quickly extricated himself from on top of the windlass and struggled to where Ling How was hanging on for dear life. Kent roughly pulled him loose from his grip on the lifeline and half carried the trembling Chinaman aft to safety.

When they finally got to the bridge, the anemometer showed a maximum gust of 72 miles per hour and the inclinometer showed a 30 degree role. No wonder it staggered them—they were lucky it didn't lift them right off the deck and toss them into the drink. Kent relieved Arlis on the helm who was struggling to keep the ship from broaching. The feeling had came back in his left arm and although he had pain in his shoulder, the flow of adrenaline made it bearable.

The low pressure cell, without any land to slow it down, swept endlessly across the open sea. Waves built up into a succession of huge swells of water as high as the bridge threatening to swamp them. They were taking the waves off the starboard bow, bursting through each crest like they were shot out of a howitzer and with each burst, green water crashed over the bow sprit and on high above the fo'cs'le, sweeping the decks clean from stem to stern. They would not have survived these waves on the foredeck. Her bow came clear of the foaming sea as she broke out of a huge wave and dropped like a stone into a valley that opened before her burying the forward half of the vessel and lifted her stern entirely clear of the raging surf. When her prop broke clear of the surface, the engine raced higher and it set up a vibration that shook the Sea Rose and the bones of the entire crew to the marrow. She then dove forward and her prop bit into the raging water again, hurtling her towards the next swell.

Kent fought the wheel for several hours before the swells lessened to about 10 or 12 feet. Even these were formidable but they were babies compared with what they had been through. Adam relieved Kent at the wheel when exhaustion completely overcame him. His whole body ached, but especially his arms and shoulders and he was dog tired. But he had a feeling of great accomplishment in the knowledge that the Sea Rose took this storm like the vessel of his dreams, and that made it all worthwhile. He was proud of her.

Later, Jacques relieved Adam on the helm since the engines were running well. Fighting the high waves was exhausting. Several days of this weather made for slow going. Turning south, as they did, put them on a course much different than the one on which they had started. But the ship was taking it all in stride, so no panic ensued and the weather radio said the seas were starting to lay down. All would be calm in a day or so. An inspection showed only minor damage from the storm. Nothing that the crew couldn't handle by themselves and they had plenty of time to work on it.

CHAPTER TWO

They were about a week out of Bali when they picked up a weak distress call on the radio. The ship in distress gave coordinates that were about 50 miles away. Captain Kent changed course to see if he could render assistance. What with the foul weather they had just encountered, some other mariner may not have been so lucky.

They soon came upon a strange looking vessel that was drifting with no power. The ship was quite old and had the lines of a Chinese Junk but had no sails. The bow had a high freeboard and was quite sharp, dropping quickly to a low point amidships where the very ornate bridge was located. It was all super structure aft of the bridge with a poop deck over the fantail. On the forecastle was a mast which housed a boom that could service the cargo hold, located forward of the bridge. It was probably an ice hold for fish storage. High Aim #6 was the name on the bow with some Chinese characters also in evidence above the name.

The crew was a motley looking bunch and the skipper was the worst of all. Kent's better judgment told him to use caution on his approach.

The Sea Rose II came along side and Kent called over the bull horn "Ahoy High Aim, how can we assist you?"

"My name is Captain Armond Yang" came the reply, "We lost engine power during the storm and have no one aboard capable of repair. We would like help to repair the engine or a tow to the nearest harbor."

Captain Kent knew that a tow would mean considerable delay. He decided to send Jacques and a crew member to trouble shoot the engine aboard the High Aim #6. If they could make a quick fix, they could be underway in 5 or 6 hours. If Jacques had a problem, Kent could radio for a sea going tug to respond to the emergency and they may only lose a day or so. Maritime law dictated that they not leave a distressed vessel.

Since the sea had calmed to 1 foot waves he opted to raft off of the High Aim with every fender on board between them, to keep from any damage to the Sea Rose. Jacques and Ling How clamored aboard the High Aim and disappeared below to the engine room.

When he saw the age and condition of the engine, Jacques knew he was in for a major job. He sent Ling How back to the Sea Rose for some additional tools as Captain Yang made an appearance.

Jacques said with a bit of disgust in his voice "I won't make any guarantees on getting this engine to run without a complete electrical rewiring. Lack of maintenance is the culprit and it's a crying shame to let a good engine deteriorate like this."

Yang replied "We have plenty of spare parts and spools of wire. All we needed was a mechanic to do the work, and it appears that we now have one. You will stay and complete the job as long as we want you to and Senor Perez will stay with you until we are satisfied with the job."

Jacques turned and looked over his shoulder directly into an automatic weapon, an AK 47, held by a very tough looking Hispanic sailor. Perez leered at him and said "I will hope for an excuse to use this on you, senor. But if you fix the engine, Captain Yang said he may give you the opportunity to extend your time on this earth. It makes no difference to me. You must decide."

The door opened and Ling How entered with the tools. After placing them by Jacques, he turned to face Captain Yang and said in very broken English "My two shipmates and I have agreed to your offer to join your crew. We will await your orders." Jacques couldn't believe his ears and started berating Ling How when he was cracked on the side of his head with a gun butt held by Perez.

"Take it easy, Perez, we need him to repair the engine" screamed

Yang. He turned to Ling How. What is your name coolie? "It is Ling How" he said. "O.K. just stay with Perez and assist on the repair. I will have further need for you and your shipmates when we make our move later."

Yang left the engine room and went into the crew's quarters where eight scruffy sailors lounged in their bunks. Yang yelled for them to pay attention. He said "We have lucked into an opportunity to make this a very profitable trip. I want everyone to arm themselves and be ready to take possession of this American ship. They don't appear to be able to put up much resistance and are short handed, but we must be able to show a state of readiness to overcome them. I will now go aboard and introduce myself and explain their position. Be ready to move on my command."

Yang went topside and surveyed the Sea Rose from his bridge. He spotted Captain Kent on the foredeck coiling spare lines. He called "Ahoy Captain, may I come aboard?"

"By all means Captain Yang. We rigged a gangway amidships for Jacques to cross over. Please use it and come aboard" said a less than enthusiastic Kent.

After Yang crossed over, he walked past Wu Chow and Ming Low and whispered to them. "I want you two to stand ready. I will be needing your assistance very shortly."

He then proceeded to the bridge where he met Captain Kent. He thanked Kent for the fine assistance and hoped that Jacques could make a quick repair. He asked "Have you had a successful fishing trip?"

"Yes" answered Kent. "In fact our refrigerated hold has about 30 Ton of bonito tuna in it."

Yang couldn't believe his ears. What a bonus this was. He can get mucho dinero for that kind of cargo in Bali or Borneo. He'd better make his move now before anyone gets suspicious.

"I saw two oriental crew members when I came aboard. How many others do you have to run this beautiful boat?"

Kent answered "Only Adam and Arlis, my two mates. They oversee the rest of the crew. My wife is the ships cook. Oh, here she comes now. I'll introduce her."

He continued "Teddi, this is Captain Yang. He's the skipper of the High Aim."

Yang turned on the charm "It is a great pleasure to meet such a beautiful lady out in the middle of the ocean."

Teddi smiled and said "The pleasure is ours Captain."

"Tell me Captain Kent, how are you able to run this vessel with such a small crew?"

"We have all the latest electronics, Captain, including a Global Positioning System that's tied into our auto pilot, the latest in a long range marine radio and of course a new radar system along with sonar for finding fish. Our engines have been completely overhauled and we have two generators for AC power. I'll be happy to show you these and other equipment." proudly bragged Kent.

"Captain Yang, may I ask you a personal question about your name?" asked Teddi.

"By all means" replied Yang. "I'm used to curious inquiries"

"I can't help but wonder about your heritage since your name is oriental but you appear a mixture, mostly Caucasian "

"My father was half Korean. The other half was Caucasian of some mixture. His mother died when he was quite young so he had no real knowledge. My mother was Portuguese."

"You have an interesting heritage Captain Yang. Is there anything else you would like to see?" said Teddi.

"No need to show me anything else pretty lady, I will have time to view them closer at my leisure." Yang continued as he revealed a .45 automatic and pointed it at Kent.

"What's going on here?" exclaimed Kent as he pulled Teddi close to his side.

"Please relax and you won't be hurt." purred Yang.

"You two coolies, come up here." Yang called.

"They won't do you any good, Yang, they don't speak English." Kent said.

"That's what you think" said Wu Chow in very broken English.

Yang chuckled and leered knowingly at Kent.

"They speak well enough to know who they'll be working for. Too bad you weren't experienced enough to know not to hire men who will work for the highest bidder, especially ones like these three that probably have done little jobs for me in the past."

"One of you, go to the crew's quarters and tell the other two that Captain Kent wants to see them on the bridge immediately. The other one stay here and take the rifle out of that rack and hold it on the good captain and his pretty wife while I discuss arrangements with them." ordered Yang.

"Captain, I will detain you and your wife in your cabin with a guard outside of the door as long as you cooperate and don't try anything foolish. If you don't cooperate, it will be very bad for both of you, especially your wife. Do you understand?"

"Yes" mumbled Kent.

Arlis and Adam came to the bridge followed by Wu Chow. "Yes Captain, you wanted….

Hey what's going on here?" said Arlis.

"Just relax, boys" said Yang as he trained his .45 on them. We have made the decision to confiscate your catch and what ever else we want to take off this ship. I will give both of you the opportunity to assist us and share in the profits or we can use you to provide dinner for the sharks tonight. Give it some thought before you make any rash decisions."

Adam and Arlis looked at each other. Arlis gave a very slight wink to Adam and turned to Yang and said "O.K. we'll stay but what happens to Captain Kent and Teddi?"

"Don't worry they may be more valuable alive as ransom. We'll find out later. First of all, we must transfer the tuna to the High Aim. You, with the rifle, take the two of them to the Captains cabin and stand guard. They are not to leave for any reason. Stay until you are relieved."

They left the bridge and Yang ordered the four of them to start unloading the tuna from the hold. He called over to the High Aim and told them to open the refrigerated hold, and load the tuna along with all the ice it could hold. They would work until midnight and then finish loading the next day.

He hoped Jacques would have the engine and the icemaker working by then.

CHAPTER THREE

Yang decided to pay Captain Kent and Teddi a visit before he returned to his ship. He walked aft to their cabin.

When he got there, he instructed the guard to let him in and he entered the cabin much to the dismay of Teddi. Kent rose up to his full height and said "What do you want Yang?"

Yang answered "Don't get excited, captain. Since you were curious about my heritage, I decided to give you a little history which may explain my actions."

"You don't have to justify anything to me, Yang. Why don't you just accept our offer to fix your engine and let us go? You're also taking our catch which is valuable."

"Humor me for a short time and we'll see what the future holds for you, Kent."

"You asked about my father. He was a sea captain by the name of Kim Yang who owned his own ship. It carried island cargo here in the South Pacific. My mother and he lived aboard the vessel and it was there that I was born. My mother died giving birth."

"This outraged my father and he felt that I was to blame. I was put off at the next port, an island called Kuralei, where a kind Polynesian woman, named Fahoutu, took me in and cared for me until I was 5 years old. It would have been ideal had not her husband, Rabaul resented me for getting more attention than the other children and the other children resented me for the same reason. The abuse came from many directions. It made me strong but very distrustful of everyone.

"So, you see I had to defend myself from an early age but even so, I suffered much abuse."

"Five or six years later my father's ship made port at Kuralei and curiosity made him visit my home. When he saw the conditions that I was living under, his hate for me was somewhat abated. He faced Rabaul, and called him every name imaginable, and a knock down, drag out fight started. My father won out and left Rabaul a beaten hulk."

"He took me back to his ship and I became a cabin boy. Conditions were somewhat better but I was to do many undesirable jobs for many years. I grew up quickly and was big for my age so it wasn't long before I became a seaman. I could climb the rigging like a monkey. Even so, my father still had hatred for me and the beatings became more frequent."

"Finally, I could take no more and I fought back. I suffered the worst beating of my life that night. I jumped ship in the next port which was Skull Island, a spot where pirate ships routinely made port."

"While working on the docks, unloading cargo, I spied a burly looking man talking to some other dock workers, offering them work as seamen. They refused and when the man left them, I ran to him and said that I was an experienced seaman. He laughed and said. 'You are just a boy. Don't bother me. I want men to be in my crew. I assured him that I could do the work of a man. He hesitated and said 'O.K. get your gear and come aboard. We'll be in port another few days and if you work hard, I'll sign you on for our next cruise."

"I ran to pick up my duffle but was stopped by the other dock workers who said "Are you crazy? That's Captain Quimby, a pirate, and his ship is a pirate ship. If you sign on with him you will become a criminal."

"But I didn't care. My life, so far, had not been a bowl of cherries. I was willing to chance it. I reported to Captain Quimby and worked harder than ever to prove that I could be a man."

"That started a long relationship with Captain Quimby. Yes, he was a pirate and yes we hijacked many ships. There were not many that got any mercy from Quimby and his crew but I had never been treated better."

"I became almost wealthy and used Kuralei as a home base. I bought a native hut on a hill overlooking the bay. It was very peaceful and when I met Liat, my Polynesian princess, I was very content. I asked her to live with me in my hut and she accepted. When I was to ship out again, I told her that it was to be my last trip with Quimby and when I returned I would find other work and stay on the island with her."

"The trip with Quimby lasted longer than I thought but it was very profitable for the whole crew. I returned 6 months later and found my shack empty. Where was Liat? To my horror I was told that she now lived with Le Trec a French plantation owner. His was the biggest plantation on the island. I was livid and I borrowed a jeep and tore up the road to Le Trec's plantation. He was once a powerful man but now he was fat and ugly, his face marked with tropical diseases."

"They had been warned that I was coming and were standing on the portico awaiting me. I said "Liat, you cannot leave me now." She cowered behind Le Trec. He screamed "GET OFF OF MY LAND OR I WILL KILL YOU." I advanced to throttle him when he drew a revolver out of his waistband."

"I stopped and eyed the revolver. It was old and dirty. It even looked rusty. I wondered if it would fire. I decided to chance it and stepped forward. He pulled the trigger and I heard an ominous click. The gun misfired. I didn't wait for a second chance. I grabbed the barrel and wrestled the gun away from him. We struggled. Liat was screaming for me to let him go but I pummeled him. He was no match for me and I flung him off of the portico. He laid in a heap and when I rolled him over, I could see a deep depression in his skull. His head had hit the stone walkway when he fell. I felt for a pulse but there was none."

"His field workers were running to the house to investigate Liat's screams. It was time for me to make haste. I sped to the docks and luckily Quimby's ship was just getting ready to get underway. I clamored aboard and told Quimby that I had just killed Le Trec. He said "Good. I never did like that Frenchman. Welcome aboard.""

"Now that I was a fugitive, there was no returning to any life, other than that of a pirate."

"I became very good at being a pirate and after a number of years I became 1ˢᵗ mate. We raided many ships and even a few small fishing villages. I had become very cynical and found that it was best for me to be that way. I had found my niche."

"We encountered a ship that looked very familiar to me and when we boarded it I realized that it was the High Aim 6. Yes, it was my father's ship. He didn't recognize me at first because I was older and had hardened into formidable man. He was quite upset with Quimby and insisted that we leave his vessel. Quimby laughed and said 'You are in no position to demand anything, Yang."

My father said "How do you know my name?"

"Quimby answered 'Let me introduce you to my 1ˢᵗ mate. His name is also Yang.'

"My father turned towards me and recognition lit up in his eyes. "Is that you Armond?" It was the first I had heard my given name for many years. I said "Yes". The venom spewed from his mouth. He poured out all the hatred that had built up for the past 35 years."

"He could contain himself no longer and he charged me. He was now an old man and I was a very strong able bodied seaman. We fought and fought and then I knew it would be a fight to the death because he would not give up until I could no longer draw a breath. I beat him unmercifully, remembering all the times he had beat me and especially that last beating. I came up from the deck with an uppercut that caught him flush on the chin, his head snapped back and I heard a sickening crunch. He slumped to the deck, a bloody mess. Yes Captain. I killed my own father."

"After we buried him at sea, Quimby said "We can scuttle this ship or I will give it to you as your own command."

"Let me see how many of this crew will stay and then I will decide. I said."

"About half of them stayed with me to spend their lives as pirates and the other half was set adrift. I doubt if they survived. We gave them no provisions. Now you see Captain Kent, I have nothing but piracy in my future. There is nothing I won't do because they can only hang me once and I've already committed more than enough crimes to hang. I hope that you remember that when I ask you to cooperate."

When Yang left them, Kent and Teddi were both speechless and shocked. Teddi said "Oh Kent, what a horrible man but I almost feel sorry for him. He's despicable."

CHAPTER FIVE

Meanwhile Jacques was working away, not aware of anything else, but he knew it wasn't good. He finally grew very tired and asked if he could sleep and finish the next day. They agreed and locked him in the bos'n locker with some food and water.

At midnight all work stopped and everyone, except for the guard outside of Kent and Teddi's room and the night watch, ate and went to sleep. Arlis and Adam finally were alone to make plans.

They decided to wait until a better opportunity presented itself but the Parker Sportster Dinghy would definitely figure into their plans. They made some preparations by removing the tie downs on both the life raft and dinghy. They would not abandon Captain Kent, but they needed to proceed with caution.

The next day dawned on the two ships lashed together. The sky was a brilliant blue and only the ocean was bluer, and it was flat as a mill pond.

After breakfast, work commenced and by early evening the tuna was all transferred. Jacques was ready to try the engine and after the first two tries it turned over. Jacques' work was done and Yang was satisfied enough to tell his guard to return him to the Sea Rose but make sure he was confined.

The sun had already set and there was a new moon so it was pitch black. The only light was from a sky full of stars. When Jacques and Ling How reached the fantail Jacques saw a chance to make his move. He swung around with his leg, taking the feet out from under Ling How. The gun went flying and Ling scrambled for it, giving Jacques a chance to leap on his back. They struggled and Jacques was the stronger. He grabbed Ling in a bear hug and suddenly the gun went off hitting Ling How in the chest. Jacques felt him collapse in his arms. It was a fatal wound. The noise roused the other two and as Ling slumped to the deck they rushed to his aid.

They pounced on Jacques as he was bending over Ling. The two of them struggled with an exhausted Jacques and they over came him, but even against those odds Jacques broke loose and using every bit of his waning strength he leaped over the side, leaving the two coolies grasping at air. He swam between the ships where he was out of sight and could gather his strength and try to decide what to do next. He supported himself by grabbing on to a scupper and tried to piece together what could be happening to the Captain and the rest of the crew. They may all be dead for all he knew.

Arlis and Adam also had come running when they heard the shot and all the other commotion. They got topside just when Jacques broke loose from the two Chinese and jumped over the side. They peered into the murky water and glimpsed Jacques making a beeline to get between the ships. They gave each other a knowing look and made their way to the life raft storage rack. When the two coolies carried Ling How away to try to tend his wound and they found themselves alone temporarily, they quickly loosed the life raft and threw it over the side, hoping Jacques would be able to use it and save himself.

Jacques heard a splash and was able to make out the life raft as it hit the water. He didn't know why or who was helping him but he thought he'd better take advantage of the situation before it got light. This might be his only chance to save himself and he had no idea what could have happened to the rest of the Sea Rose crew but could only expect the worst. He silently paddled away in the dark of the night. The life raft was fully provisioned with food and water so he knew that he could survive for weeks if only he could get out of sight of the two ships before first light.

When Yang came over with Perez to investigate the trouble, they instructed the coolies to throw, the now dead, Ling How over the side and then Yang berated them severely. He said "What the hell happened to the mechanic? Is he somewhere on the ship?"

"No boss! He's gone in the water, we take care of him, he no bother you any more, he disappear under water, make splash, splash and go under." Both then started jabbering in Chinese and Yang yelled "Okay, okay shut up."

"Perez, take a look around with a light to make sure he's not swimming around somewhere."

"I'll look but it's a waste of time in these shark infested waters" and he stomped off.

They did not notice the missing life raft so Arlis and Adam were still safe. Tonight they must make their move. Time is running out.

Yang then instructed Adam to relieve the watch that was guarding Captain Kent and Teddi and cautioned him to be aware of trickery. His watch would be until morning when Arlis would relieve him after the breakfast meal. Yang and Perez returned to the High Aim after double checking on the security of the prisoners.

As they were leaving the Sea Rose, Yang turned to Perez and said, "I don't fully trust those two Polynesians. Maybe you should stay here in hiding and observe them. My survival instincts are sending signals and we're too close to ending this caper to let something go haywire."

"Aye, Aye Captain. Nothing would give me more pleasure than sending one or both of them to Davie Jones Locker. Don't worry I'll keep a weather eye on them."

Several hours later, when he was sure every one was bedded down, Arlis rounded up as much food and water that he could find and stowed them aboard the dinghy. He then quietly, with muffled manual tackle, lowered the Parker Sportster dinghy over the side into the calm ocean. He hung a knotted line over the side securely made fast to the rail.

Perez was quietly observing all of this. Yang's instincts were correct and that's why he was good at what he did. He decided to wait and not encounter Arlis yet. In his bloodthirsty little mind he wanted to wipe out all who were involved in this little scheme. Yang will reward him greatly and besides a massacre was more his style and would satisfy his own craving for a good shootout with his AK 47.

Arlis quietly went below to the Captains cabin and told Adam that all was ready and to rouse Kent and Teddi. He said, "Be very careful, Adam. Yang may have posted a lookout to watch us from the High Aim. I felt very uneasy but I don't think anyone saw me lowering the dinghy. At least no one stopped me and I saw no activity over there. Hurry let's get out of here. Now."

Adam had already prepared the two of them for the escape so they were awake and set to make a break for freedom. They silently stole topside and made their way to the fantail being careful not to make any noise. When they reached the fantail, Perez stole out of the shadows and yelled, "Freeze."

Teddi stifled a scream as the three men turned on their heels and came face to face with Perez who said in a sinister voice, "I will welcome you gentlemen to try something silly." He sneered, his face reflected shear meanness as he said, "You have no idea the pleasure that I would get to see your bodies writhing in pain while I pumped you full of lead and then mercifully ending it with a killing shot. Captain Kent, you would go with the knowledge that I will not kill your wife. We have other plans for her. Both Captain Yang and I fancy her as I'm sure the crew will after we are done. You were so silly to try this fiasco. Did you think we were amateurs?"

As he was railing on about what he would do to them, Adam noticed that Perez was standing on a coil of dock line and the bitter end was draped over the rail just a short distance from his right hand. He slowly inched his hand towards the line, but Perez noticed and yelled, "Stand easy or I'll cut you down."

Arlis was watching what was happening and he suddenly threw up his hands to draw attention away from Adam. Perez quickly swung the automatic rifle towards Arlis and squeezed the trigger to cut him down—Arlis hit the deck as the shots went wildly over his head. In that instant Adam grabbed the line and gave it a hard pull. A single coil leaped free and wrapped around Perez' ankle and as Adam deftly jerked the line again, the tightened single coil jerked Perez' feet from under him. As he fell the gun flew into the air out of his hands and clattered to the deck. Kent lunged towards it and grabbed it before Perez' could recover.

Adam and Arlis, acting as a team, both made a leap and landed on top of Perez, slamming his head to the steel deck with a sickening thud. He was out like a light but still breathing.

The four of them silently looked at each other with a sigh of relief. They sat for a few minutes, listening for any movement or activity from the High Aim or from the two coolies on board the Sea Rose. All was quiet.

Adam said, "We should give him the same medicine that he was going to give us and feed him to the sharks."

"We can't do that, Adam, and you know it. Let's tie him up, gag him and stow him in the bos'ns locker. Yang's wrath will be enough punishment," said Kent. "And who knows Yang may do the job himself."

Adam and Arlis, none too gently, trussed up Perez with the most abrasive line that they could find and then they jammed a dirty oil soaked rag into his mouth before wrapping duct tape around his head so he could not spit the rag out. They both chuckled as they tossed him into the bos'ns locker.

One by one they climbed down to the dinghy on the knotted line and when all four were aboard, Adam shipped the muffled oars and silently rowed them away from the rafted ships. Kent gazed back at his beloved boat and silently made an oath to get revenge for this atrocity. Yang has not seen the last of him.

The Sportster could be rigged for sailing. After a few hours of rowing, a gentle breeze came up. Kent and Arlis stepped the mast and rigged the mainsail. It caught the wind and they started sailing. When they rigged the foresail, the boat picked up speed. The two ships were now out of sight. They were in the clear—at least for now.

A south course towards a small group of Pacific islands that Kent had spotted on the chart offered the best chance for rescue. There was no other land any where near them. So, that's where they headed. They had no compass so the Polynesians steered by the sun and the stars just as their ancestors had done centuries before when they migrated all through the Pacific Ocean.

CHAPTER SIX

When dawn broke over the High Aim 6, Captain Yang ate a hearty breakfast and was feeling very content with the progress of his hijacking. He sent a messenger to summon Perez, the most devious of his henchman, to come his cabin.

The messenger returned to report that Perez was not in his cabin. Yang growled "Where the hell is he? Find him and if you need help, grab the two coolies from the Sea Rose."

After he awakened the coolies, the three started at the bow and worked their way aft. They were not successful in finding Perez, but when they finally got to the fantail, they heard a muffled sound and thumping coming from the bos'ns locker. There he was, all trussed up and fuming mad.

Meanwhile, Yang was planning his next move. He will bring the prisoners over for further questioning and find out if there is anyone that would be willing to pay a ransom for their release. And if so, how much he should ask? If there is some potential he will take them back to Skull Island and make some demands. Even if he succeeds in collecting, he's not confident they will survive the treatment he's planning for them.

If he finds that collecting a ransom is not likely or too difficult, he'll turn them over to Perez and his motley crew to do with them as they please. "I may detain the "fair Teddi" a day or two, myself, before I release her to Perez." He mused to himself, "after we decide what to do with them, I'll strip the Sea Rose and scuttle her or maybe I'll refit her for my own use at Skull Island."."

Yang sat back and relaxed, planning a few hours of entertainment for both he and Perez.

Suddenly, Perez came bursting into Yang's cabin with Wu Chow in one hand and Ming Low in the other he threw them to the deck and screamed "THEY ARE GONE! THEY ARE GONE! And these idiots were in their bunks, peacefully sleeping and dead to the world while I was in the heat of battle doing as you bid me to do."

"What are you saying you imbecile?" yelled Yang "WHAT DO YOU MEAN GONE?"

"Captain, their cabin is empty and the two Polynesians are no where to be found. They overcame me with sheer numbers after I had the drop on them. If only I would have had some help from these two idiots we would still have them. Let me take care of them now."

"Wait, Perez, we may need these coolies for other duties. It is doubtful that four people in a dinghy will survive this tropical ocean for long, and we have much to gain with what we have here. Who knows, our paths may cross again some day then we will get our revenge. But for now let's finish up here before something else happens."

"They laid their plans pretty well, Captain, both the life raft and dinghy are missing. It also appears that some provisions have been taken."

"Then we must proceed in haste. If, by some stroke of luck, they get picked up by a passing ship, we could be in for some trouble."

"Perez, I want you to take these two coolies back to the Sea Rose and prepare it for sailing. By first light I want the three of you to get underway to Skull Island. With all the fancy electronics and the automatic pilot, even you three should be able to handle it without much difficulty. You should reach Skull Island in 4 or 5 days."

"In the meantime I will need all of my crew to unload the tuna cargo in Nusa Dua on Bali where I should get top dollar. When I get to Skull Island we will split the booty. You and the coolies can start stripping the Sea rose of any thing of value until we get there. Don't scuttle her. I may decide to use her myself later."

"Wu Chow and Ming Low go start making preparations to get underway. Perez, wait here with me and we will plot your course" said Yang.

The Chinese left the cabin and Yang said "O.K. Perez, when you get to Skull Island, we will no longer have need for those two men. Dispose of them at your convenience and we will deep six them when I get back. That will make two less shares and all the more for us. Now get those charts down and we'll plot a course"

Unknown to Yang and Perez, Wu Chow and Ming Low were crouched down outside of the porthole, listening to their conversation. They gazed at each other with frightened eyes. Ming quietly motioned to Wu to follow him to the Sea Rose.

When they got to their quarters they jabbered back and forth incoherently. They were in a panic. Finally when they settled down they decided to make a plan. There was no way to escape from the ship. "Why don't we overthrow Perez, after we get underway, and kill him. Then we can take the Sea Rose to Indonesia and strip it for ourselves." There were several ports, where pirate ships docked, and they could negotiate a deal. Even if they were not successful in selling the parts at least they would be alive.

The next morning at first light both ships got underway and Perez set the course on the auto pilot to Skull Island. He called the two Chinese sailors to the bridge and laid out their duties.

"We will stand eight hour wheel watches which should be very easy with the auto pilot engaged. Only in an emergency or to change course will it be disengaged. Wu Chow will stand the first watch until 1600. Ming Low will relieve him and stand the next watch until midnight when I will relieve him. Mine will be the first dog watch so Wu Chow will relieve me at 0400 and stay on watch until 0800. That brings Ming Low on until 1600 and I will have the next watch until midnight. This way we can rotate and no one will have the same watch from day to day."

"The two of you will keep the same quarters that you previously had. I will occupy the captain's cabin and while I'm sleeping, the hatch will be locked. If either of you want me you must call me on the intercom or on the ships phone. I will have the only key to the cabin."

This means a change in plans for Wu Chow and Ming Low. They

had planned to subdue Perez while he was sleeping. They knew that he was much stronger than either of them and a face to face struggle would be difficult. They would need to carefully plan the overthrow to their advantage.

After several days at sea Ming Low was standing wheel watch, when he noticed Perez and Wu Chow on the foredeck stripping some brass fittings. Perez was bending over when Wu Chow sneaked up behind him and smacked him over the head with a two by four, sending him sprawling and out like a light. Wu was beside himself with glee. He pranced around like a monkey waving the two by four and screaming for Ming to come and help him.

Ming Low ran down to assist and the two of them quickly dragged Perez to the bosn's locker before he woke up. They tied him up and when he stirred and gave a moan, Wu smacked him again and spewed out a torrent of Chinese gibberish. They were both laughing as they locked the door.

Later, they decided not to go to Indonesia because they might encounter Captain Yang. They thought they would be better to locate a yard and try to sell the whole boat making up some story of being hijacked and the owners being killed. They knew of a large salvage yard at Willie Creek in Australia. They knew that they could find someone a little less reputable so not too many questions would be asked.

Their plan still was not solid but they changed course towards Australia any way and would make a decision when they got closer. In the meantime they must dispose of Perez and neither one relished doing this task.

They both armed themselves and started towards the bos'ns locker.

Perez was by far more experienced in skullduggery than either Chinamen so it wasn't surprising that he had escaped and was lying in wait for them. He was hiding just outside the hatch leading to the fo'c'sle and when they emerged he leaped on them. He was much stronger and knocked both of them to the deck. He wanted revenge for those two lumps on his head.

They had been too surprised to draw their weapons and Perez was beating on both before they could react. But Ming Low drew his weapon and fired missing Perez but hitting Wu Chow in the shoulder and he started bleeding profusely. He fired again and this time hit Perez but it was not a killing shot. Perez knocked the gun from Ming Low's hand and it flew over the side. They grappled and banged up against the lifeline which had been weakened by the storm. The lifeline buckled but did not part. They rolled around on the steel deck and Perez was on top of Ming.

Wu Chow could see that Ming Low was in trouble against a much stronger man. He grabbed Perez from behind trying to choke the life out of him but he was weakened by the bullet in his shoulder. The three struggled as a group and again banged up against the weakened lifeline clinging to each other. This time the life line parted and the three went over the side, grasping at each other, hoping to grab something to keep from falling overboard, but the only thing to grab was falling bodies. It was a mass of flailing arms and legs.

All three hit the drink and were spitting and coughing salt water when they came to the surface. Perez and Wu Chow were still bleeding from their wounds and swimming only made the blood flow faster. The water turned pink around them.

Sharks have an extremely sharp sense of smell. It is said that they can even detect one drop of blood in the water around them. There was much more than one drop present here.

A Great White Shark was the first to arrive and he attacked Perez. The first strike severed his body almost in two with the Great White ripping loose a mouthful of abdomen. The Chinamen both screamed and started swimming wildly but by this time a school of sharks arrived and the feeding frenzy started. The water boiled with each shark biting on to a man and shaking him like a dog shaking a rabbit. The water now turned red with blood which made them even more frenzied. Soon it was over and all that was left was a few scraps of the three men. A young shark was making short work of those pieces.

The Sea Rose sailed on at full throttle with the auto pilot set for a course to take it into Australian waters in the Indian Ocean. The only sound on board was the deep, steady drone of the engines and an occasional creaking as the ship pitched and rolled on a steady course to Willy Creek.

CHAPTER SEVEN

Meanwhile Captain Yang had made port at Nusa Dua in Bali and sold the cargo of tuna to the highest bidder. He was well pleased with his haul and made way for Skull Island in the Solomon's to meet up with Perez and the Sea Rose. He was anxious to install some of the modern navigation gear on his own ship.

When he anchored at Skull Island, he was surprised that the Sea Rose was not moored or anchored there. He was contemplating on his next move when a dinghy pulled along side with several men aboard.

He saw that it was Captain Konka and two of his crew. Konka was a fellow pirate and they sometimes joined forces when need be.

Konka yelled "Ahoy Captain Yang, may we come aboard?"

"Come aboard" answered Yang "But tell those thieves with you to keep their hands in their pockets. I don't want to see anything missing when they leave, like the last time. You owe me a set of binoculars"

"No worries" said Konka "I've already instructed them to be on their best behavior"

Konka climbed up the Jacobs ladder and his two henchmen followed him.

"I have a proposition for you Armond, but first tell me about your latest coup"

Captain Yang was only too happy to tell about the tuna cargo on the Sea Rose and what he planned for the electronic gear.

"Did you say that the Sea Rose is a long line trawler of Taiwanese manufacture?"

"Yes" replied Yang

"Armond, I hate to tell you but we saw this vessel and it was not headed towards Skull Island. We thought it looked like a likely prospect and tried to hail it but they did not respond to our distress call. We came about and attempted to chase it down but it was heading south at a high rate of speed. The course was towards Australia and the strange thing was that we saw no activity on the decks or in the wheel house. My crew got nervous and thought it might be a ghost ship. We gave it up and came here."

"That damn Perez" said Yang. "I'll have his head if he's double crossing me" Yang dismissed Konka and retired to his cabin to plan his next move.

Meanwhile, the crowded dinghy continued sailing south with its four passengers. None of them complained about the uncomfortable conditions because they all knew what would have been in store for them and they were happy to be alive in spite of their discomfort.

They were able to catch some edible fish which provided much needed nourishment even though it was difficult, especially at first, to choke it down raw.

"Raw fish! I can't eat raw fish," Teddi said. But her growling stomach was telling her that she could—that she must.

"Think of it as sushi, sweetie," cajoled Kent. "Look, Adam and Arlis like it, don't you boys."

"Oh, yeah," they said in unison as both stripped off pieces and chewed heartily, grinning as if they were downing filet mignon."

"See, honey, it's not so bad—and we have to get some nourishment" pleaded Kent.

"Yea sure" mumbled Teddi "why don't you try it?"

Kent flinched but he took a piece, placed it in his mouth, began to chew and then gagged, spitting out the contents back into water where it had come from.

Teddi giggled and said "I think I can manage to stay on my fast a little while longer."

"I think I'll go on a fast too," Kent said after he had spit a few more morsels into the water. But Arlis and Adam ate merrily along. "More for us," said Arlis, and with that he opened his mouth wide and let another slab slide down his gullet.

It rained after three days out. They rigged canvas to catch the rain and were able to supplement their water supply which they knew was important to do for survival.

One night they saw the lights from a ship on the horizon. Kent attempted to light a flare but they had gotten wet and were useless. It was very discouraging.

The fresh breeze had died and their sails were slack. The sun seemed white hot and beat down on them mercilessly. The water was so calm it looked like an oil slick on the surface. The sails provided a little shade but not enough to help.

Suddenly the surface was broken with shark fins. They were all around the boat, swimming underneath and then breaking the surface on the other side. One aggressive T-head rammed into the side of the dinghy. Thank God he didn't take a bite out of the freeboard. But he might on the next try. Adam was swinging a paddle at the closest ones which only aggravated them further and they started thrashing the water around them.

All of a sudden something happened. A lot of activity was going on under the surface that they couldn't see. The fins decreased in numbers and then disappeared all together.

"They're back" screamed Teddi as fins and sleek bodies broke the water. "Wait, those are not sharks, they're dolphins. They seem to be fighting off the sharks."

"You're right, Teddi" said Adam. "The dolphins will drive the sharks away by butting them with their heads. They have tremendous power and the sharks know that. My people have many stories about dolphins saving lives at sea."

"They are marvelous creatures, swimming around us, leaping and splashing and grinning up at us."

Later, that night a breeze came up and they were able to sail on. After another week the provisions and water were getting in very short supply. They cut the rations even more and were in dire straits. There were periods of delirium with dreams of rescue and the sighting of mirages which looked like land but were only heat waves.

All four were restlessly sleeping, going in and out of consciousness. Teddi stirred, half awake, she mumbled "I hear strange singing—it must be angels—maybe we're dead. Another angel is answering with that strange sounding tune—KENT! KENT! Are you with me—are we dead—I hear angels singing."

"Teddi! Wake up. It's not angels singing. Look out there. It's a pod of humpback whales calling to each other. That big one is almost on top of us with one eye looking right at us. I think he's calling to us with his eerie song."

"This is good luck" said Arlis. "I knew our luck would change when I woke up and saw that albatross soaring over us yesterday".

They all watched the huge whales, some of which were 40 or 45 feet long and had to weigh as much as 40 tons. They were extremely acrobatic. Often they would throw themselves out of the water and swim on their backs with both flippers in the air. Others would slap the water with their tails as a signal to the young not to stray too far from mama and auntie. It was quite a show. And then — they were gone.

But Arlis was right. A rain cloud appeared overhead and a squall provided them with drinking water. The cool rain felt so good after days of sweltering sun. It rained for two or three hours and stayed cloudy after that which meant a fresh wind to sail in.

They slept peacefully that night while the boat steadily sailed south.

The next morning at first light, Kent awakened and by habit scanned the horizon. Was that another mirage? Probably so. He stared and stared and the mirage seemed to become clearer, as the sun broke above the horizon.

"Hey you guys!! Wake up!! Look just off of our starboard bow. Tell me what you see"

They both sat up and looked out. Arlis rubbed his eyes and looked again. "Yes—yes, I think its land!" he exclaimed.

"That's not a mirage, Kent. I think I can make out two distinct mountain peaks. Tighten up the sails and let's get the paddles. We are saved!!!" said Adam.

Teddi had awakened and was speechless. She was crying for joy but no tears were coming because she was so dehydrated. Slowly the distant spot grew larger, until a shimmering emerald island materialized.

The island was still a long way off and it was after dark when they reached it. Luckily there was a full moon so they could keep it in sight. Soon they were close enough to hear the waves breaking over the coral reef which surrounded the island. It could be dangerous trying to go in at night. Coral was as sharp as the sharpest knife.

They reefed the sails and drifted for the rest of the night.

In the morning, they surveyed the reef and decided that they should travel parallel to it until they could find an opening. They only flew the mainsail so they would have more control. They went west for several hours with no likely spot discovered so they came about and went east. Sure enough shortly after they passed the starting point, they spied an opening. It wasn't very wide and the waves were breaking high on each side of it. They discussed whether to search further or chance it to enter here. They could see a lagoon with a beach on the other side of the reef.

After many weeks at sea in the small dinghy they decided to go in. The breeze was on their beam so they left the mainsail up and with the makeshift rudder steered the boat towards the opening.

Everything was going as planned and they were in the opening when, as happens so many times when you approach a land mass, the wind shifted slightly and a gust came from the beam. It heeled the dinghy close to capsizing and all four shifted their weight to try to right the boat. It made steering impossible and they rammed upon the coral with a great force from the gust and an incoming wave. There was a screeching sound as the dinghy's hard bottom scrapped across the sharp coral ripping it to shreds. The next wave lifted them clear of the reef but flipped them all the way over and all four went flying into the surf. The dinghy came down on the reef upside down and was torn asunder.

The four were fortunate not to come down on the coral except for Adam who almost made the lagoon but one foot caught a razor sharp piece. He didn't even feel the cut and was not aware until he saw the blood and felt the sting from the salt water.

They all swam for the beach in the placid lagoon and lay there for a time until they could catch their breath. They saw pieces and parts of the dinghy and some gear from onboard floating in the lagoon. As tired as they were, they knew enough to salvage as much as possible for survival. There was no sign of human habitation as yet, maybe there was none at all.

Two of the things salvaged were the first aid kit and the fishing box so they could dress Adam's foot which could easily become infected from the coral and they could catch some fish to eat. Hopefully, they could start a fire and have cooked fish tonight. Kent and Teddi still found it hard to chew the rubbery texture of raw fish, and although they had done so in order to survive they were looking forward to a fire to do some cooking.

CHAPTER EIGHT

Arlis went fishing and Kent's job was to start a fire. Teddi and Adam started to gather palm fronds to build a lean to. Kent gathered some kindling and dry twigs and put them in a shallow pit that he had surrounded with small rocks about the size of your head. In the survival kit was a flint and everything else needed to start a fire. He had one going in a short time.

By the time he added a few nice sized logs and had a good cooking fire going, Arless showed up with several fish, one was hog snapper at about five lbs. They cleaned the fish and speared them with sticks to start cooking them.

After feasting on the fish, Adam and Arlis said they'd better take a look around to see what the island had to offer. Teddi and Kent finished constructing a lean to for them to sleep in tonight.

When the two Polynesians returned, they had found nothing unusual in the rain forest or on the beach. They found nothing that would indicate people living within several hours of walking. The forest showed signs of animals, probably wild boar so they might be able to trap one and have some meat. Coconuts were plentiful and would provide good nourishment. They even found a banana tree. So they knew that they wouldn't starve.

They would explore a little further each day. The twin peaks were in the middle of the island. It would take a major trip to scale one of them so that might have to wait a while until they got some strength back. A view from there would tell them what else was on the island, hopefully people.

After exploring the next day, Adam ran back to the camp and excitedly said "We found fresh water. It's a stream flowing down from one of the peaks. There's a 20 foot waterfall leading into a small pond and Arlis is already swimming in it. Come on, before he soaks it all up."

They hurriedly ran to the spa and dove in clothes and all. They splashed and played in the water like a bunch of kids and drank until they could hold no more. After laying up on the bank in the cool shade they decided that this would be an ideal spot to make a permanent camp. So for the next few days this was their project. It was an ideal camp site and still near enough to the beach so they could fish and gather crabs. Arlis and Adam built a trap after they heard a wild boar, rustling around the pond, coming in for a drink of water. Sure enough they trapped one which set up terrific howling and grunting.

"O.K. boys, you caught it, now butcher it" said Kent. The meat was a little gamey but it was the first meat for any of them for a long time. Now that they were getting stronger, it was time to climb the mountain to observe the island. They decided that Adam and Arlis should continue with the exploring. Teddi packed enough provisions and water to last three or four days and the two Polynesians started out.

The first day was mostly hiking through the rain forest, but by the end of the day they started getting to some higher ground. By noon of the second day they reached the top of a hill which gave them a better view of the island but still only high enough to see the shore from which they had just left.

They must get higher to see a bigger part of the island but it would be impossible to reach the top of one of the twin peaks, at least on this trip. It was very rugged and massive rocks prevented a straight climb. They decided to go as far as they could tomorrow and then return to camp.

From what they could tell at this point, travel across the island would be difficult because of the thick forest in the valley below them.

But why even cross if there was more of the same. They could gather brush and kindling for a signal fire up on this hill so if a ship passed close by they could light it to draw their attention.

They were able to make it about half way up the mountain, just about where it split into the twin peaks. They decided to make camp and observe as much as they could and return to the main camp the next day. Travel down hill would be much easier.

During the night, Adam could not sleep. He climbed up and sat on a huge boulder reflecting on the beauty of the night. As he gazed to the south he thought he saw a flickering way off in the distance. Yes, it was a fire but very faint and very far away. But it meant that someone else was on this island. He awakened Arlis and he also saw the flicker of fire. As the night wore on the flame died out but now that knew that they were not alone.

The next morning they got started before sunrise to return to the camp where they could report the find to Captain Kent. There were other people on this island. Who were they? Would they be friendly? What if they were pirates? How would they travel across the island? These questions and more would face them and weigh heavily on the decision of what to do next.

When they reached the main camp along side the pond, it was very late and the married couple were, already asleep. They decided to turn in and get a good nights rest before the arduous task of deciding how to approach the next move. Maybe Captain Kent would come up with a solution. He was the one that always made good decisions. They both fell fast asleep.

When Teddi and Kent arose the next morning they were so happy to see their two friends safe and back in camp. They were still sawing logs so they let them sleep and get some deserved rest. Teddi prepared a feast for them when they awoke, because she knew that they'd be famished.

Later, when they finally stirred, Kent said "O.K. you lazy louts, heave out so you can eat and give us the lowdown on what you found."

They both chuckled and Adam said "We're starved alright, but first of all the good news is that we're not alone on this island"

"That's great news, Adam. Tell us more" said Kent.

"As soon as I fill my belly, I'll give you the bad news" laughed Adam.

They both dug in to the pork and crab meat that Teddi had fixed them.

As they were eating they explained to Kent what they had found. They told him about the fire on the far side of the island and what might be a village or at least some people. They also told him about the very rough terrain as you got higher on the mountain which was very close to being impassable unless you went around at a lower elevation. And then about the valley on the other side which was a very thick jungle and looked like it would be very difficult to pass through.

Kent was deep in thought. "Well boys you've given me some things to chew on. First and foremost, getting to the other side of the island is where we must go. That's without a doubt even if we take the chance that they are not friendly. It's our best hope of rescue. Next, the best way to get there is not necessarily the shortest route. The mountain and the jungle are formidable obstacles and we might not make it."

"Why not go around? The beach is flat and from what we've seen so far it looks like it stretches for quite a ways. We could encounter some obstacles but as a last resort we might be able to swim around them. At least I think we should give it a shot"

They discussed it, giving each one a chance to give some input and an opinion. Finally they decided to take the time to explore each direction on the beach to see if one or the other would be better. Kent volunteered to do the exploration since it was his idea to try traveling on this route.

He started early the next morning, planning to walk until nightfall or until he met an impassable point and then return the next day. He found that the beach widened and narrowed at times but he was always able to move on without any problem until he reached a point where the coral reef disappeared and there was no longer a lagoon.

The beach was no more. He reached a point where a sheer cliff came down to the waters edge and waves came crashing into the base. There were huge rocks in the surf that looked like they had at one time been part of the cliff and had fallen into the water. The rocks stretched out into the boiling ocean for several hundred yards.

He couldn't see how far the cliff extended but it looked pretty formidable. A swim out into the ocean and then around the rocks might be more than what they could do, especially Teddi. He decided to camp for the night and head back in the morning.

When he got back that next afternoon, he explained what he had found and the decision he made not to try to scale the cliff or to swim around it.

The four of them sat around the camp fire that night discussing their options. Finally Kent said "We know we can't go over or around that cliff. Why even explore the other way? Let's make our preparations and the four of us start out until we can go no further or until we arrive at the village. If we meet an obstruction, we'll decide what to do at that point. We can't just sit here waiting for something to happen. The other three cheered and said "Let's do it".

The next few days were ones of preparation. Water was the major item that they would need. They knew they could fish and gather crabs for food, but fresh water would be in short supply. They would carry only the necessary survival gear and what they couldn't find on the way. They would need the few waterproof containers that they had salvaged from the dinghy in case they had to swim. In these would be the medical kit and fire starting material.

They all hydrated themselves on the morning they started and struck out on the beach. They tried to stay on the hard packed portion for easier walking and also it was a lot cooler on the feet than the soft, blistering sand. The first day was easy and even kind of pleasant. They could see nothing ahead that would deter them. At sunset they stopped and made camp.

They all slept very soundly that night even though they could hear the rustling of wild boar in the brush. Teddi was a little apprehensive about it though, so she snuggled up against Kent. This made her feel better. Kent kind of liked it, too.

Clouds had formed the next day which was welcome since it made it less unbearably hot. They might get a thunder storm this afternoon. It would be good for cooling off and for collecting water. They trudged on and got the expected thunderstorm. They stopped for the day and again slept well after a meal made from fresh caught fish.

The third day saw a changing terrain. A little less beach and a little more brush. Then as they came around a bend they saw a small river emptying into the ocean. This may have been the outlet of the stream and pond where they had made their camp. Anyway it was fresh water to replenish their supply and after walking up stream they took a well needed swim.

After playing in the water awhile, Kent said "O.K. let's push on" They crossed the river and made their way back to the beach where they moved on until dusk.

They had several uneventful days and were starting to wear down when suddenly they spotted two young naked boys playing in the surf. Kent waved his arms and called "HELLO". The boys looked up with startled expressions and took off running the opposite way. Kent said "Well I guess we're going to find out if they are friendly."

They decided to wait where they were and prepare to meet the inhabitants of their island.

It wasn't long before the two young boys appeared, this time wearing loin cloths, and with them were four very formidable looking Polynesian men. One of the men, in a language of the South Pacific islands, yelled some very guttural sounding words. Adam brightened up and answered him in the same manner.

"What did he say, Adam?" queried Kent.

"He wants to know who we are and where did we come from" said Adam. "I answered him saying 'We are friends from a ship that was raided by pirates. We escaped in a small boat and are now lost. Can you help us?"

The island Polynesians were mumbling to each other and one was gazing menacingly at the lost group while he gestured with his formidable looking spear.

"Tell them we mean no harm and ask them if they speak English, Adam" said Kent.

Adam did so. The one who appeared to be the leader, surprisingly, answered "Yes, I speak English very well" Kent breathed a sigh of relief. At least they could communicate.

"My name is Captain Kent Allison, this is my wife Teddi Allison and our first mate and second mate Arlis and Adam. Our ship was the Sea Rose, a long line fishing boat. We were hijacked about a month ago and escaped in our dinghy. I have no idea what has happened to the rest of our crew and to our ship itself. Probably stripped and scuttled by now. Can you help us get to another island where we can get to the Australian authorities and make a report?"

"We are very sorry to hear of your plight, Captain Allison. If we look apprehensive it's only because we have heard of pirate raids on small fishing villages like ours and we don't want attention drawn to us by outsiders. Please come with us to our village. You can rest and tell us the whole story. We will help you all we can, but we are limited in what we can do. After you rest I'll explain how we can go about this."

The small group turned and started the short trek to the village itself with the Sea Rose crew following behind.

As they were walking, Kent called ahead to the leader of the group "What do we call you?"

He answered "My name is Ben Fletcher Adams. I was named after my great, great, great grandfather, Fletcher Christian and I am a direct descendant of John Adams, one of his crew."

Teddi was startled and whispered to Kent "Oh my God, Kent, he's a descendant of the H.M.S. Bounty mutineers, Fletcher Christian and John Adams. I've heard that his and other mutineers of the Bounty have descendants in these and other islands in the South Pacific."

"This should be a very interesting visit." said Kent.

CHAPTER NINE

They soon got to the village and Kent was somewhat surprised to see that at the center point of the settlement was a large Quonset hut with two other smaller ones in close proximity. There were several cement block buildings that resembled barracks. And then, in contrast to those buildings, were a number of thatched roof huts that surrounded a fenced corral in which children were playing with a herd of pigs.

There was also a larger hut with a high thatched roof apparently for use by someone of importance. Not surprisingly this hut belonged to Ben, now recognized as the chief of this village.

"Ben, this almost looks like an old military base" said Kent.

"You're right, Captain, this was a P.T. Boat base during the big war against the Japanese" said Ben. "You will notice, our harbor, although it is small, is well protected and not very visible from the ocean side."

"Did your people live here before the war?"

"No. My father, along with other descendants of the mutineers came here during the last few years of the war. They came from Noumea as volunteers to help the American sailors establish a base. There was a village already here but the people were quite hostile. You've heard of the cannibalism sometimes practiced by some of the more ancient tribes? Well, this one had been one of those. They had stopped doing that kind of thing in recent years since it was frowned upon by some of the younger ones. However the Japanese occupied the island early in the war and were brutal to them. They enslaved the men and raped the women. This enraged the local men and soon there was an uprising. The locals had a history of never giving quarter when fighting a battle and they soon won out and escaped. Although many were killed because of the superior fire power of the Japanese, they were able to harass them with night time raids. When they could do so, they would capture some of the soldiers and revert back to the old customs. The Japanese soldiers were filled with revulsion at this and when the war was not going well for them they abandoned the island. When the Americans came, they were very distrustful and although they did not fight them or practice their ritual, as they did with the Japanese, they refused to cooperate and kept to the hills. The Americans needed help to build and maintain the base and the skipper knew of our people in Noumea so he asked them to help. My father's people had also suffered in the hands of the Japanese so they were only too happy to accept the offer to help to defeat the enemy. The Americans also furnished food and lodging along with payment and needed protection. "When the war was over and the base was no longer needed the Americans turned everything over to my father and the rest of the workers. Most of them, rather than go back to Noumea, formed this village along with the old villagers.

"That's quite a story, Ben" said Kent. "I'd like to hear more, but first do you have any ideas on how we can get to civilization?"

"One of the pieces of equipment left by the Americans was a short wave radio but I'm afraid it may be beyond repair. It hasn't worked for many years. You may take a look if you like. Other than that, the only contact that we have with the outside world is the supply ship Kon Tiki which is not due for another month or two."

"When it comes, it will bring goods that we have ordered on the previous trip and also supplies that we can't produce here. We pay for these goods with island products that we make here such as hula skirts, boars tooth necklaces and other souvenir types of things."

"The boat will carry passengers only when it has room. Usually Father Tom McCann, a Jesuit missionary, will make his visit while the boat is here or sometimes he'll stay with us while the Kon Tiki makes a short run to an island close by. He, almost always, performs a wedding or two while here."

As they approached the larger thatched roof hut, Ben said "This is my home. Please come in and meet my family."

As they entered the hut, they found it quite pleasant inside. "You've already met my two sons" said Ben. "This is my wife Teio".

Kent said "We are very happy to meet you, Teio, and most grateful to Ben for his hospitality. Do you have any other children?"

"Yes, we have two daughters, Mareva is our oldest child. She has left the island and now lives on the island of Tahiti where she works at a hotel and is doing quite well. She has met a young American man and they plan on marrying in the next year. Our youngest daughter, Marte, is still here on the island and runs a school for the children. She was in a convent until last year when she decided to come back home. She had gotten a good education in the convent and is very happy teaching the children here."

"Let us get your party settled in, Captain." said Ben. "One of the small Quonset huts is broken up into several rooms and has a small galley and a head with a shower. It hasn't been used for a while and if you don't mind cleaning it up a bit, it's yours and your crew's to use while you're here."

All agreed to do the work and were extremely overjoyed to be treated so well. They also were happy for a chance to rest up in a real bed tonight. As they were leaving, a young Polynesian girl walked in. Ben said "Marte, I want you to meet these people. They have come upon our island in a small boat after being hijacked. This is Captain Kent and his wife Teddi. Adam and Arlis are their crew members. This is my daughter Marte."

Marte was stunning. She was a small girl and slender with very black hair. Adam was speechless. He had gasped when she entered the hut. It was a very audible intake of air and held for what seemed like an eternity. Kent, Teddi and Arlis expressed their happy salutations but Adam just gawked, his mouth moving but no sound emerging. They then headed for the place that was to be their home for the next month or so.

The Quonset hut was not bad at all. They spent an afternoon of cleaning and made it presentable for the time being. Teddi asked for a few alterations for the near future and the men all agreed to make things as comfortable as they could. Both of Ben's boys, Minarii and Niau, came calling with some grilled abalone for the evening meal after which they all crashed and had a good nights sleep, the first for many days.

The next day, Ben stopped by and offered a tour of the village and the surrounding area. All four agreed to this because they were very curious how such a small village so remotely located could survive so well. They first stopped at the large Quonset hut where the women and a few of the older men were busy making island goods. They were not just making grass skirts, they were weaving, quilting, carving wooden sculptures and bowls, making drums and hand-dyed pareu.

During their walk, they passed by the school house which was in the second small Quonset hut. The children were outside playing the games that all school kids play at recess time. Marte was standing off to the side of the playground watching the games when she saw her father with the group of strangers. She was dressed very conservatively with a Frangipani flower over her left ear. She approached them to give a greeting and offered a tour of the school. They accepted.

This time Adam was able to compose himself and enjoyed in some lively conversation with her in both English and Polynesian. They seemed to hit it off rather well. He told her that the frangipani, a white waxy flower, very sweet like dogwood, was his favorite flower and that someone as beautiful as she should wear it all the time. She blushed, but it was obvious that she was enjoying it very much.

As they left the school, Ben said "Marte will be one of the dancers at tomorrow nights luau. In fact she is one of the leaders here on our island. The young men and women put on a very good exhibition of the dances that have been passed on to us from our Tahitian ancestors. No one knows how long our people have been doing these dances but it must be many hundreds of years. This luau is in your honor and will last most of the night, so rest up tomorrow, it will be a long day."

"This is a great honor, Ben" said Kent. "What can we do to help?"

"Nothing at all." said Ben. "In fact, we look for a good excuse to have a luau. The men are already digging the pits for roasting the pigs. There will be plenty to eat and drink."

"Ben, we are very curious about your history on the Fletcher Christian side." said Teddi. "Could you tell us a little about it?"

"Certainly." said Ben. "Let's go back to my home for some refreshing drinks and I'll tell you all that has been passed down to me."

When Kent and Teddi arrived at Ben's hut, they relaxed and Teio served them a refreshing drink that tasted like a combination of pineapple and coconut. Surprisingly it was cool and very soothing. Later they discovered that it was somewhat fermented and that's why it relaxed them. Adam and Arlis had decided to go fishing with the group of island men who were gathering food for the luau.

Ben started his story "It all started in England when the collier ship Bethia was converted to take a voyage to the South Seas to bring back easily grown breadfruit plants needed for cheap food for the slaves in the West Indies. King George III had been petitioned to start this expedition and have the breadfruit transplanted there."

"The ship was renamed HMAV (His Majesty's Armed Vessel) Bounty since it carried four four-pounders and ten swivels. Later, after the mutiny, it became known as HMS (His Majesty's Ship) Bounty."

"The ship sailed from Spithead, England on December 23, 1787 with Captain William Bligh and a crew of 45 men bound for Tahiti via Cape Horn. Fletcher Christian was acting Lieutenant and second in command."

"When the ship approached Cape Horn it was impossible to get through to the Pacific Ocean. Bligh and the crew of the Bounty tried for thirty days, fighting terrible storms with at least hurricane force winds, snow and rain with very high seas. They were forced to turn east and head for the Cape of Good Hope at the southern tip of Africa. They had to refit the ship at False Cape which took another thirty-eight days. They finally arrived in Tahiti on October 26, 1788. More than ten months had passed and they still had no cargo."

"The bounty stayed in Tahiti nearly six months in a luxury most of the crew could never imagine. They were never cold or hungry. The beautiful flora was only surpassed by the women of the island, and they were gorgeous, so it was considered a paradise."

"During the stay in Tahiti, conditions deteriorated. Christian had been made commander of the shore party to collect the breadfruit plants and lived ashore for most of the six month stay. Living arrangements were set up ashore and there is conflicting evidence as to all the many relationships that were developed with the Tahitian women."

"Fletcher Christian was about five feet nine inches tall with a dark complexion and well muscled. He was sometimes described as swashbuckling, a slack disciplinarian, a great favorite with the ladies, conceited but also mild, generous and openly humane. It is not known how many of his descendants may have resulted from this shore duty but several were claimed."

"When HMS Bounty finally left Tahiti, on April 6, 1789, there were 1015 breadfruit plants onboard, and a very unhappy crew. Many crewmembers left behind strong attachments. There had been cases of desertion but Bligh was able to capture all the deserters and flogged them without mercy."

"They were back to the harsh realities of shipboard life. Bligh's reaction was ranting and raving. The crew and officers reacted with disgruntled compliance. Christian was affected the most and seemed to be the recipient of most of Bligh's abuse. At first, Christian had decided to desert but after discussing a plan to steal a boat and sail away with Midshipman Edward Young, Young suggested that they should take over the ship and do away with Bligh."

"Christian then put the idea to Adams Quintal, William McCoy, Alexander Smith, Charles Thompson, John Williams and Burkitt. In the early morning of April 28, 1789 Bligh was awakened and brought out on deck in his night shirt, and with his hands tied, he was held abaft the mizzenmast. No person was killed or seriously injured during the mutiny. Christian saw to that."

"Captain Bligh and 18 men were cast adrift in the South Pacific Ocean in a 23 foot boat. Bligh proceeded to make one of the most heroic voyages in history, he was an excellent seaman. First they made it to the nearby island of Tofoa, but the natives were hostile and they were lucky to get away with only the loss of one man. They eventually made the heroic voyage in 48 days, landing in Timor on June 12, 1789."

"After the mutiny, the Bounty first returned to Tahiti. Christian was elected captain, and the ship set off to find a place to live. The mutineers started and then abandoned a settlement on the island of Tubuia, and the ship again returned to Tahiti. Nine of the Bounty mutineers with six Polynesian men, twelve women and one baby again left Tahiti on board Bounty.

They searched for and found, Pitcairn Island, which had been incorrectly charted years before. They found the island on January 15, 1790. After they took everything of value off the ship, HMS Bounty was burned and the mutineers set up life on Pitcairn."

"The little colony was not a happy one, in great measure due to the inequality between the British mutineers and the Polynesian men regarding sharing the women and the land. Dissention and then murder were the result. On September 20, 1793 Fletcher Christian and five other mutineers as well as six Polynesian men were killed in a tragic fight to the death. During the following several years, most of the mutineers died or were killed."

"Only John Adams and Ned Young remained and then Ned Young died of asthma in 1800. The only male survivor was John Adams. This was his real name. When he had signed on the Bounty, he was hiding from the law so he gave his name as Alexander Smith. He had been a violent person, but had changed dramatically. Ned Young had taught him to read the bible and it became his saving grace. He went on to become the respected leader on Pitcairn, and died on March 5, 1829. He was the last of the original mutineers."

"The mutineers that stayed on Tahiti when the Bounty left for Pitcairn faired no better than the rest. Captain Edward Edwards was assigned to take HMS Pandora to find and capture them. When he arrived at Tahiti on March 23, 1791, he located fourteen of them. Two had been murdered, eight gave themselves up right away, and others took off to the mountains only to be caught and brought back to the ship in irons. They were all put in a cage on the main deck called "Pandora's Box"

"The voyage to England was a treacherous one. When the ship hit a reef near Australia four drowned in their chains. Fourteen escaped but were recaptured. The surviving crewmen were tried by court martial in England, were found guilty of mutiny and hanged at Spithead onboard HMS Brunswick on October 29, 1792. Several of the unwilling participants were found innocent and were pardoned."

"Pitcairn Island became a part of the British Empire in 1831 and the people were moved to Tahiti. The experience was a failure, and the people quickly returned to Pitcairn. In 1856 the population had become overcrowded, and all of the people were moved to Norfolk Island. This also didn't last and most moved back to Pitcairn."

"Since then the fortunes of the Pitcairn people have ebbed and flowed, depending on each other, the weather, the passing of ships, the sale of postage stamps, and the sale of island made products."

"The descendants of the Bounty mutineers and their Tahitian wives still live on Pitcairn Island, Norfolk Island and many other islands here in the South Pacific. The small group here, on Tongolo Island, are mostly mutineer descendants with a few of the original inhabitants also living with us. We are a very peaceful people and live apart from the rest of the world except for an occasional visit by the Kon Tiki and sometimes an island hopping sailboat looking for a tranquil anchorage for a few weeks."

"We survive with what we can raise and the fish we can catch. We trade island made products for other staples that we can't grow. The large Quonset house is where we make and store the products that we trade when the Kon Tiki arrives."

"That's about all I can tell you Teddi. I think that should give you a pretty good idea of our history. It has been passed down from father to son and will continue to be as long as there are mutineer descendants."

Kent and Teddi returned to their quarters feeling very good about their situation. What good luck to land on Tongolo. Staying here for a month or longer will not be hard to take. They rested to prepare themselves for the luau tomorrow.

The next day was spent traveling around the village and meeting the local people. They were a wonderful and friendly group. Everyone they met offered fruit or drinks and asked what help they could give.

At the luau, Ben asked that all four sit with his family. The food was excellent and the drinks gave everyone a feeling of joyful exuberance. It was noticeable that Adam and Marte sat very close to each other. When the entertainment started, Marte excused herself and left to be part of the dancing.

All of the dancers, both men and women were very exciting, dancing at a furious pace that made your head whirl. It seemed like there bodies were made of rubber, they were so supple.

When Marte came on, she was part of a group that told a story by dance and drums. She was magnificent. The story was of a princess that was to marry her lover but a suitor fought and killed her lover. She grieved to the point of death but she and her lover were joined again in the after death. It was all done with beautiful costumes and resounding drums and dance. It was worthy of a night club show in Hawaii. Adam was transfixed.

As soon as Marte came back, everyone wanted to talk to her and tell her what a wonderful performance it was. After she thanked everyone for their kindness she sat down next to Adam and waited for his words which were many and very private. Everyone then knew that something special was happening with Adam and Marte.

CHAPTER TEN

The next month passed very quickly. Teddi helped Marte teach the children in the little schoolhouse. Kent worked with Ben showing him ways to improve living conditions in the village. Adam and Arlis worked with the men on many jobs but mostly fishing to keep the village larders filled. It was very compatible and everyone was very contented. Life was good.

One afternoon a great commotion was heard in the bay. The children of the village were running and laughing and calling "Jolly is here!!! Jolly is here!!!" Sure enough off shore a mile or so was a beautiful sailing ship.

"It looks like a schooner" said Kent.

Ben walked up behind him and said "Yes, it is a schooner. It's the Kon Tiki. There will be much celebrating for several days. It is bringing staples like sugar and flour and many other goods for trading. The skipper is Captain Roger McNulty, a genuine Irishman. The children have nicknamed him 'Jolly", because his name is Roger. But don't worry, he is not a pirate. In fact you won't find a more honest man in the whole of the South Pacific."

"Well I'm sure glad to hear that since it looks like he's our only way to get back home." said Kent.

Teddi said "Oh I'm so excited. Can we go down to the dock and watch him come in?"

"Let's go." said Ben. "I like to welcome him and get an idea of his route on this trip. Also see if he brought any passengers."

They got to the dock just before the ship was made fast to the bollards. It was a beautiful schooner with solid rigging and sleek lines. It had the appearance of an old sailing ship but the main deck was laden with modern equipment. Upon closer inspection Kent discovered that the hull was fiberglass and not wood which meant that it was not old but fairly new construction. The sails were furled and the mainsails were stowed within the mast. When the ship came into the dock it was under power and a bow thruster was used to bring it close to the dock. From the sound of the engine, Kent determined that it was diesel and at least 450 horsepower, maybe more. Kent could hardly wait to meet the skipper of this elegant ship.

After the lines were made fast and a gangway lowered to the dock, Captain McNulty came down to the pier. His face looked like the map of Ireland, his hair was dark brown, he was about five feet nine inches tall, strong made and a star tattooed on his left breast. His knees stood out a little and he might be called a little bow-legged. Yes, he was an Irishman. No doubt of that.

"Ben, you old whipper-snapper, top o' the morning to you. It's good to see your smiling face again." said McNulty, in an Irish brogue, as he nimbly stepped to the pier.

"And it's always good to see you, Captain." said Ben.

"I'd like you to meet another sea captain and his wife." said Ben. "This is Captain Kent Allison and his wife Teddi. They landed here on our island in a dinghy after their ship was hijacked. They and two of their crew were fortunate enough to escape the pirates and used exceptional seamanship to sail the small boat to Tongolo Island." continued Ben.

"It's always a pleasure to meet a fellow sea faring man Captain Allison. And might I add the lass you call your wife is like a bright sunny day breaking above the horizon. She is indeed a fine lassie to be proud of."

Teddi said "Thank you for your kind words sir and I also might add that it is obvious that you've kissed the Blarney Stone."

With that, they all had a good laugh and it was plain to see that getting along with Captain McNulty was not going to be a problem.

"I've brought the good Father with me this trip and he'll be staying for awhile. After we unload your cargo I'm booked to take a hold full of stores to Konora. I'll be back in about a month to pick him up and I'll then have room for your island goods to take to Bali."

"When you have time, Captain McNulty, I would like to discuss booking passage for my wife and I as well as our crewmen." said Kent.

"Let's do that later, captain." said McNulty. "I have cargo to unload and a terrible thirst to quench. I also want to hear about your adventure with the pirates. They are a scourge here in this area. I try to keep up with all that happens so we can compare notes and try to defend ourselves some how."

As McNulty clamored back aboard the Kon Tiki, a neat looking, conservatively dressed, white haired, older gentleman walked down the gangway. "Hello, Ben." He said.

"Hello Father Tom." said Ben. "Welcome back to our island. We will have a few weddings and a few baptisms for you this time Father. Also we have a few new folks for you to meet. Captain Allison and wife and two crew members have happened on the island. You can get the details later after you get settled."

"It's a pleasure to meet you Captain. And I assume this pretty lady is your wife?"

"My pleasure also, Father. Yes, my wife's name is Teddi." said Kent.

"I'm so happy to see a priest, Father." said Teddi. "Will you be saying Mass soon?"

"Yes, my dear lady, I say Mass each morning at 8:00. There is a secluded spot just outside of the village that offers a perfect place for prayer and contemplation. We call it Natures Cathedral. It's beautiful and has enough room for many of the villagers. I'll also be giving absolution for about 15 minutes before Mass. I'd be very happy if you and your husband could attend a few of the services."

"Now if you'll excuse me, I'll get settled in. Will I be staying in the same hut as always Ben?"

"It's reserved for you each time you visit us Father." said Ben.

As the group dispersed, each going to their quarters, Ben yelled to them "Don't forget the luau tomorrow night to celebrate the arrival of the Kon Tiki."

The next morning, Kent and Teddi attended Mass at Natures Cathedral and were surprised to see that many of the villagers were also there. It was thrilling to hear them sing hymns in that special Polynesian way. You could sense their love of God and also their respect and love for Father Tom.

The day was one of preparing for the luau. All the visitors pitched in and really looked forward to another night of revelry. Teddi said to Kent "I almost feel like we are a part of the village. They are such a kind and thoughtful group. I'm going to hate to leave here."

Kent just smiled.

That night, as before, the luau was a booming success. The food was great, the dancers were intense and everyone was in a celebrating mood.

"And now" Ben said, "the next dance will tell some of the history of our Tahitian ancestors. The mutineer side of our culture is but an infant when compared to our Tahitian side. We have little written word but some say that around 4000 BC the great migration started from Southeast Asia across open water to settle the Pacific Islands. They say that Tonga and Samoa were settled around 1300 BC and from there colonization voyages were launched to the Marquesas and the Tahitian Islands in about 200 BC. Centuries before the Europeans concluded that the world was round, the great voyagers of Polynesia had already mastered the Pacific Ocean aboard massive, double-hulled outrigger canoes. They navigated by stars and sun."

"Music and dance has always been a very important part of Polynesian culture. The beauty, power and drama of today's Tahitian dance testify to it's resilience in our culture. We dance for joy, to welcome a visitor, to pray to God and to challenge an enemy. We still use the same traditional instruments, the thunderous drums, conch shells and harmonic nasal flutes. The story tells of our ancient traditions and competitions."

"Oral history recounts the adventures of gods and warriors in colorful legends where javelin throwing was the sport of gods, surf riding was favored by kings and Aito strongmen competed in outrigger canoe races and stone lifting as a show of pure strength."

"Our Temples were called Maraes and were once the center of power in ancient Polynesia. These huge stone structures once hosted all the important events of those times. We now celebrate Heiva each year in July in Papeete which is a pure display of Polynesian festivity. We are a very proud people."

After Marte finished performing this different Polynesian tale, which was even more beautiful than before, she and Adam moved to the fringe of the large group of people. It wasn't long before they stole away altogether and were strolling on the beach. The moon was full. The ocean was calm. It was a scene of tranquility. They stopped under a banyan tree to look at the silver path that the moon was creating on the surface of the water.

Marte looked up at Adam and he bent and gently kissed her ruby lips. He said "Marte, when I'm with you, the world seems to stop."

Marte smiled up at him "I am very happy when I'm with you too dearest Adam."

Adam said "I would so much like to be with you more and talk to your father about staying here in the village—so that some day—uh, if you would think about it—uh, we could go further—I mean—you know—oh Marte—I'm not saying this very well and I'm very nervous—maybe I should just keep quiet—maybe you would need more time—maybe…"

"Anymore time and we might die of old age." said Marte. "Yes, Adam please go to my father. Ask him if you can join the village and above all ask him if you can have my hand. I've fallen in love with you."

Adam couldn't believe his ears. He just stared at her and suddenly he embraced her and smothered her with kisses. She looked up at him with tears of joy in her eyes and before long both were crying with happiness.

"Oh Marte I'm so happy. I love you so much."

CHAPTER ELEVEN

The next morning, Kent and Teddi were resting after breakfast since it had been a late night at the luau. There was a knock on their door and Kent answered with "Yes, who is it?"

"It's Adam, Captain Kent. Could I speak with you for a moment?"

"Sure Adam. I'll be right out." said Kent.

After telling Teddi to continue her resting, Kent left the room and said to Adam "O. K. Adam, what can I help you with?"

"Captain, I have come to ask if I can be relieved of my duty to you. It is not that I am unhappy being on your crew. You and Teddi have been fair and very kind to me. I have grown to love this island very much. It is much like Vanicoro, the island where I grew up. But there is nothing on Vanicoro for me to return to. All my family has left there. I want to ask Ben Fletcher Adams if he will allow me to become part of the village."

Kent smiled and knowingly asked "Is there some additional reason you'd like to stay here Adam?"

Adam blushed and said "I guess it's pretty obvious that I have special feelings for Marte. Yes, we have fallen in love and she has accepted my proposal—as crude as it was. I also must also ask Ben for his permission to marry his daughter."

Kent embraced Adam and said "I hate to lose such a good seaman but I'm very happy for you and I treasure the friendship we have found with each other. When I get back to civilization and have access to funds, we'll work out a way to get you the money you have coming."

"Thank you Kent. You have made me very happy. And now for my next stop. I'm very nervous about this one." Kent smiled with the thought of this huge, strong man quavering with fright on his next encounter.

Adam slowly walked towards the hut with the high roof, muttering to himself all the way. When he finally reached Ben's hut, he called "Ben, are you there?" He waited "It's Adam."

In a few seconds, Ben emerged through the doorway. "Yes, Adam, I am here. What can I do for you?"

"Ben, I want you to know that I have come to feel very happy and content in the last month or so that I've been here on Tongolo Island."

"I'm happy for you Adam. Is there something else?"

"Yes. I also want you to know I'm a good fisherman and a very hard worker."

"Okay Adam. I have seen that with my own eyes. You have done more than your share and have never refused when asked to help. But why are you telling me this now at this time?" Ben said with a slight lilt to his voice and a grin slowly creeping across his mouth.

"Ben, I would like to ask if you would accept me into your village. I would like to make this my home."

"You need not ask Adam. It is good, hard working and moral young men like you that we need to keep this village intact. My answer is yes. We will be pleased to have you. Now is there anything else you would like to discuss with me?"

Adam shuffled his feet and looked Ben in the eye and blurted out "I have fallen in love with Marte and would like your permission to have her as my wife."

"Well now" said Ben. "This is a different matter. There are some things I must do before I can answer you Adam. It's not like in the old days where a father arranges his daughter's marriage. In today's modern times it is more a decision made by the girl in question. Of course a father does what he can to influence his daughter one way or another. I will discuss this with Marte and give you an answer."

"Thank you, sir. I will anxiously await your decision."

Adam then turned to walk away.

Ben yelled after him "Hey Adam, don't look so worried. I think I know what Marte will say."

****

Later that afternoon Kent and Teddi were walking on the dock where the Kon Tiki was tied up. As they passed by the schooner, Captain McNulty stuck his head out of the companionway and shouted "Captain Allison would you and your fine wife like to come aboard and share a wee bit of Irish whiskey with me?"

"That would be very nice Captain McNulty. I haven't had the opportunity to sample any for many a moon." said Kent, as they approached the gangway.

After they were aboard and resting comfortably on the fantail, McNulty said "I keep a few bottles of a very good single malt, Captain. Although I have some ice in my ice maker I prefer my scotch neat. How about you, neat or on the rocks?"

"Scotch neat is fine for me Captain McNulty, but Teddi may prefer something with a little less bite."

"Of course, my dear, I have a very nice sherry. Would that suit you a little better?"

Teddi said "It would suit me very well Captain. With just a little ice please. Ice right now would be a great luxury."

McNulty called to his cabin boy, gave him the drink orders and the young Polynesian scurried off.

McNulty said "That young man is an orphan whose mother and father were killed in a terrible typhoon several years ago. His father had crewed with me and had asked me to be the boy's Godfather. After the death of the parents, I decided to take him under my wing instead of sending him to an orphanage. He's like the son that I never had."

"Oh. What a touching story. What's his name?" said Teddi.

"His name is Tararo." said McNulty as the boy reappeared with a tray of drinks.

McNulty said "Tararo I would like you to meet Captain Allison and his wife."

Tararo said, in very precise English "I am very pleased to make your acquaintance sir and madam." And then he gave a slight bow and asked "Can I get anything else sir?"

"No, that will be all Tararo." said McNulty as Tararo scurried away. "And don't forget, young man you have studies to do." McNulty chuckled "He's not always quite so formal. I think he may have been showing off just a bit."

"Okay let's hear your story Captain Allison but first please call me Roger."

"Thank you Roger, we will and please call us Kent and Teddi." said Kent.

"First of all, this was our very first fishing voyage after we picked up the boat in Taiwan." said Kent. "Things started so well and I never expected it to go sour so fast. We picked up a good crew in Bali and made a great haul of Tuna just west of the Marshalls. We were heading back to Bali when I picked up a weak distress signal and I headed for the coordinates to render assistance. We soon came upon the High Aim No. 6 captained by Armond Yang." Kent went through the details of the overthrow, the theft of the cargo and the eventual escape.

"My Chief Engineer, Jacque Chenier, tried to escape but was lost over the side. The three Chinese defected to join Yang. Teddi and I and my two mates escaped on a sailing dinghy and with the superior seamanship of my two men we were able to sail here to Tongolo Island. I imagine the Sea Rose was scuttled after they stripped her."

"That's quite a sad story, Kent but not the first one I've heard with similar piracy tactics. You are lucky to survive. Most victims are not quite so fortunate." said McNulty. "The pirate, Armond Yang is notorious and has quite a price on his head. The reward is now $350,000 Australian."

"Did you say that your ship was the Sea Rose and it was a Taiwanese built Trawler which you used as a long line fishing boat?"

"That's correct Roger." said Kent.

McNulty silently thought for a moment and said "Now I don't want to get your hopes up but I heard of a similar type boat that was found drifting in Australian waters under very strange circumstances. It was towed somewhere on the northwest coast of Australia. I can't remember all the details but I do know that there was no crew aboard."

"My God, Kent." Teddi said excitedly "could it be the Sea Rose?"

"As I said" repeated McNulty "I don't want to get your hopes up but I think it bears checking into. I'll be leaving in a few days for Norfolk Island where they have good communications. Give me all the specs on your ship, the documentation number, your insurance company, anything you can come up with. I'll find out everything I can as well as calling your insurance company. They will be pleased to hear that you're still alive and will start their own investigation."

"Roger you have no idea how much hope that you've given us. I'll start documenting all the information that Teddi and I can remember and get it to you by tomorrow morning. Let's go Teddi. I want to get started right away."

Teddi jumped up. She gave Roger a big hug and said "Thank you, thank you, thank you."

Roger smiled and said "It was indeed my pleasure madam."

Back at Willie Creek, Robert Craig was getting very impatient just thinking about all the bureaucracy involved with salvage rights. He knew there were other ways, without going through legal channels, to profit from his windfall. And one sure way was to contact Armond Yang to whom he had sold contraband previously.

The other alternative was to find out who the insurer was and strike a deal. But it would be so much easier to contact Yang. Besides he had lived on the wrong side of the law to long and had too many other suspicious dealings to be drawing attention to himself, by an insurance adjuster or some legal authorities.

Contacting Yang by radio or by satellite phone, directly, was too dangerous. Too many unknown ears could be listening. It would be best to get word to him by word of mouth and set up a meeting on the island of Bali, the same way we did on our last venture.

Through a seaman on a visiting fishing boat he was able to get a message to Yang that he would be staying at Rachel's Inn at Nusa Dua in about three to four weeks and would like to meet with him. When Yang got the message he confirmed by the same seaman that he would travel to Bali and would meet with Craig at the bar in Rachel's

Inn four weeks from today. His message to Craig was "This better be worthwhile."

Craig was sure that he made the right decision. Dealing with Yang was always dangerous but he felt he had the upper hand here. He was already counting the money and feeling very good about it.

Meanwhile, Yang mused thoughtfully to himself "This suspicious meeting must have something to do with the Sea Rose. Konka said he saw it heading towards Australia. I wonder if Perez and Craig are working together. No matter. If I can work a deal for that ship, it will replace the aging High Aim No 6. And with a little help from Konka it may cost me very little, if anything at all."

Chapter Twelve

After Captain McNulty left for Norfolk Island, things quieted down to a regular routine. The excitement consisted of Marte assuring her father that she indeed was in love with Adam Mauatua and wanted to spend the rest of her life with him. Ben invited Adam to his hut and officially gave him his and Teio's blessing, wishing them much happiness and hoping for a house full of grandchildren.

They all hugged and kissed and cried a little bit and then Ben said "Okay now let's talk about practical matters. I'm sure that Marte would like Father McCann to perform the ceremony so that means a marriage in about a month or wait another three to six months or possibly longer."

Marte blurted out "Now, we want to be married now, don't we Adam?"

"Now child just relax, there are some preparations to be made. First of all, where will you live? The small Quonset hut is only to be used as temporary quarters for guests. I doubt if you or Adam would want to live here in the big hut, or at least not for more than a night or two. Adam, have you given any thought to this? What are your plans?" said Ben.

Adam had a thoughtful look on his face and said "If I had a small piece of open area somewhere in the village, I could build a hut. I have done so several times back on my island and with some help I know I could have it completed in two weeks or so."

Ben said "I have already spoken with my counsel and they agree that a section on the fringe would make a suitable spot for an additional hut. Adam, you must agree to become a member of the village and join the fishing fleet in order to acquire this property."

"I accept" Adam loudly acclaimed. "I can't believe what a lucky man I am."

"Okay" said Ben. "Let's you and I take a walk Adam and I'll show you the spot. I think Marte's mother may want to have some private conversation with her."

The two men along with Marte's brothers Minarii and Niau walked to the future home site. On the way the older boy, Minarii said "Adam, my brother and I would like to help you build your hut. We will work hard and we don't want any pay. You will soon be our brother-in-law and this will be our wedding present to you and Marte."

"Well thank you both. That is a very generous offer and I accept. I'm going to need all the help I can get to meet the deadline. Which reminds me, Marte and I must speak to Father McCann, just to make sure everything is okay with him."

After Adam and Ben laid out the basic parameters for the hut, they started back to the center of the village. Ben went to report the decision to the counsel members and Adam wanted to discuss his plans with Kent and Arlis. The two boys decided that it was a good time to take a swim.

Adam returned to the Quonset hut where Kent and Arlis were discussing the possibility that the Sea Rose might still be afloat. He told them about the meeting with Ben and the agreement he made.

Kent said "Adam I'm sure that you are going to be very happy and have a great life with Marte. It looks like they consider you a part of the family already."

"That is true, Kent." said Adam. "But I've got a lot of work to do if I want to be married on this trip by Father McCann."

"Arlis and I have strong backs and are both willing and able to help." said Kent. "Why don't we take the next day or so to draw up a plan and start lining up materials for the hut."

"Sounds great, Kent. I knew I could count on you guys. I want to get Marte and show her where her new home will be. I'll be back in about an hour." said Adam as he skipped off.

"He's as happy as a kid at Christmas time" said Kent. "Let's get started Arlis. We're going to have a busy couple of weeks ahead of us."

And that they did. But with the five of them and some other volunteers from the village they made good headway. In two weeks time the hut was livable enough for Adam to move in. It was now time for Marte, Teio and Teddi to make it a home. Under their supervision and labor provided by Adam and Kent the hut took shape and was almost ready for the married couple to move into after the wedding.

While the hut was being built, the wedding plans were also underway. This wedding feast would be bigger than any luau they have ever had here on Tongolo. The marriage of the daughter of the island chief was an important event and would be celebrated as such. All 100 plus villagers would attend this wedding feast. Teio and her extended family worked and planned constantly. Ben observed and smiled. He had a good feeling about the union of his daughter and this Polynesian giant.

As the happy day got closer, the schooner Kon Tiki sailed into port, returning from Norfolk Island. Captain McNulty was pleased to hear of the upcoming celebration and agreed to delay leaving by a few days so as to keep the planned date of the wedding. After he made the arrangements to have the outgoing cargo loaded starting the next day, he asked Ben "Where is Captain Allison? I have information and good news for him."

Ben answered "He's probably with Adam making final touches to the new hut. I'll send Niau to fetch him." He called Niau to run and get Kent and the boy scurried off.

It wasn't long before Kent came to the dock and Teddi was not far behind him.

"Come aboard you two. You'll be happy to hear what I have to say." said McNulty.

They clamored aboard.

"I'll start from the beginning" he said. "When I reached Norfolk Island, I ran into an old shipmate and told him your story. He went on to say that a 127 foot fishing trawler was indeed found drifting in Australian waters and was towed in and docked at Willie Creek.

He couldn't remember the name but when I mentioned Sea Rose, he thought that sounded familiar."

"This gave me great hope and I was able to talk to the authorities at Coast Watch a division of the Australian Customs Service in Canberra. They had sketchy data on this event but referred me to Commander Eric Lawson of the Australian Navy stationed at Broome. This Naval Station is very close to Willie Creek."

'Unfortunately Lawson was at sea but expected back very soon. I briefly told my story to his yeoman and asked that the Commander contact me on the marine radio."

"A few scant hours before we got underway, I got a call on my radio from Lawson. After I repeated the hijack story, he became very interested. Yes, it was the Sea Rose at Willie Creek and it was towed in by a "not so honest" man named Craig. He and his crew were holding it at a detention center. Lawson had gotten word through an informant that Craig was looking to make some kind of deal on the black market and possibly with the notorious Armond Yang."

Kent was beside himself with excitement "This is good news, bad news Roger. What can we do? Can the Navy do something? Can my insurance company do something? How can I get my ship back before this guy dismantles it? I've got to move fast."

"Hold on, Kent, I'm not finished, I contacted your insurance company and made a report. I also gave them Commander Lawson's name. When Lawson contacted me, the insurance people had already contacted him. Needless to say, the insurance company will fully cooperate in any plan to get the ship back to you. Commander Lawson would like to communicate with you to get your assistance in not only getting your ship back but ridding the South Pacific of the scourge of Armond Yang once and for all."

"Of course I will cooperate, Roger. I'll do anything, but what?" said Kent.

"I'm not sure but it involves some kind of a sting. He has asked that I get him on the radio as soon as I get in range of Broome. I am confident that he will want you in Broome as soon as possible. Time is of the essence."

All the while the men discussed the situation, Teddi sat there with look of panic on her face. "Kent I don't want you doing anything dangerous, yes we want our boat back but I don't want to lose you in the process. Those pirates are without mercy."

"Let's not worry about that yet, Teddi, I want to hear Commander Lawson's plan first. At least we know that the Sea Rose is still afloat and the Australian Navy is willing to help us. Let's get this wedding planned so we can get underway as soon as it's over."

They went to find Adam and Arlis to give them the good news and when they did it was a happy group of survivors. Arlis assured Kent that he was available to help in any way he could to get the Sea Rose back.

Adam said "Do you need me skipper? I will help if you need me. Marte will understand. She must understand."

"I know you would help Adam, but you deserve the happiness you've found here. You can be a great asset to this village. I want you to stay. We'll have the whole Australian Navy behind us. Stay here with your bride."

CHAPTER THIRTEEN

At the Australian Naval Base in Broome, Commander Eric Lawson was meeting with several agents from Coast Watch a division of the Australian Customs Service. Lawson explained to them that he had a paid informant at Willie Creek who was a crew member of Robert Craig's.

"It seems that this guy Craig has contacted Armond Yang about buying some contraband, specifically a derelict fishing trawler moored at Willie Creek. Yang and his pirates have been terrorizing ships in this area too long. I'd like to put him away and rid the South Pacific and Indian Ocean of this scourge. Along with him, we might also get rid of Craig, someone closer to home. He's small potatoes and a real pain in the ass."

"Both of them are known drug runners and deal in some gun running as well. I've got a plan but I'll need the law enforcement cooperation of the Custom Service. Will you listen to what I have to say?"

"Of course Commander, we'd like to see those two out of business as well as you"

Lawson spent the next several hours laying out a sting and explaining that hopefully Captain Allison would participate. It also will involve talking turkey to Robert Craig and applying legal pressure that the Customs people could enforce. This would be the iffy part of the plan. If something goes wrong it will probably be here. The Custom boys agreed to help but emphasized that they hadn't fully prepared to interrogate Craig so they'd have to do some bluffing. Lawson agreed to back them up where he could.

"Okay let's go see Mr. Craig."

As Lawson, with the Customs officials, walked to the helicopter pad, he said "Anticipating your cooperation, I had the local law enforcement office pick up Robert Craig and detain him at the local lock up. He has no idea why he's there but he also knows there are a variety of charges that he could be brought up on. At about this time he's probably screaming like a wounded eagle and insisting that he see an attorney. But the local Constable has suddenly become hard of hearing. We should be there in a few hours."

When they arrived at the lock up, Craig was in a cell. The guard said that he had quieted down after ranting and raving all morning. Lawson asked that he be brought in the office for an interview.

The guard brought him into the office in hand cuffs and leg irons. He was quite put out and said he wanted to see a lawyer. Lawson said "Just calm down for a minute Craig. I'm Commander Eric Lawson of the Australian Navy and these two gentlemen are from the Customs Service. We want to discuss something that may be of interest to you."

"What interest would the Navy have in me? I didn't do anything to them."

"We're investigating into a known ring of drug smugglers and gun runners. Your name has popped up more than a few times." said the senior Customs man. "We'd like to hear what you've got to say about it."

"You've got nothing on me" said Craig "I want my lawyer."

The Customs man read off a laundry list of offenses and names of offenders and all the while Craig squirmed in his chair. "Several of these incarcerated men have agreed to turn states evidence and have given us facts and figures. Would you like to hear the ones you have been implicated in? Or would you like to hear a proposition from Commander Lawson?"

Craig's eyes darted from the agent to Lawson and back again

as he slowly looked up and nervously mumbled "What kind of a proposition?"

"First of all, let me tell you what we already know" said Lawson. "We know that you and a crew of sorts got word, through illegal and unknown means, of a derelict ship drifting in Australian waters. After locating the vessel, you took it in tow and moored it at Willie Creek. It happens to be in excellent condition and was probably hijacked and the crew murdered. Not wanting to get involved in legal means of salvaging for various reasons including your own rap sheet, you contacted a notorious pirate called Armond Yang."

Craig turned a bright shade of red and then slowly as the color drained from his face he turned a ghostly white. "I don't know where you heard all of that. Yes, I've got the ship but I got it legal, I have salvor's rights and I never talked to Yang. How could I?"

"We know that you communicated through a third party and you've made arrangements for a rendezvous in Bali at Rachel's Inn. The only thing we are not sure of is the exact date but we know it's in about three or four weeks. Is that close enough for you?"

"Even if all that would be true, and I'm not saying it is, I haven't done anything that you can hold me on. You've got no proof."

"You're probably right but the Customs Service in Canberra is requesting that you be transferred there and will be faced with an arraignment for seven different offenses ranging from smuggling to assault with a deadly weapon. Do you want to hear how you can get most, if not all, those charges reduced to the point of probation?"

Craig was now sweating heavily. "Can I have some water? I'm not feeling very good."

Lawson nodded to the guard who left the room to get a bottle of water for Craig.

"We'll wait for your answer, Robert" said Lawson in a low well modulated voice. "You do some thinking while we go make some phone calls. When we come back you decide if you want to leave for Canberra with these two gentlemen or if you want to listen to what could be a turning point in your life." And the three of them got up and left the room.

Outside in the courtyard where the three were hydrating their parched throats they reviewed the interrogation. All three had a good laugh when they thought of the squirming, uncomfortable Robert Craig.

"I think we did pretty well considering we didn't have a lot of concrete evidence to present to him. Good thing there was no attorney present. He must really have a guilty conscience." said Lawson. "Let's go back in and present our plan."

As they all settled in around the table Lawson said "Okay Craig, made up your mind?"

"I've got to hear what you want me to do first. Yang doesn't mess around. Some hard time in jail might be better than going to Davie Jones Locker." mumbled Craig.

"Okay, here's the deal. We want you to keep the meeting with Yang in Bali just as you would have before. Make a deal to sell him the Sea Rose and tell him he must take it to Skull Island to strip it or what ever he wants to do with it. You cannot do the stripping at Willie Creek. Tell him you will deliver the ship to a point just outside of the 200 mile zone and he can take it from there. Your own fishing boat will pick you up at that point and take you back to Willie Creek."

"Here's the difference. My men will be manning the smaller boat which will look like a fishing boat on radar but in fact will be a heavily armed frigate. The Sea Rose will have a crew of Navy Seals and Customs Service men, all armed and disguised as regular seamen. We hope that Captain Allison can also be with you to provide assistance in identification and whatever else he can help with."

"We are hoping for the element of surprise. The best case scenario will be that we don't need to fire a shot however we won't depend on that, given the circumstances. I hope to take Yang and his whole crew prisoner and charge them with piracy. After we get him to Canberra the indictment will include murder as well as many other charges that will certainly put him away for life or possibly the death penalty."

"Your job will be to make the arrangements for the sale and then be on board when you are to exchange the ship for money. You should be in no danger. We will take care of the capture and the arrest. What do you say?"

"I haven't heard what I'm getting out of this yet." said Craig.

The senior Customs man said "I can have a legal document drawn up—it will state for your cooperation on this sting and for testimony against Yang, all pending and past legal charges will be dropped providing that you obey the law while under probation for a period of five years."

Craig hesitated and then said "When will the paper be ready?"

"We can have it all signed and notarized and back here for your signature the day after tomorrow. You will have to stay in the lock up until we get back. You'll be under close scrutiny after that, so don't get any funny ideas. Should you take off or change your mind they'll probably lock you up and throw the key away. There are ways for a prisoner to get lost in the system and never surface again."

"Okay it's a deal, but I want a guarantee that I'll be safe from Yang."

"You got it. Do as we say and you'll be safe. The men in my group are some of the toughest in Customs"

Lawson and the Customs Agents left the building and headed back to the copter. They all shook hands and congratulated themselves on a job well done.

"That was a stroke of genius saying…there are ways for a prisoner to get lost in the system and never surface again. Where did you come up with that one?"

They all laughed and the senior man said "It comes with experience Lawson. It comes with experience."

"Well I think it probably erased all doubt as to what he was going to do." said Lawson.

"Let's get this whirly-bird back to Broome."

CHAPTER FOURTEEN

Wedding preparations on Tongolo had reached the final stages and everyone was getting nervous. The only calm one was Father Tom McCann. He had been through many, many of these and although this one was special he remained calm. Father had known Marte since she was a baby in fact he had baptized her. He thought for a while that she was going into the religious life but alas that wasn't to be. She's a wonderful teacher and loves her students. She will make a great wife and mother. Along with this new villager, Adam, they will be a wonderful asset to the community. This was indeed a marriage that he was very pleased to officiate.

Although they have known each other a short time, they both have wisdom beyond their years. Father had spent several hours talking to them, both together and individually. There was no doubt in his mind that this was the right thing to do. In his conference with Ben and Teio he assured them of this fact.

And so the happy day had arrived.

Natures Cathedral was filled to capacity. The people of the village had added even more flora to the already abundant blossoms. Flowers were everywhere. There were orchids, frangipani and many other tropical plants that would only be so abundant in a tropical paradise like this.

As the guests filed in and silently found places to sit, most of them on the large, soft, grassy area before the altar, a lone harmonic nasal flute played old Tahitian music. The melody was quietly serene and gave a feeling of peaceful repose. When anyone in the crowd spoke it was in subdued whispers. Holiness and great respect was very evident.

The flute stopped playing and it was so quiet you could hear the surf which was hundreds of yards away. Father McCann and Adam stood on the altar with Marte's two brothers slightly to the rear of them.

The flute started playing a slow almost mournful melody as Marte and Ben slowly walked towards the altar. Marte was even more stunning than the first time Adam had seen her. She was dressed like a Tahitian Princess and carried herself with an air of royalty. When they reached the foot of the altar the music stopped and Ben turned to his beautiful daughter and kissed her lightly with tears streaming down his cheeks. He then presented her to Adam. There was not a dry eye in the congregation.

They bowed before Father McCann and sat on high backed chairs to the right of the altar.

Father began the Mass and the children's choir, mostly Marte's students, sang in Latin.

> Kyrie e-le-i-son
> Christe e-le-i-son
> Kyrie e-le-i-son

The children were singing their very best in tribute to the teacher that they had so much love for. The Mass continued.

After the couple said their wedding vows, Marte carried a small bouquet of flowers to the side of the altar to the statue of The Blessed Virgin Mary. As she knelt before Mary and prayed and wept, a teen age boy with a beautiful tenor voice sang Ave Maria. His voice was as clear and pure as a silver bell. He put his heart and soul into this touching hymn. Again there was not a dry eye in Natures Cathedral.

When Marte and Adam again joined hands at the altar, Father McCann introduced them to the congregation to a resounding round of applause. Then as they walked up the aisle the Tahitian drums and conch shells played an intense rendition. The celebration was now beginning in earnest and would last until the next day. There was no doubt as to the importance and love that everyone attached to this wedding.

At the luau that evening, the food and drinks were plentiful. The dancing and music was non stop. Teddi and Kent were so very happy for the newly weds and promised that some day they would return to this island paradise to spend some time with them.

Captain McNulty wanted to get underway as soon as possible and late into the evening he took Kent aside and said "Captain Allison, I would like to get underway the day after tomorrow at first light. I suggest that you and your lovely wife make all final preparations, not yet made, tomorrow. You'll have time to rest a bit before we make port so stay and celebrate with your new found friends and the newly weds."

"We'll be ready Roger. We're very anxious to hear how we're going to get our boat back and to get busy doing it."

The day after the wedding was one of peaceful quiet. It was a day of rest and relief. The whole village was taking this day to regroup and prepare to go back to the regular daily routine the next day.

Captain McNulty was making ready to get underway on the following day at first light. The night before he had discussed his plan with Kent and they agreed it was best to leave as soon as possible. The plan was to set a course for Bali in Indonesia. This would be a convenient spot to hop a flight to anywhere and Roger could make preparations for his next extended cruise.

As soon as they reached radio range they would patch in to Commander Lawson at the Naval Base in Broome. Kent could be brought up to date and determine his next step.

In the meantime, preparing to go was hard. It wasn't the fact that they had so much to get ready it was the difficulty saying goodbye to the many friends and newly found loved ones. Teddi was especially emotional. She cried every time she embraced someone that had played a part in making them feel so much at home here on this island. By evening she was spent and had to lie down and rest.

Soon, Ben, Teio and the two boys came to see them. It was very emotional and they sat and talked for hours. Teddi looked at Kent with tear filled eyes and said "Can we come back some day?"

"Of course we can honey. This has become a home for us. The first thing I must do is get our boat back. Then we can regroup and even possibly make this a routine stop on our fishing expeditions. Since I heard that the Sea Rose is still afloat and where she is, I got to thinking how we might even make this our home port. It's closer to the fishing grounds than is Honolulu."

"Could that be possible, darling? Oh that would be so wonderful. Can we build a hut like Adam and Marte's? I've got some wonderful ideas."

"Easy, easy there Mrs. Allison, let's get our boat back first. We've got a few things to clear up before we can make those kinds of plans. First things first.

Teddi laughed and said "Okay I'll wait but I'll also remember what you said and I have witnesses." Ben and Teio laughed along with her.

The next day Teddi and Kent were at the dock waiting to board when Arlis arrived with all the gear he managed to collect during their stay on the island. Roger and his crew were making the final sailing preparations when a shout was heard.

Adam and Marte came running down to the dock. "You can't leave without a bon voyage from us" said Adam as he and Marte embraced each of them.

Adam looked at Kent and said "You are the finest man I ever worked for Captain Allison and I will never forget you. I count you as the best friend a man could have and I will always be there if you need me. Just say the word."

"Thank you Adam" said Kent. "I also count you as someone that I could always trust to be there for me. Be happy in your new found life my good and loyal friend. We hope to see you on a regular basis."

They boarded the schooner and cast off the lines. As they pulled into the harbor towards the open sea a canoe with half a dozen shirtless men rhythmically muscled spade shaped wooden paddles through the water driving the canoe swiftly forward. It pulled along side and for awhile was able to keep pace with the schooner. But slowly as the gap grew larger, separating the two, the canoe turned and stopped.

The Tahitian men saluted the passengers by raising their paddles and cheering them with guttural sounds.

As the schooner cleared the mouth of the harbor, Roger killed the engine and raised the sails settling into a 10 degree heel. The quiet was only broken by the soft rustle of the wind in the sails and the sound of the hull silently cutting through the surf. If you listened intently you could still hear the beautiful goodbye singing of the villagers back on Tongolo Island.

Roger set the charted course for Singaraja in Bali.

CHAPTER FIFTEEN

Robert Craig checked in at Rachel's Inn. He arrived at around noon. It was now early evening and he had waited in the bar most of the afternoon. He hadn't seen hide nor hair of Yang but a steady flow of Captain Morgan's Rum had calmed some of the nervousness, which was evident when he first arrived. He was glad that Yang was late.

He had just settled back and was admiring a comely young lass sitting at the bar and was thinking about making a move to start a conversation when he was suddenly startled back to reality by a rough shove from behind. There was Armond Yang and another tough looking ruffian standing behind him, both with ugly smirks on their faces.

"She's too high class for the likes of you Craig, let's sit over here in the corner" said Yang. "Meet Captain Konka who is joining us. We both want to hear about this big deal that you have for me. And as I said before, it better be good. Bring that bottle of rum and a couple more glasses."

Craig told Yang about getting word from an informant about the drifting Sea Rose. Yang listened intently and said "Are you telling me that no one was aboard the vessel when you took her in tow?"

"That's right. And everything looked intact. There was some slight damage on the port lifeline and a splatter of blood but nothing that indicated storm damage other than there was no dinghy or life raft. They could've been washed over board.

"Hmmm" said Yang. He turned to Konka and said "I wonder what happened to Perez."

"I don't know about anybody named Perez. I'm telling you that the ship was abandoned and I was lucky that the Navy boys didn't want to bother with it. Anyway, I've got her and I'm ready to give you the whole kit and caboodle for a token of the value. I've checked and Allison paid just under a million U.S. for the boat but his insurance value is 1.2 Million. I'm willing to let it go for 25% of the value."

Yang and Konka burst out laughing. "You must be out of your mind Craig. We know why you can't make a legitimate claim on this vessel. I'm willing to make you an offer of $50,000.00 Australian and you'd better be thankful that I'm feeling generous today. If I wasn't ready to retire the High Aim, I'd walk out of here after I stuck a knife between your ribs."

"Come on Yang, I've been square with you. You were the only one I contacted. At least give me $100,000 US. It's well worth every penny and more."

"You sniveling little piece of sheep dung. Who do you think you are, negotiating with me?" He leaped to his feet tipping over the bottle and spilling rum all over the table and on the floor.

Craig grabbed the bottle before it could roll on the floor and screamed "Geez, Yang don't get excited."

"Listen punk" Yang's voice was threateningly low and dripping with peril "I'll make my final offer of $100,000 Australian and it's only because I don't want to waste a trip here with only your slit throat as an accomplishment. Understood??"

"I don't suppose it would be a good time to ask if I could think about it" said a cowering Craig in a quivering voice.

"You've got a lot of balls you little twerp. No pissing contest here, take it or leave it. And I want it delivered outside of the 200 mile Australian fishing zone."

"Okay Yang, you've got a deal."

"Good. Meet me at these coordinates on the 15th of next month. Konka will bring me and my crew. You can arrange your own passage back to Willie Creek. You'll get the 100K when I take possession if everything meets what I'm expecting."

Craig extended his hand to shake with Yang and it was left dangling. Yang said "You've got my word piss ant. You don't need a hand shake." And he stomped out.

When Yang and Konka were alone, Konka said "I think you could have gotten it cheaper Yang. He was very nervous and my first offer would have been even lower."

"Don't worry" said Yang. "I'm very suspicious of this deal. When we make the meet, I want you to have a full crew to run your ship because I'm using all my men to board the Sea Rose and they will all be armed to the teeth. We will make short work of Craig and whoever he might have with him to greet us. Do you still have the two 3 inch guns operative on your ship?"

"I have the two 3 inch guns as well as a 40 millimeter and two 20's. What's the deal?"

"If we're going to do away with Craig, we'll also sink his return vessel so there are no witnesses to any of this." said Yang.

"Well I hope you know what your doing" said Konka "seems like a lot of risk if Craig is hooked up with Perez. He's pretty ruthless."

"Don't worry about Perez. I know his drawbacks and the biggest one is that he bites off more than he can chew. I want that ship. It can easily do 15 knots cruising speed and I bet she'll top 18 or 20 flank speed. She's got 1850 H.P. in the main engine and two auxiliary engines of 265 H.P. each. Her fuel capacity is 140,000 liters which will easily give us a range of 13,000 miles. And that's not counting all the fancy electronic gear that Allison so graciously showed me. Yes, Konka, it will be well worthwhile."

CHAPTER SIXTEEN

The Kon Tiki was finding almost ideal sailing conditions with the wind blowing 15 to 20 knots directly off of the starboard beam. Seas were running 3 to 5 feet and the Kon Tiki was humming along at 7 to 8 knots. McNulty could see that Kent was dying to take the helm so on the second day out he said "It sure would be nice if we had someone aboard that knew something about sailing so he could relieve my helmsman."

Kent smiled and said "You Irishmen really know how to hurt a guy. I know that your helmsmen have been on auto pilot for the last two days and not much steering has been required but I'd sure like to take a crack at the helm without the auto pilot for about an hour or so. Do you think you could accommodate me?"

"Please be my guest Kent" said Roger. "Every once in awhile I do the same thing. There's just no other feeling in the world like taking the wheel of a sailing ship in a fresh breeze off of the beam. Helmsman, turn the wheel over to Captain Allison. Your course is 186 degrees Captain."

Kent relieved the helm and turned off the auto pilot. He immediately felt the wind trying to turn the boat to port and he gave it a little starboard rudder. The boat responded after a slight lag but he over corrected and had to come back to his course of 186. After a few more corrections he settled in to the course and now anticipated each gust or wave that tried to push or pull him one way or the other. This is what sailing the seas is all about. Some day he and Teddi would be at a point in life that they could sail the world in their own cutter. That's a dream that seems pretty far distant given his present unknown circumstances.

The next day Roger tried the marine radio and after a few unsuccessful tries he was finally able to contact Commander Lawson. He called to Kent to come into the radio shack to have some conversation with Lawson.

"Hello Commander Lawson, This is Kent Allison speaking."

"Good afternoon Captain Allison, it's good to finally get to talk to you."

"Thank you, sir. I hope you've got some good news for me."

"Yes. I think the best news is that I've seen your ship and it seems to be intact and is docked at Willie Creek."

"That is good news but tell me, what is the status of my retaking possession? I'm not real familiar with maritime law or what can be done."

"This situation is a bit complicated and to give you all the details over the radio is not wise. I can tell you this. We have a plan to return the vessel to its proper owner. I have received permission from your insurance company, your mortgage holder and Australian authorities to proceed with arrangements but we need your cooperation to finalize the plan. I can fly to Bali when you arrive there and give you the details if that's okay with you."

"Yes, it's absolutely okay with me Commander I think we are due in Bali in about a week. Captain McNulty has one stop to make in Borneo and then next is Singaraja. We can call when we're a few days out to let you know our ETA" replied Kent.

"That's a roger. I'll be quite anxious to meet with you Captain. This could be a very good thing for many people. Lawson out."

"Well, Captain Allison, it sounds like the outlook is getting better each day" said McNulty. "You've got to keep me informed as to the final result of this intriguing adventure. It's almost like a fiction story. I think you and I should celebrate with a dram of single malt. The sun just went behind the yard arm and the cook just told me that dinner will be ready in about one hour."

The two captains relaxed. When Teddi joined them, Kent told her about his conversation with Lawson. Again she was happy but had reservations about the danger that Kent could face.

She said "Call it 'women's intuition' or what ever you want, but I just don't have a good feeling about the whole situation. Darling, you mean more to me than anything in this world and if it meant starting all over again from scratch just to keep you safe, I would do it."

"Don't worry honey, I'm not about to do anything foolish but I want our boat back and we've got the whole Australian Navy behind us so I feel pretty good about it. At the very least, I want to hear his plan."

Teddi just sighed and stared off into space. Why did she have this feeling of impending doom? Maybe she was overreacting. Whatever. She will hear the plan along with her husband and influence him all she could to go back to Tongolo. Yeah sure. Lots of luck lady. "I think I know how far I'd get with that" she thought to herself as she lovingly looked at the man in her life. "I know my husband better than that."

When they were two days out, Kent radioed Commander Lawson and made arrangements to meet him at the Royal Palm Hotel where he, Teddi and Arlis would be staying. The Kon Tiki made port on the 5th of the month at Singaraja, right on schedule.

They said their goodbyes to Captain McNulty, after a trip to the Royal Bank of Scotland where the insurance company had wired funds. Fortunately they had cargo coverage which they lost during the hijacking. These funds would pay for the debt they had accumulated to this point and would hold them over until the final disposition of the Sea Rose.

They checked into the hotel and found that Commander Lawson had not yet arrived. Kent left word for him to contact them after he checked in and they went to their rooms for some well deserved rest.

****

Kent and Teddi were napping when the phone rang and jolted them from a deep sleep. It was Commander Lawson. He had just arrived and asked if they could meet him for dinner in the hotel dining room at 7:00. Kent agreed and said that he was quite anxious to finally get some direction as to when and where they were headed.

LATER THAT EVENING

"Good evening Commander Lawson. I'm Kent Allison and this is my wife Teddi."

"Good evening and it's a pleasure to finally meet with both of you. Hopefully this can be the start of solving this seemingly hopeless dilemma the two of you have been facing for these last several months."

"We certainly hope so Commander" said Teddi "but I'm very concerned about my husband's safety. Will this be dangerous?"

"Now Teddi" said Kent "I'm sure the Commander will explain everything in detail. Let's just listen."

"Well Captain Allison, your wife has every right to be concerned. These are very dangerous people as I'm sure you've already experienced. The plan to get your boat back in your hands and to rid the seas of Captain Yang and his merciless crew is not going to be easy. In fact if everything doesn't go as planned it could be very difficult. I want you to know that right up front. Your participation would be helpful but not vital."

"I didn't figure that this was going to be a cakewalk Commander. The good things don't come easy. I'm willing to take some chances with the backing of the Australian Navy. Let's hear your plan."

"I knew it!!! I knew it!!! He's going to be right in the face of danger" said Teddi.

"We'll do everything possible to keep Captain Allison out of harms way Mrs. Allison. Now let me lay it out for you. First of all the four of us will fly back to the Navy base at Broome. I assume your First Mate is still on board with helping you."

"Arlis insists on helping where ever he can." answered Kent.

"After we are back on the base, I will set up quarters for you and the Mrs. in a bungalow in the dependents area. It will be temporary quarters as long as you are acting as an unpaid consultant to the Australian Navy. Your mate can stay in the barracks with the Navy Seals who will be accompanying us on the mission. We'll travel to Willie Creek and you can check out your ship. I've taken the liberty of sending a repair group to make any necessary repairs or upgrades so she should be ready to sail."

"We'll make contact with Robert Craig and make sure he's still cooperating. Craig has met with Yang and under our direction has set up a rendezvous on the 15th. The squad of Navy Seals will arrive as well as six sailors in civilian garb to act as crew members. We'll get underway in plenty of time to make our rendezvous with Yang. When we reach the coordinates my ship, the Stuart, a Navy frigate, will be far enough out of sight so that it will only be a blip on their radar screen. They won't be able to tell that it's a Navy warship. She can do 35 knots at flank speed so when we need her she'll be there pretty quick."

"Also as further back up, the Intrepid a Missile Cruiser with a helicopter gun ship on board will be just out of radar range. The copter will be warmed up and crew ready in a minutes notice. We're assuming Yang will come aboard from his ship the High Aim No 6 with a crew to take over the Sea Rose. That's when we'll make our move with the Seals and once they are subdued the Stuart should arrive and neutralize the High Aim No 6."

"The High Aim is pretty much of a scow with not much fire power so there shouldn't be a problem taking her over. After that we'll take the whole kit and caboodle back to Broome and turn them over to the feds."

"As a bonus Captain, there is a good sized reward offered which we, as Navy, cannot accept but you can, although you'll probably have to split it with Craig."

"Sounds like a plan, Commander" said Kent. "When can we leave? I've waited long enough and I'm anxious to get rolling."

"First thing in the morning" said Lawson "I've already arranged the reservations to fly us to Broome."

Teddi was very quiet.

CHAPTER SEVENTEEN

The next morning the four of them traveled to the capital city of Denpasar. The airport there had direct flights to Broome. When they landed in Australia, a Navy bus picked them up to transport them to the base. After they got settled in their bungalow, Teddi asked if it was possible to go into town the next day to reestablish her wardrobe. It was kind of meager since many of her things were left on the Sea Rose and she wasn't sure what was still there. Kent agreed and reminded her that this was going to be her quarters while he was away and she should make herself at home as much as possible. She became very quiet again and reflected on the dangerous mission that her husband was going to face in the near future. Maybe a little shopping trip would get her mind off things and make the day a little brighter. Shopping always gave her a lift.

The next day while Teddi was shopping, Kent, Arlis and Lawson took a copter ride to Willie Creek. They met Robert Craig at one of the ram-shackled shacks where he headquartered and also lived. Kent's first impression of Craig was not a good one. He could feel a sense of insincerity right away. He was anxious to get aboard the Sea Rose to see what was missing and the overall condition.

Craig said "I'll meet you at the boat in a few minutes. I've got some other business to clear up this morning."

On the way while walking to the boat Arlis said "I don't like him boss. I'm going to make it my main job to keep an eye on him while we're underway."

"That's probably a wise decision, Arlis." said Lawson. "He's not one of my favorite people either."

After they boarded the Sea Rose, Kent relaxed and felt better. She seemed in good shape, at first glance, and he almost had the feeling that she was also glad to see him, as well. He started his inspection on the bridge, checking all the navigation instruments and controls. Everything seemed to be shipshape. Next he toured the main deck, checking the anchor windlass on the bow, the bow thruster and worked his way astern checking all the running rigging. He noticed that a repair had been made to the lifeline on the port side. It looked solid.

Next he went below to the engine room. He mentioned to Arlis who accompanied him "Boy I sure wish Jacques was here to look at these engines and the generators. Let's take a quick gander and then we'll run them if the oil and filters look okay."

"I'll climb down and check the bilges and the bilge pumps while you doing that, boss. Looks a little dirty down there. I'm probably going to spend some time cleaning especially that forward bilge" said Arlis.

After a few hours in the engine room and bilges they checked the cargo holds and the three blast freezers. The freezers might need a tune up, maybe Freon, before they did any serious fishing. But for now they would be okay.

After that the living quarters and galley were next. Some clean up was needed but all in all it wasn't too bad. They needed provisions, of course, but they would only get what was needed for the trip coming up. What with Kent, Lawson, Arlis, six sailors and 10 Navy Seals they would need food for nineteen men for at least four days to be safe.

Kent thought it would be a good idea to check the bottom and the running gear. He located his scuba gear and was about to strap on his tank when Arlis appeared with his already on.

"This is my job boss. You can be the topside man in case I need anything. I need a scraper and wire brush. Is there one in the tool box?" Arlis said in a firm manner.

Kent chuckled "Okay I'll defer to you on this one. Just be careful and don't try to get every barnacle scraped off."

Arlis went over the side. Kent followed the bubbles from the bow back to the stern as Arlis made his bottom inspection. Then he could hear scraping and tapping under the stern where the props, prop shafts and rudders were located. No doubt they were covered with barnacles from sitting idle for so long. Scraping was necessary for the props to run true without vibration at high R.P.M.

Arlis then worked on the bottom, getting the heaviest concentration off but the rest would have to wait until dry dock time. Fortunately Kent had insisted on a good bottom paint in Taiwan so it wasn't as bad as it could have been. The boat was sound.

When they met with Lawson later they agreed that one more day of cleaning and a few minor instrument settings and they'd be ready to sail.

They planned on leaving the next evening for the Navy Base and start briefing the crew and the Seals. Lawson will turn over temporary command of his ship, the frigate Stuart, to his executive officer, Lt. Commander Tim Gates, since he will be on the Sea Rose with the main occupational force. The frigate will play a large part in this plan in neutralizing the High Aim No 6 but the main area of contact will be on the Sea Rose.

After a day of cleaning up odds and ends, Kent and Arlis were happy with the ship. They took the copter back to Broome and decided to take it easy and have a final evening of complete relaxation. The hard part was coming up.

The next few days were filled with briefing, planning, coordinating with the Stuart and reestablishing contact with the Intrepid. All vessels must be on split second schedules in case the plan went awry. Weather will play a factor as always but the outlook for calm seas was in the forecast. There were no lows in evidence for weeks. The occasional tropical afternoon shower was the only foul weather in the forecast and that presented no problem.

Kent and Teddi spent a quiet evening at home in the bungalow the night before the strike force was to leave. They were reminiscing about where they would visit when they start sailing on the Cabo Rico after they rebuild their resources from commercial fishing.

Teddi said "Honey, do you think we could go to that spot in Borneo where we stopped briefly on the Kon Tiki? It was so beautiful. We could put in there and then go overland to Papasena where, I heard, is a good jumping off spot to take a helicopter into the Foja Mountains. Back in those mountains there are spots where there have been no humans for hundreds of years. There is no big game or snakes. Maybe this is where the Garden of Eden was."

"That sounds like a good place I'd like to be right now, my dear. It certainly would be better than where I'm going the day after tomorrow." said Kent.

"Oh Kent, I'm so afraid for you. Please promise me that you'll be careful."

"I promise, Teddi. I want to get back to you as quickly and as safely as possible."

The next morning at day break, Lawson, Kent and Arlis joined the sailors and the Seals on Pier 12 where they boarded a small troop ship to be transported to Willie Creek. All their gear including automatic weapons and ammo had been loaded the day before. By 8:00 A.M. they were underway. Teddi and the other wives were all on the dock bidding their loved ones good bye.

They arrived late that afternoon and spent the rest of the day and into the evening loading every thing on the Sea Rose. The sailors and the Seals spent the night on the transport since there wouldn't be enough bunk space on the Sea Rose for all of them.

The Sea Rose got underway at first light the next day. Seas were calm and no rain was forecast. They should make good time and probably arrive at the coordinates before morning. The trip was uneventful so far. The Navy crew was efficient and handled the Sea Rose very well.

Kent was asleep in his cabin when Arlis gently awakened him at about 5:00 A.M.

"What's up Arlis?" said Kent.

"Commander Lawson thought I'd better wake you, sir" said Arlis.

"You sound concerned. Is something wrong?" asked Kent.

"Well we're not sure. But a thick blanket of fog has settled in. It may lift at day break but as of now it's pretty bad. And we're very close to the coordinates."

Kent quickly pulled on a pair of pants and he and Arlis made tracks for the bridge.

The fog seemed so thick that it could be chopped into chunks like cheese. The Sea Rose groped her way into it like a blind man in an unfamiliar room and all around her the fog seemed to press closer. The fog mesmerized Kent and he felt a bit of vertigo, but he forcibly rejected the sensation and stared ahead. He ordered idle speed and stationed a sailor on the fog horn with orders to sound it every 30 seconds. He knew the High Aim was in the area and he didn't want a collision. He would rather that they knew that he was in the area and hopefully let him know where they were.

The quartermaster was intent on the radar screen when he reported. "Captain I have a blip."

"Where away sailor?" said Kent.

"Two points off the starboard bow at a distance of about 300 yards." said the quartermaster.

"Stop engines and let's keep very quiet. Listen for any sound."

As they listened, the sun broke over the horizon and the fog very slowly seemed to get a little less dense.

The lookout reported "I see a ship, Captain."

"Where away?"

"On the starboard beam. Looks like she's dead in the water."

Kent and Lawson looked starboard with night binoculars.

"If that's the ship we're meeting it looks a lot different than the High Aim No 6" said Kent.

"Your right" said Lawson. "That ship has some fire power. Look at those three inch guns, one forward and one aft. Seems to be quite a few men aboard also. This may not be as easy as we thought. Let's hail them. Do you see any name or identifying numbers?"

"You won't find any identification on that vessel" Craig piped up. "Not many ships are painted black as night and have a profile like that one."

"Do you know it Craig?" said Kent.

"Unfortunately I do, Captain" said Craig. "It's a pirate ship under the command of Captain Konka. He was with Yang when I met them in Bali. I didn't expect that they would use his ship but since they are, they must have other plans than to just take the Sea Rose and gently fade away."

"She looks fast and heavily armed" said Lawson. "Do we have a location on the Stuart, quartermaster?"

"I've got nothing on the radar sir."

"We don't want to break radio silence, it will just alert the pirates on what we have planned."

"The pirate ship is not as fast as your frigate, Commander, but the Stuart would have a tough time catching her if she decides to run. It is said that Konka is not afraid of a sea battle either." said Craig.

As they watched the black ship come out of the fog and pull along side, Yang appeared on the wing of the bridge with a bull horn in his hand.

"Heave to Sea Rose. We are coming aboard." he called.

No sooner did he say that when four crew members from the black ship threw grappling hooks, with stout lines attached, across the open water between the ships. All four hooks caught and held on the life lines of the Sea Rose. Two were aft and two were forward. The sailors hauled them in using winches and when the ships were close enough other sailors jumped aboard the Sea Rose and threw a bight of a hawser on the bits and made them fast to their own ship. The Sea Rose was in effect married to the sleek black ship.

When two of the Australian sailors attempted to resist the boarding, they were swarmed under by the pirates and knocked to the deck. If there had been any doubt before, there was none now. This was a forceful boarding and it was happening very fast and very efficiently. It was not quite going according to plan.

The Navy Seals were poised to react but Lawson held them back. He didn't expect this bold action so quickly. Yang had taken the element of surprise away with his very fast and well planned boarding almost as if he anticipated this. Next, Yang and his pirate band swarmed over the rail. All carried AK 47 automatics. There were eight of them plus Yang. They meant business and they were very experienced at this type of business.

CHAPTER EIGHTEEN

Yang and two of his men raced to the bridge. Three pirates went aft and three forward to neutralize the crew. When Yang got to the bridge he spied Craig and said "What ever you and Perez had planned for me Craig will not be enough to thwart me from taking this ship."

"What are you talking about Yang?" said Craig. "I told you before, I don't know any Perez."

"You know exactly what I mean. Wait a minute… that's Captain Allison. Who is this other fine gentleman? He doesn't look like any of your scurvy crew. In fact the whole crew is a little too clean cut for the likes of you. I knew you had something up your sleeve but I had it figured all wrong. I thought it was Perez—what's going on?"

"We can still make a deal Yang" said Craig. "I was forced into this by Commander Lawson here. I tried to reach you to warn you but couldn't get through."

"Hmm, yes I knew were trying to reach me" said Yang. "I was confused, but now—Okay. Allison you and Lawson, stand over there and keep your hands in sight.

You!!! Take our good friend Mr. Craig over to speak with Konka. Tell him I said to loosen Mr. Craig's tongue in any way he sees fit."

"No. No. Yang. I'm with you" screamed Craig as he was being dragged away. He was in great distress and whimpering as the pirate roughly threw him across the rails to the pirate ship and into the waiting arms of leering pirate crew members. He knew his fate."

"Now gentlemen it appears we must make plans of what to do with you two" said Yang.

But Yang's words were cut short by the din of violent conflict suddenly splitting the calm. There was a fusillade of automatic gun fire from the stern. It sounded as though a real fire fight had broken out. Several guns were discharging multiple rounds of ammo.

Screams were heard and they were followed by groans.

Yang screamed "What's going on back there? You two get back there and see what's happening. I'll watch these two."

But when Yang's attention was drawn away by the gun fire, Lawson and Allison dove through the hatch and out on the bridge wing. Yang saw the movement in his peripheral vision and fired several shots at the movement but was too late to do any great damage. He heard a yelp so he may have hit one of them. As he started to follow them out of the hatch, Lawson got off a shot in Yang's direction, missing him but enough to slow him down.

"Lawson, are you hit?" said Kent.

"He nicked my shoulder" said Eric. "No problem, it wasn't a direct hit. I've had worse."

Yang was trying to position himself for a better shot when all of a sudden he was knocked from his feet by a huge Polynesian body hurtling through the air that hit him from behind.

Arlis had been below since he had stood the mid watch and had gone to his cabin after he had awakened Kent. He thought he'd catch a few winks before the rendezvous with the pirates but before he could drift off to sleep the activity started up on the bridge. He quietly stole up the interior ladder leading to the bridge when calamity broke loose on the stern. He got to the bridge just as Yang got off a few shots. That's when he sprung into action, rushed in and slammed Yang to the deck.

Yang's gun went flying and Arlis pinned him down screaming "Captain, Captain I've got him."

Kent and Eric peered around the bulkhead and saw what Arlis had done. They clamored back onto the bridge just as one of Yang's pirates entered the bridge from the other side. As the pirate pointed his AK 47 towards Kent, Lawson got off two quick shots and both hit home. The pirate flipped over the rail and was dead when he hit the water.

Lawson grabbed his hand held radio and called the Seals leader. "This is Lawson, Lieutenant, what is your status?"

"I'm on the fantail with four of my Seals. We've neutralized the pirates back here. All are dead or wounded except for one who ran forward. Three of my seals went forward to the fo'c'sle. I don't know their status" replied the lieutenant over the radio.

"We took care of the one pirate that ran forward and we have Yang in custody" said Lawson. "We know of three or four other pirates forward. They had captured and locked the crew in the forward Bo'sn's locker. Tell your men to use caution. They are ruthless."

Suddenly shots rang out up forward and the three Seals took cover. They were pinned down and reported, to the lieutenant, over their self contained radio, of their predicament. Lawson heard the report over his radio and said "Come on Arlis let's give them a hand."

"Here Kent, take this AK 47 and hold Yang here while we help those guys."

Kent grabbed the gun and pointed it at Yang. He said "Don't give me an excuse to use this Yang" as Eric and Arlis headed for the fo'c'sle.

With all his attention on Yang, Kent did not hear a pirate sneaking up on him from behind. The pirate swung the butt of his gun and hit Kent from behind with a smashing blow to the head. Kent saw a blinding light before he slipped into oblivion.

The pirate ran onto the bridge quickly followed by the other two. They had scurried down one deck after they pinned down the Seals with a barrage of bullets and worked their way up to the bridge the same way Arlis had.

The first one bellowed "Let's get back to the ship. These guys are pros."

"Give me a gun first" said Yang. "I want to finish off this pain in the ass Allison."

"No time captain, here they come and it looks like Konka is cutting the hawsers. He's going to make a run for it and leave us if we don't jump for it."

Konka's intention was to run. He knew that the operation had suddenly turned sour. He saw the frigate coming hard and knew he'd better move now or be captured before he could move away from the Sea Rose.

Yang was the first to jump just as the ships were separating. He made it easily. The next pirate also made it but his feet slipped and he was hanging on with two hands on the lifeline. The next one jumped, he hit the side of the black ship but was too low to grab the lifeline. He plunged into the water just as Konka gunned both engines and turned away from the Sea Rose. The stern of black ship swung towards the Sea Rose and bounced off just as the man hit the water. The port screw was churning the water in an effort to get the big ship moving and created a suction that pulled him under the stern. The water turned a bright red as his body was chewed up by the fast turning screw. The third pirate decided not to jump when he saw the fate of his shipmate. He threw down his gun and raised his hands as Lawson and Arlis returned to the bridge.

Yang easily climbed over the lifeline and headed to the pirate ships bridge. His cohort yelled "Help me Captain, I'm slipping."

"To hell with you, idiot. You and your men have caused me to lose a prize. Help yourself or die." said Yang as he left the man barely hanging on.

The ship started to gain headway which caused a rolling and pitching. It soon was enough to loosen the pirates grip, he screamed and splashed into the wake of the black pirate ship, flailed helplessly in the turbulent water and then slipped below the surface to drown.

Back on the Sea Rose, Arlis grabbed a wet towel and gently swabbed the cut on Kent's head. Kent started coming around but was disoriented. Arlis told him that everything was okay and just try to relax until he felt a little better. Kent sat up and had a glazed look in his eyes but stayed quiet as Arlis suggested.

Lawson gathered his men and asked the lieutenant for a condition report. The lieutenant said "Two of my seals are badly wounded sir and are in need of medical help. Three more have minor wounds which we can take care of. The sailors are in good shape. Three of them were roughed up by the pirates but just need first aid. It looks like you caught one yourself sir. Better have the medic look at it."

"I'll have the Intrepid send a copter for the two badly wounded men and any one else you feel should go, lieutenant" said Lawson. "But we still have work to do."

"Radioman, get the Stuart on the radio and patch it up to the bridge" said Kent.

"I've already got them on the horn sir. They are awaiting your orders."

"This is Commander Lawson, who have I got?"

"This is Gates, Commander we have the pirate ship in sight. The fog has lifted and she's going hell bent for election north northeast."

"Chase her down Gates and make a request that she heave to." said Lawson.

"Will do sir but do you think she will?" came the answer.

"Probably not but you must do so before firing on her."

"Aye, aye sir. Do we have permission to engage her in combat if we get no response or if she fires upon us?" said Gates.

"Permission granted. Sea Rose out." confirmed Lawson.

"Quartermaster do you have the Intrepid on your radar screen?" yelled Lawson.

"Yes sir and she's in radio range" came the answer.

"Intrepid, Intrepid this is the Sea Rose. Come in please." Lawson spoke into the marine radio.

"Hello Sea Rose. What is your status?" answered the Intrepid.

"We have engaged the pirates and subdued them. We have two badly wounded Navy Seals that need evacuation and are in need of immediate medical attention. Can you send a copter with a basket to retrieve them?" queried Lawson.

"Wilco Commander. The medical copter will leave immediately. Do you have need of the missile carrying copter?" answered the Intrepid.

"That depends on your location and if you are in range with your missiles," said Lawson.

"We have the pirate on our scope. He is presently out of range but if he holds his present course he's coming right at us and will be within range shortly."

"Okay. Let's hold that copter until the Stuart makes contact. Sea Rose out" said Lawson.

ABOARD THE STUART

"Sea Rose, Sea Rose this is the Stuart, we're gaining on them sir. Should I contact them?" said Gates.

"Yes. Tell them to heave to by order of the Australian Navy" ordered Commander Lawson.

Suddenly, the stern three inch battery of the pirate ship fired on the Stuart. The shell whistled over their heads, missing, but not by much. They fired again and the next one was even closer. They were finding the range.

Lt. Commander Gates quickly grabbed the P.A. system mike and screamed "Commence fire. Commence fire."

All forward batteries fired, lobbing shells at the black pirate ship. Two of them made hits but not in a critical spot. It didn't slow the pirate down.

The pirate returned fire and one of their three inch shells made a direct hit on the Stuart's forward battery and killed the gun crew. Shrapnel wounded several others.

"Intrepid, Intrepid this is the Stuart. Come in." called Gates.

"This is the Intrepid. Go ahead Stuart" came the reply.

"We've taken a pretty solid hit and both forward batteries are inoperative. Can you assist with missiles?" requested Gates on the Stuart.

"We just got in range. Missile number one will fly in about 30 seconds" answered the Intrepid.

"That's a 'roger'. We'll back off a little." the Stuart came back.

"Missile number one away. Missile number two stand by" reported Intrepid.

"I see the vapor trail of the missile sir" said the Stuart Officer of the Deck "It's coming this way and coming fast. I'm glad we moved when we did."

The missal made a direct hit and created a gigantic explosion on the pirate ship. A huge fireball surged up from the doomed ship and lit up an already bright sky.

"Looks like they hit her in a fuel tank sir— My God look at her burn" said the Officer of the Deck as he gave an uncontrolled shudder.

Suddenly the second missile hit, immediately after the first one, and it made a direct hit in an ammunition magazine. The explosion shock wave rattled the glass on the Stuart and the resonance was felt and heard back on the Sea Rose. The pirate ship was obscured by smoke and flames. It was obliterated.

When the smoke cleared, the ship was in two distinct pieces. The bow had already settled and sank slowly from sight. The stern stayed afloat a little longer but then it too disappeared below the surface.

Debris floated in a wide arc, thrown clear by the gigantic blast. A few bodies were evident, some were slowly trying to swim, others were missing body parts and not moving.

"Stuart. Stuart. Lower the zodiacs and stand by to pick up survivors" called Lawson on the radio.

"Aye, aye sir. I'll report what we find. Can you send the medical copter here after they pick up your wounded? I've got some wounded here that need more help than what we can give them" requested Gates.

"Wilco. It should be there shortly. Sea Rose out" quietly answered Lawson.

Lawson slowly turned to Kent, who sat glassy eyed in the captain's chair, and in a quivering voice he said "I'm sorry, Captain, there has been a terrible loss of life, as well as some badly wounded men. None of us anticipated this. Some of my own men and of course most of the pirates have been killed. We had to use maximum force to subdue the black pirate ship, which was formidable. We had no idea it would be present. We've sunk her and Zodiacs from my ship are now checking for survivors."

"I know how you must feel, Commander, even though the pirates brought it on themselves, it's still human lives that were wasted and you can't help but feel remorse."

CHAPTER NINETEEN

The two Zodiacs from the Stuart were lowered into the water with the boat davits. As soon as they splashed down, the 100 H.P. outboard motors were started and they shoved off to search for survivors.

The first boat found four pirates floating in a group. Two were badly burned. The other two had minor scrapes and slight burns and the four were loaded into the boat. The coxswain immediately headed back to the Stuart to give the burned survivors medical treatment and to confine the other two.

The second boat could only find two survivors. Both were burned but not seriously. The coxswain circled the area where the ship went down but found no others alive. There was one dead body in a life jacket afloat but nothing else except debris from the sunken ship. The bow hook and coxswain lifted the dead man aboard and they headed back to the ship.

On the way they passed Number one Zodiac who said that he would take one more look around for possible survivors. Number one scoured the area and was ready to turn back when the bow hook yelled "I see something just dead ahead. Might be a dead body. It doesn't appear to be moving."

"Grab him with the boat hook and pull him along side. We can take him back and at least he'll have a proper burial" said the coxswain.

After he was along side, both men grabbed on to the life jacket and hoisted him aboard.

"This guy's still breathing" said the bow hook. "Just barely, but he is breathing. Let's get him back in a hurry, he's burned pretty bad but he might make it."

Back on board the Stuart, the medical helicopter had just lifted off with the wounded men from both the Sea Rose and the Stuart and was en route back to the Intrepid where there was a fully equipped sick bay with doctors.

After the Navy corpsmen examined the pirates he determined that at least three of them needed further medical help, one was still unconscious. After consulting with Commander Lawson they decided to hightail it back to Broome where they could all be treated and the less severe confined in the brig. The more serious ones could be treated and admitted to the base hospital where they could be under guard until the Customs Division could direct the Naval Command as to what to do next.

Back on the Sea Rose, Arlis took command since Kent was still feeling woozy. He obviously had a concussion and the medical corpsman ordered him to rest, checking him periodically to make sure he was conscious.

Arlis charted a course back to the Navy base in Broome. The Stuart would get back at least eight hours before them.

Commander Lawson reviewed the casualties for his report, to be submitted when they docked in Broome. He counted three sailors dead on the Stuart. No fatalities on the Sea Rose. Three seriously wounded on the Stuart and two Seals on the Sea Rose. The minor wounds included Captain Allison with a concussion, Commander Lawson with a wounded shoulder, two Sea Rose sailors with abrasions and two Seals with minor gun shot wounds.

The pirates did not fare so well. The state of the art pirate ship was sunk, all High Aim pirates were dead and there were six survivors from the black pirate ship. Three of them seriously injured or burned. The fates of Captain Yang and Captain Konka were unknown but they were presumed to be dead.

The Sea Rose suffered some damage from stray bullets but nothing serious. The Stuart had some major damage from the one direct hit that she suffered forward of the bridge. She would be in the yards for awhile with that damage. Commander Lawson would not be going to sea, for some time, on his command.

The Sea Rose docked at the base the next day. Teddi was among the wives waiting on the dock. When she saw Kent walking down the gangway she started crying. And when she saw the bandage on his head and the pallor on his face her knees buckled and Kent had to grab her to keep her from falling. He hugged her to him as she sobbed with happiness.

"Oh my darling" she blubbered "are you okay? I was so worried. Are you hurt?"

"I'm fine" he said "It's over now sweetie. Time to stop worrying. Let's go home and I'll tell you everything."

As they were leaving the medical corpsman said "Captain Allison I'd like you to check in at the base hospital and let the doctors take a look to make sure there's no fracture. Sometime this afternoon will be fine."

"Okay Doc. Will do" replied Kent.

They went to their bungalow and Kent kicked back in the Lazy Boy. He said "Grab me a cold beer Teddi and I'll brief you on the trip."

"Sorry Mister. You'll only get a cold iced tea until after the doctor examines you and then only if he says it's O.K." said Teddi.

"Okay, okay, then sit down and let me tell you about it so we can get over there and get a clearance. I'm dying for a beer."

Kent went over the whole saga and Teddi moaned and groaned all the while.

Kent reported to the Navy doctors on the base hospital and they pronounced him fit. No fractures were found and the concussion was only slight. He still had a slight headache but no more dizziness or disorientation. The doctors suggested that he curtail any rigorous physical activity for a few days but that was the only restriction.

While he was there he saw Commander Lawson who had stopped in to have his shoulder wound looked at and dressed.

Lawson said "Oh good. I was going to get in touch with you Kent. It appears that we got a break on the pirate ship survivors. One of the ones they fished out was none other than Captain Yang himself."

"That guy must lead a charmed life Eric. Do you have him in the brig?" said Kent.

"No. In fact he's right here in the hospital. He's still unconscious and under guard. They thought he was dead when they fished him out." said Lawson.

"Well what happens now?" said Kent.

"First of all we'll have to see if he's going to survive. He's burned and in pretty bad shape. And then if he's physically able he'll be confined in a federal lock up until he goes to trial. I'll estimate that the trial won't take place for another year, if we're lucky. The wheels of justice turn slowly." answered Lawson.

"I'll abide by my agreement to testify at his trial but your people will have to give me plenty of notice. I've got to get back to making a living catching tuna as soon as I get the Sea Rose seaworthy again. I've got some debt to pay."

"There's more good news, Kent. The Customs Division is going to submit your name to receive the entire $350,000.00 reward for the capture of Yang. And no split with anyone, since Robert Craig is dead and of course Australian Naval Personnel are not eligible. Can you use the money?"

"I'm speechless Eric" said Kent. "You have no idea on how relieved I am. I can hardly wait to tell Teddi. This will also give me a chance to show my appreciation to Arlis and Adam. I just wish Jacques was here to benefit from this."

"Let's have dinner at the officers club tonight, Kent" said Eric. "Lieutenant Commander Gates may join us. We can celebrate a job well done."

"Sounds good to me Eric" answered Kent. I'd better get back and give Teddi the good news."

The next day dawned sunny and bright and typified the attitude of the Allison couple. It was great to be alive and well, and to have their beloved Sea Rose back.

Kent said "Let's go to the boat and take an inventory of what needs to be done. Then I've got to make arrangements with the Navy as to what part of it they will be responsible for and what we may have to arrange with an outside contractor. Arlis and I can handle some of it ourselves. I'd like you to take a look at the galley and stores."

"I'm ready' said Teddi. "In fact I'm anxious to get back into the safe and sane routine of commercial fishing again. Let's go."

Once aboard the Sea Rose, they felt at home again and Arlis was already on board checking the fishing gear. He said "Captain, if it's alright with you I'd like to bunk back here on the boat now. I can get more done and I just feel better on something that floats."

"I think that's a good idea Arlis" said Kent. "In fact Teddi and I and will probably join you very soon."

As they were busy checking the well being of the Sea Rose, they didn't notice a jeep that pulled up on the dock. It was a Security Patrol Vehicle and a Security Sailor was walking up the gangway.

When he reached the main deck he saluted smartly and said to Kent "Permission to come aboard sir."

"Permission granted, sailor. What can I do for you?" said Kent.

"Sir, a man showed up at the Main Gate asking to come aboard the Sea Rose. He claims to be a crew member." said the sailor.

"That's strange" said Kent. "Did he identify himself?"

"No sir, but he's standing on the dock right next to the jeep." answered the sailor.

When Kent gazed down at the dock, he saw a familiar figure standing there. He cried out "Jacques, Teddi it's Jacques." And he ran down the gangway onto the dock and grabbed Jacques in a huge embrace, laughing all the way.

Shortly behind him was Teddi, tears streaming down her face, she squeezed herself between them hugging Jacques as tight as she could. Jacques couldn't contain himself and the tears of joy flowed from him also.

They were still entwined in a three way embrace when Arlis came down the gangway and hugged the whole group. He said "I guess you must have found the life raft we threw over."

Jacques said "That was what saved my life Arlis and I will always be indebted to you."

"That's okay partner. The next time we get hijacked you can save me."

Kent said "Let's go aboard. We've all got a lot of catching up to do."

As they were going aboard, the Security Sailor said "Well I guess that answers my question. Have a nice day folks."

The four of them went aboard and relaxed in the salon. Teddi got the men a round of beers and some snacks and Kent said "Jacques tell us what happened and how you managed to get here."

Jacques said "My only escape was to jump over the side to get away from those Chinamen and I thought I was a goner until all of a sudden here comes the life raft flying through the air. I had no idea how or who threw it but it saved my life. It was pitch black that night so I paddled the raft as fast and as far as I could all night long."

"By morning I was exhausted but I was out of sight of both boats so I slept. When I awoke the sun was beating down on me unmercifully. Thank God you equipped the raft with survival food and water and the equipment I needed to keep going. I lost track of how many days I drifted but I got by with fish that I caught and rain water to drink."

"Finally after a week or longer I was picked up by a tramp steamer heading to Darwin, Australia. I was able to recuperate on the way and when I got there I contacted the local authorities and told them my sad story. They were very apprehensive as to how true it was since at that time the Sea Rose had not yet been found."

"I got a job on the docks since I was broke and figured I would work my way back to Bali. One day several weeks later, a policeman that I had made a speaking acquaintance with, stopped me and asked what ship I had been on. When I told him about the Sea Rose, he told me the story about the sting and your encounter with Captain Yang. That was the first I knew that you guys had escaped.

I took the few belongings and money that I had and made my way here. You don't know how happy I am to find you guys well and the ship in one piece.

The next few hours were spent bringing Jacques up to date on the rescue of the Sea Rose crew and capture of Armond Yang.

CHAPTER TWENTY

The refurbishing of the Sea Rose was well underway and Captain Allison was considering making a plan to continue with commercial fishing. He asked Arlis his opinion on the bottom of the boat.

"What do you think, Arlis?" said Kent. "You took a look before we went out. She seemed to be a little sluggish to me. Do you think we should go into dry dock?"

"It might not be a bad idea Captain. She had quite an accumulation of barnacles that were too heavy for me to scrape off" said Arlis.

"I'll check with the Yard Master for availability today" said Kent.

As Kent was walking towards the yard office he saw Eric Lawson. "Hi Eric" he called.

"Hello Kent" replied Lawson "I was just coming to see you. I have good news. The Customs Group has approved the reward money and they want to know where you want it sent."

"Wow. That's as timely as you can get. My finances were depleting quickly. Have them wire it to my bank in Honolulu. I've got the routing and account number back on the ship."

"Sure. I can walk back with you. Where are you headed now?" said Lawson.

"I'm on my way to the yard office to arrange for a dry dock. I was wondering how I was going to pay for it. Bottom work is to be paid by me. Now I know I can handle it okay."

After Kent made the arrangements and found that he could make the move in a few days, they went back to the Sea Rose.

"Good news Teddi. The Customs boys have approved the $350,000.00. I'm instructing them to wire it to our dwindling account in Honolulu. The balance was getting close to overdraft after the next couple of automatic withdrawals for the boat payment."

"Are you going to set up the accounts for the men like we discussed?" asked Teddi.

"I am, honey" said Kent. After we pay the expenses which should be less than $25,000.00, I'll divide the rest in five equal parts. You and I will each have a share and one share each to Jacques, Arlis and Adam. I'll set up a money market account for each and it will be theirs to draw on as they see fit."

"You're a fair man Kent" said Eric. "Give me the routing and account and I'll take care of it today."

After Eric left Kent said "Let's get the boys up here so we can tell them. They'll be happy to hear it, I'm sure."

Kent was right. They were overjoyed. They discussed an itinerary. Both Arlis and Jacques had suggestions.

Arlis said "Captain, after the ship goes into dry dock, I'm not going to be of much use. Would it be okay if I went to Tongola to tell Adam about his share and possibly recruit some villagers as crew members?"

"I think that's an excellent idea, Arlis" said Kent. "We could probably pick up some crew here and steam over to Tongola to pick you up and the rest of the crew on the way to the fishing grounds. See what kind of arrangements you can make with Captain McNulty on the radio."

"Captain, if you want to look for crew here I became acquainted with an Italian family that has three sons that are strong, young seamen and they are available. Do you want to talk to them?" said Jacques.

"Another good idea. I'm going to be a little more cautious this time" said Kent. "When can they come aboard?"

"I can check it out today" said Jacques.

The following day, Arlis came to the bungalow and knocked on the door. When Kent answered he said "Okay Captain, I was able to get Captain McNulty on the satellite phone. He's going to put in at Singaraja on Bali in three days. He'll be making port on Tongola in less than a month. He said I can have passage at no charge if I work as crew. I agreed. I'm catching a flight to Bali tomorrow morning."

"That sounds great Arlis" said Kent. Adam will be glad to see you and hear about our windfall. I'm going to talk to the young men that Jacques knows this afternoon. With any kind of luck we'll have us a solid crew by the time we leave Tongola in about a month or so."

Arlis left to get his sea bag packed.

When Kent got to the Sea Rose later that afternoon, Jacques was already there with three handsome, strapping young men.

Jacques said "Captain Allison I'd like to introduce you to the three young men that would like to join our crew. The oldest one is Matteo, next is Giuseppe, and the youngest but the biggest and probably the strongest is Antonio."

"I'm happy to meet you boys. Well, you certainly all look healthy and strong enough to be seamen. What kind of experience do you have?" said Kent.

Matteo said "I have my Able Body Seaman's papers, sir, Giuseppe is a certified diesel mechanic and has his Fireman's papers, Antonio is still an apprentice but he is very strong and has been around fishing boats his whole life, as all of us have. We are looking for a permanent berth on a commercial fishing boat and we are available now."

"You come highly recommended by a trusted friend and crew member. You understand the amount of pay is predicated on the size of our catch. I will be fair with you as the rest of my crew can tell you. We can work out those details later."

"We are familiar with the pay that commercial fishermen work under and we have heard what a fair man Captain Allison is" said Giuseppe.

"Okay then, come back tomorrow with your gear and we'll get you signed up. The next day we will get underway for a test run of the engines for a half a day and when we return we will go right into dry dock for a good bottom cleaning and painting. Prepare yourselves for some hard work. We should be ready to get underway in about ten days for Tongola, where we pick up our First Mate and the rest of our crew and then off to the fishing grounds."

"I have two requests Captain Allison. May I speak?" asked Matteo.

"By all means, Matteo. We don't stand on much formality here. I'm available for any reasonable request. What are they?" answered Kent.

"Our father has been very ill with cancer for several years. The doctors are quite optimistic about his recovery but he needs another year before he can work again. My mother who is a registered nurse has her hands full taking care of him, she can only work part time, and their finances are critically low. Can we have 75% of our pay transferred to their account when we get it?" asked Matteo.

"All I need is the account information and when we unload our catch in Bali or Tahiti, I can send the funds anywhere you want. But are they in dire straits now?" said Kent.

"Yes. They have borrowed the maximum on the house and it's close to foreclosure but my brothers and I have scraped up enough to make the next payment which should hold them over for now." answered Matteo.

Kent said "We've had some good fortune with finances of late. I'm going to give you guys an advance of $10,000.00. Would that help them?"

The boys couldn't believe their ears. They whooped and hollered and jumped up and down screaming and thanking Kent profusely.

"Who do I make the check to?" asked Kent.

Matteo answered "Make it to my mother, Theresa Pastecherio."

After they calmed down, Kent asked them "Okay boys, what's the other request?"

"We have a sister who is an excellent cook and as hard a worker as the rest of us. Do you need some help in the galley and mess hall?" said Antonio.

"That's your department Teddi. What do you think?" said Kent.

"Why don't you bring her along tomorrow and let me talk to her. What is her name?" said Teddi.

"Her name is Rosa Maria but we call her Rosie" said Antonio

"and she makes all the good pasta just like our mom who brought the recipes from Italy."

"I think I like her already" said Kent.

Chapter Twenty One

The next day the three Italian boys came aboard with their sister. She was a beautiful young girl with bright eyes and a winning smile.

Matteo said "Captain Allison and Mrs. Allison this is our sister Rosa Maria. She would like to talk about hiring on as a cook and helper in the mess hall."

"We're very happy to meet you Rosa. Why don't you and I go down to the galley where we can talk without interruptions" said Teddi.

"I am very happy to meet you and the Captain, Signora Allison. Yes the galley will be fine. I'm very much at home in a galley. Perhaps I can show you."

As they left the quarter deck, Kent said "Okay boys let's get your gear down to the crews quarters and then come back up to the mess hall and we'll fill out the paperwork. After that you can look around the ship and get acquainted. Giuseppe I want you to meet Jacques who will show you the engine room and freeze blasters."

After an hour or so, Teddi and Rosa Maria came into the mess hall. Teddi said "Kent I've decided to sign Rosa on as my assistant. She's no stranger to a ships galley and I sure would welcome a chance to talk to a lady once in a while when we're on one of those long cruises. We've worked out a pay schedule and she also wants 75% sent to her mom and dad. She said she has her gear with her and we can give her Adams cabin. She said she'd like to prepare tonight's meal but we need a few more ingredients. Can we go to the Ships Store on the base and buy a few provisions?"

"That's your call Teddi. Get what you need" said Kent

The evening meal was all that was needed to determine that Rosa was a permanent member of the crew of the Sea Rose. It started out with lightly deep fried Calamari and marinara sauce, a green salad with Italian dressing and gorgonzola cheese, Italian garlic bread, angel hair spaghetti with marinara sauce and veal parmesan all washed down with Chianti wine. It was one happy crew. There wasn't even room for desert.

The next morning after breakfast the Sea Rose got underway for its shake down cruise to check out the engines. Matteo was at the helm and Kent was gazing seaward at the rolling Pacific waters that seemed to shine with an exotic intensity from its blue depths. His love of the sea had never dampened from the time he first saw it as a toddler.

As they cleared the harbor entrance, he called Jacques over the intercom. "Prepare to do your thing with the engines in about 15 minutes Jacques. I know you want to give them a good test but I want to get into the dry dock before 1300 today."

"Aye, Captain. I shouldn't need more than three or four hours especially now since you've given me an assistant." replied Jacques.

"Very well Jacques. Let me know what RPM you want and which engine you want it on" said Kent.

The next several hours were spent running engines fast, slow, forward and in reverse together and individually. Jacques made his adjustments and was soon satisfied that they were tip-top. They headed back to the ship yard and eased their way into dry dock by noon.

The next day the bottom was found to need a sand blasting and new bottom paint. Replacing the cutlass bearing will help with eliminating the sluggishness that Kent experienced. The new crew members worked very well and at the end of each day were very happy to rest and eat some of Rosa's good chow.

The hard part was soon over and after 10 days the Sea Rose was back afloat. They started the final preparations to get underway for Tongola. Teddi said she would need at least three days to stock up so Kent scheduled departure for Monday of the following week.

The day before the Sea Rose was to get underway, Commander Lawson and his Executive Officer Tim Gates came aboard to wish them Bon Voyage.

Lawson said "It's been a privilege to work with you Captain Allison. I'm sure our paths will cross again some day. If nothing else we'll see you at the trial. I understand that Yang will need some recuperation time since he was quite badly burned during the battle. The Customs people will keep you advised since your testimony is going to be critical to put this guy away for good."

"It was our privilege to work with you and your crew Commander. I'll be waiting for the Customs notification and hopefully see you in Canberra at the trial."

The trip to Tongola was easy and without incident which gave all the new crew members time to get acquainted with the ship and for Kent to determine their duties. He was very happy with their seamanship and their work ethic.

Their arrival at Tongola was well after midnight so Kent decided to anchor just off of the harbor entrance rather than chance an accidental grounding on the coral surrounding the island. Also the crew could get a full night sleep.

He was peacefully sitting on the bridge when Teddi arrived with a pot of coffee and two cups. He smiled and gave her a kiss. They both leaned back and enjoyed a cup of the steaming brew. The delicious smells of the nearby flora wafted from the lush island. This was perfect contentment.

In a few hours the tropical sun climbed slowly over the hills of lava and coconut palms until it bathed the anchored Sea Rose in rays of golden light.

There was a flurry of activity as the crew awoke. Teddi said "I'd better get below and give Rosa a hand with breakfast. I know you'll want to get underway to tie up right away."

"Yes I do. Make it a light breakfast so we can weigh anchor in about an hour" said Kent.

After a quick breakfast of coffee, juice and sweet rolls the crew took their docking stations and the Sea Rose got underway.

As they entered the harbor they could hear the happy Polynesian singing coming from the shore. Just barely at first but gaining volume the closer they got.

Several canoes had already left the shore line and the spade shaped wooden paddles wielded by six shirtless men propelled them through the water. As the first canoe approached them a tall, smiling Polynesian man waved frantically.

Kent said "That's Adam. Antonio put the Jacobs ladder over the side so Adam can come aboard."

As soon as Antonio lowered the ladder, Adam leaped from the canoe and clamored up to the deck. He hugged Kent and Teddi and said "Welcome home Captain."

Kent said "It's good to be back, Adam. Let's get tied up. We'll be here a while and we've got a lot of catching up to do."

After the Sea Rose tied up at the dock, it was one mad scramble of happy people both on the ship and on the dock. Marte had been furiously waving from the dock as they approached. Adam jumped off and swooped her up in his massive arms. He carried her aboard so she could hug and kiss Teddi before anyone else could get to her.

The gangway was placed on the deck and Kent left the ship into the outstretched awaiting arms of Ben Fletcher Adams. Next it was Teio with hugs and kisses and then Teddi came down the gangway and following Kent joyously accepted greetings from everyone.

"Come to my house after you secure your ship Kent. Adam and I have great news to tell you" said Ben. And then the celebrating went on for hours before every one calmed down.

Arlis finally was able to make his way to the ship and also greeted Kent. He said "I was able to recruit four strong young seamen Captain. I'll bring them aboard when things settle down a little. In the meantime introduce me to the men you were able to hire."

"Sure thing Arlis, I think you'll find them more than satisfactory. The two seamen are securing all the mooring lines now and the fireman is down below with Jacques. Let's go back to the fantail."

Kent and Arlis made their way aft and Kent said "Men, I want you to meet the First Mate Arlis Teraura. You'll be working directly under him from now on. Arlis this is Able Body Seaman Matteo Pastecherio and his brother Apprentice Antonio. You can meet Giuseppe later after Jacques and he finish shutting down the engines. I'll leave the three of you to get acquainted while Teddi and I visit with Ben and Adam. Ben said he had news for me."

Teddi and Kent walked to Ben's hut, taking longer than expected since everyone they met wanted to pass the time of day with them. When they finally arrived, Ben, Teio, Adam and Marte were all there.

Adam said "Captain, we want to thank you again for the generous share of the reward money and that's what Ben wants to talk to you about."

"Yes, Captain Kent we want you to know what a great impact this windfall will make on our poor village. Adam came to me when Arlis gave him the news and asked "What can we do with this money to help the villagers be more comfortable and have a better life?" As you know we are quite happy with our tranquil lives away from the hustle and bustle of the outside world but it can also be a detriment without communication and health facilities. Adam and Marte have agreed to give the entire amount to the village. We plan to buy a generator large enough to power a clinic and to hire the same installation technicians to restore the radio left here by the P.T. Boat sailors. The money left will be used to buy fuel to run the generator. We will also attempt to bring in a medical person to run the clinic. None of this could have happened without your generosity and so with your permission we would like to name it The Allison Clinic."

"Ben, I'm speechless. Of course you have my permission. It's a great honor and I'm very happy for your village" said Kent, struggling with emotion throughout his answer.

"Good. Then we will celebrate with a luau tonight. That's one tradition that will never change no matter how modern we get" said Ben.

That night, the luau lasted even later than usual. The dancers and musicians gave it their all and the food was plentiful and delicious.

But soon the time came when the Sea Rose left for the fishing grounds. They became one of the best boats in the commercial fishing fleet. Month after month they would bag the limit of the refrigeration hold. Their regular stops included Bali, Tahiti and they even made it to Honolulu on one trip. Of course they would stop at Tongola at every opportunity but it wasn't often enough.

About a year later, when they put into Pandang Bai on the island of Bali, a message was waiting for Captain Kent Allison to contact the Customs Division at Canberra, Australian Capital Territory with reference to the trial of Armond Yang.

Kent called them immediately and was told that the trial was scheduled to start on the 25th of the following month and that the Prosecutor would issue a subpoena for him and for Teddi to appear as witnesses for the Prosecution. Kent agreed to testify and told them his location so he could be served.

This gave them about 6 weeks to prepare. They had planned to be in port about two weeks for some periodic maintenance before an extended trip. After discussing it with Teddi they made a plan.

They would remain on board until the work was done to Kent's satisfaction. The ship would then leave port under the command of the First Mate Arlis Teraura for an extended trip to catch tuna for delivery to Sidney, New South Wales. Kent and Teddi would fly to Australia to spend some time touring until time for the trial. This should put the Sea Rose in port at Sidney at about the same time the trial is over to pick up the Captain and Teddi.

Teddi was very excited. This will be their first real vacation. They will have at least two weeks to tour before they had to be in Canberra to discuss their testimony with the prosecutor before the trial. She had some shopping to do.

Chapter Twenty Two

Kent and Teddi caught a flight into Sydney and then took a cab into the downtown area. Kent spared no expense. He booked a suite in the Vulcan Hotel which was very close to the Opera House. The accommodations were luxurious and dinner that night was exquisite.

Then next day was reserved for shopping and that evening Kent got second row seats at the Sydney Opera House to see Dame Joan Sutherland singing The Merry Widow Waltz.

Teddi was in her glory.

After a few days in the big city they decided to relax in a bed and breakfast. The B&B 101 Addison Road came highly recommended so they relocated there. It was in the town of Manly on a quiet tree lined street on the town's popular Eastern Hill. There were several beaches within 3 to 5 minutes walk and they took advantage of these.

Manly Wharf had a ferry that crossed the magnificent Sydney Harbor. On the way across they met a very friendly couple that offered to show them the city in their car. Kent said "That's very kind of you but we don't want to be a bother to you and besides the cost of gasoline is out of sight."

The gentleman replied "Look, you Yanks saved our bacon in World War II and I don't forget it. Please join my wife and me for an afternoon ride around the city."

Teddi said "We'd be happy to and it's a privilege to be with you."

The next day they rented a car and drove to Adelaide, South Australia, touring the countryside and acting like tourists. South Australia is wine country and wine connoisseurs are not disappointed here. A short drive from Adelaide is the Barossa Valley where wineries abound. After a few days of sampling some very good wine they were ready to get to Canberra to prepare for the trial.

The flight from Adelaide to Canberra was uneventful and upon arrival they checked into the Bentley Suites on the Parliamentary Triangle. This was convenient to the city centre.

Their appointment with the prosecutor was for 10:00 AM the next day. This evening would pretty much wind up their vacation.

When they got to the prosecutors office the next day his reception was very sedate and this was surprising since Kent's telephone conversations with his office had always been upbeat and optimistic.

When they were seated across from him at his desk he very glumly said "I've got very bad news. Armond Yang and the remaining pirate crew member have escaped."

"When did this happen and how could it happen" queried Kent.

"It was during the transfer from the Federal lock up to the local Federal Holding Cell where they were to be held during the trial. They were in a secure van with a driver and two guards. There was a five car pile up on the freeway and they were involved. The driver was killed and the guards were both injured. One was unconscious and the other badly injured. It appears that both prisoners only had minor injuries. They were able to get the keys from the injured guard and unlock their manacles. The also took the guards guns and headed for the woods" explained the Prosecutor.

"Surly they can't stay free for very long with no place to go, can they?" asked Teddi.

"This happened late yesterday afternoon and I'm afraid it was quite late last night that anyone realized that dangerous criminals were on the loose. They've already made a move. Yesterday evening a lady and her daughter were car jacked at a shopping mall. The two men forced them to drive to an ATM and draw out $750.00. They dumped them in a remote area and drove the car into the city. Fortunately the woman and her daughter were only slightly hurt. It was definitely Yang according to the description."

"What do we do now?" said Kent.

"Let's give it a few days. If the authorities don't capture them quickly it probably means that they've left the area. We know that you must return to your ship so we can have you and Teddi give a deposition in case you are not available when we finally do bring him to trial" said the Prosecutor.

"Alright, we'll be at the Bentley Suites if you need us" said Kent

As the three of them left the offices of the Prosecutor and were walking down the walkway a television crew stopped them. "Mr. Prosecutor, may we ask some questions?" said the news cast lady.

"I'll answer what I'm able to but this is an ongoing case please remember" he said.

"Is it true that Armond Yang was the carjacker last night?" she asked.

"Evidence indicates that is true" he said

"Are there any leads as to where they might be?" she asked.

"I can't answer that. And that's enough for now" he said.

"Who are these people? Are they involved in the case?" she asked.

"They are witnesses for the prosecution and as I said the interview is over" he said as they hurried away down the walkway.

The news cast lady was signing off as they left "This is Linnie Handle of WKCY News signing off."

Kent and Teddi caught a cab and stopped for lunch before going back to the hotel. As they were going into the hotel the same news crew was waiting outside the lobby door. As the cameras panned them in front of the hotel, Linnie Handle said "Captain and Mrs. Allison, can we ask you some questions?"

Kent said "Wow, we didn't expect this. I don't think we are able to answer any questions pertaining to the trial."

"Aren't you the Captain of the Sea Rose, the derelict ship that was docked in Willie Creek?"

"Yes, I am but please. I really can't answer anymore questions. I'm sorry" Kent said as they ducked inside.

Teddi said "I think we'd better stay in the suite this evening and have room service send up dinner.

"Sounds like a very good idea" said Kent.

The next day Kent and Teddi ventured down to the hotel restaurant for breakfast and lunch with no more encounters with the television people so they decided that dinner out in a fine restaurant would be safe.

They dressed in their finest clothes. Teddi wore a new dress that she had bought in Sidney and hadn't had a chance to wear yet and Kent had made reservations in a fine French Restaurant that came highly recommended.

As they left the hotel lobby to hail a cab they noticed that the doorman was not there and the only cab available was sitting off to the side. Before Kent could wave the cab pulled up to the curb.

As he opened the door for Teddi he glanced at the driver who looked a little familiar, he hesitated and said to Teddi "Hold it a minute hon."

She said "What's the matter?"

Suddenly Kent felt a hard jab in his rib cage and a gruff voice said "Please get in Captain. You and the pretty Teddi are going for a little ride."

Kent turned and saw the evil leering face of Armond Yang. He roughly shoved the off balance Kent through the open door and onto the back seat of the cab. As Kent raised his head he was staring into the muzzle of a Glock held by the cab driver. Now he recognized him as one of the pirates.

Yang then shoved Teddi into the cab and pushed her up against Kent on one side of the cab. He then got in and sat on the jump seat facing them so he could keep his gun trained on them.

He said to the driver "Get moving." And the cab peeled out from the curb.

"That was very good television coverage Captain Allison and right in front of the hotel where you were staying. That was very thoughtful although I don't think you meant it to be" said Yang.

"Let us go Yang. You're in enough trouble already without kidnapping added to it" said Kent.

"I'm not worried about that Captain. After I take care of you two I have some very good friends who will get me back to Skull Island and no one will bother me there" said Yang.

"Where are you taking us?" said Kent.

"My friends have a quiet little cottage outside of town where no one will bother us or hear any screams or other noises we may make. It's not far. Here in Australia you can be in the wilderness very quickly" said Yang with an evil grin.

After 30 or 40 minutes the cab turned up a bumpy dirt road and soon they pulled up next to a ramshackle hovel overgrown with weeds. Yang said to the driver "Get out and open the door next to our good Captain. Keep him covered and I'll take care of covering the sweet lady. I'll keep her very close to me" he said with a wicked laugh.

As they were making their way up to the shack two glaring spotlights came on, one from the right and one from the left and lit up the whole area around them. All of a sudden a helicopter appeared overhead with another spot light.

A bull horn screamed "This is Post Commander Ken Filigno Jr. of the Australian Provincial Police, Yang. We've got you covered with SWAT team sharp shooters. Give up now or suffer the consequences."

Yang screamed "Not as long as I've got these two hostages. The only way they will survive is if you provide us with a safe way out of here. We will kill them and don't think I will hesitate to do so. We'll let them go if you get us out of here."

"Don't be a fool Yang" said Filigno. "Give up while you can."

"We're going into the shack" said Yang. "Make arrangements to get the four of us safely out of here and on a helicopter to a prior arranged spot where a ship will be waiting for us. I'll give the details to the pilot."

As they were walking, Kent whipped is left arm forward in midair, knocking the pirates gun to the side before tumbling into him with his full weight. They fell to the ground together and Kent drove his shoulder into the pirate's chest, the pressure cracking two ribs and knocking the wind out of him. Kent's right fist crashed into the side of his neck and knocked him out before another warble could leave his mouth.

When Kent made his move, Yang was taken by surprise. He fired off a quick shot in the grappling Kent's direction but it went wide. Teddi quickly pulled herself free from his grasp and fell to the ground and rolled as she fell.

Yang then took aim and his teeth were bared in a satisfied murderous grin. He was a devil and was going to take Kent with him since he knew he was a goner. Before the final click, as he pulled the trigger a shot rang out from a snipers 30.06 rifle. Yang stood for an instant with disbelief in his eyes as a bloody hole, the size of a penny appeared on his forehead. As he fell and rolled over the damage to the back of his skull was evident. It was a mass of brain tissue.

Kent ran to Teddi and scooped her up in his arms. She was trembling and mumbling incoherently. "It's okay honey. It's really over this time. He will never bother us again."

CHAPTER TWENTY THREE

18 months later

Man oh man, what a good catch this is Captain" said Arlis. "We must have 45 tons of tuna in the refrigeration hold."

"You're right Arlis. In fact it may be a little more than that. It's time to head in. I've promised this catch to be delivered to the cannery at Darwin in the Northern Territory. They've promised me top dollar, so set a course for Darwin and we'll get underway" answered Kent.

"Aye, aye Captain. The boys could use a break" said Arlis.

"You're right, mate. After you set the helm watch and lookout, grab Jacques and meet Teddi and me in the mess hall for a cup of coffee. We'd like to discuss something with you two" said Kent.

About 30 minutes later Arlis and Jacques entered the mess hall. After they filled their coffee cups they sat down at a table with the Captain and his wife.

Kent said "Men, we've been hitting it pretty hard for the last 18 months or so and we've had fantastic catches. It's time for a little break. When we land in Darwin, I'm going to give the boys and Rosa leave to go home and visit their mom and dad. I understand that Mr. Pastecherio has made great progress with the cancer and is expected to make full recovery. I'm sure the kids would like to spend a month or so at home. When we leave Darwin we'd like to head up to Tongola and just kick back for a while. If you would like to go to Bali, Arlis or if Jacques would like to go to Honolulu, we can arrange it."

Both men agreed that a break was needed and they would give some thought on the visit to Bali and Honolulu and they got up to leave.

"Wait one minute" said Kent. "We have more to talk about. Our plan from the beginning was to fish commercially for ten years and then buy a sail boat and sail around the world at a leisurely pace. We've got about three and a half years into it and are doing better than we thought. A lot of it is due to the outstanding job you two have done. If we continue for about another three years at this pace we can hang it up and go sailing. We would like to make you two an offer. With the reward money and other insurance payments we were able to make a big dent in the mortgage and soon it will be paid off. We will turn ownership of the Sea Rose over to you in three years in return for fifteen percent of the profits for a ten year period. I'm sure you'd like to discuss this with each other and there will be a lot of detail to work out but do you think you'd be interested?"

Jacques and Arlis sat there in awe and said "Kent you are an amazing man."

Kent replied "No, I'm just lucky to have friends like you two."

Chapter Twenty Four

Three years later

As the Sea Rose steamed into Tongolo's natural harbor, Kent and Teddi felt a surge of remorse that this will be the last time that they will make this trip into this beautiful island on their beloved trawler. It was time to take the next step and travel to Fort Lauderdale to pick up their brand new Cabo Rico Cutter. Also it was time to follow their plan and turn the boat over to their faithful crew, who have worked so hard, to help them fulfill their dreams.

Of course, Tongolo will still be their home and they will return here to live when their cruising days are done. But it's the closing of a wonderful chapter in their lives and it makes both of them very sad.

The Sea Rose will continue as a commercial fishing boat but with a different skipper at the helm. Jacques will now be captain with Arlis as his first mate and both will be equal partners in ownership. They will keep the same crew with the Pastecherio brothers holding the positions of second mate, chief engineer and leading seaman. And, of course, Tongolo will always be a regular port of call for the Sea Rose so when the cruising couple returns they will still be able to have an occasional visit with boat and crew.

As always happens when a familiar boat enters the harbor of this beautiful island, the villagers were at the waters edge waving, singing and offering a welcome to the seagoing travelers. The ever present canoes were paddling out to greet them with, laughing, young men and girls calling to them. But they always gave a special welcome upon the arrival of the Sea Rose whose owner and crew gave so much to this island paradise and made life so much easier and added many more comforts to their village.

They now had a fully staffed clinic and electric power which allows them contact with the outside world by radio. They still maintain the old ways in many things which allows them to still hold on to the tranquility that they have enjoyed for many years. They have not been discovered by the large cruise ships yet so the hustle and bustle of civilization has not entered their lives.

Ben Fletcher Adams and Adam were on the dock to greet them when the crew disembarked. Kent and Teddi explained to them that this will be a short visit and the last one for them for a long while. The Sea Rose has a hold full of fish which must be unloaded in Jayapura on the island of New Guinea. They will leave the vessel at that point and catch a plane to Sydney and make plans to fly to Fort Lauderdale and pick up their new boat.

Adam invited them to visit his hut to see Marte and his children. And later they could prepare for the inevitable luau which was planned for tonight. He explained that Marte has turned over the dancing to younger girls now that she is a mother of two children and is very happy to just be an instructor.

When they arrived at the hut, Marte welcomed them with open arms and eyes filled with tears of happiness. She was glowing and it was obvious that Adam was making her very happy. Teddi couldn't wait to hold and cuddle the newest addition to the family, a sweet smelling chubby little baby girl. She was oblivious to any thing else and was lost in the cooing and baby talk which was emanating from both baby and adult.

Kent and Adam just rolled their eyes and Adam said "Let's go outside, skipper, I want to show you the boat I'm working on."

When they got outside Adam said "Did you see the look on Teddi's face when she held the baby?"

"Yea, she certainly was contented" answered Kent.

"I don't know, skipper, you may have a discussion coming up. I've seen that same look on Marte's face and we now have a boy and a girl. Women can get very domestic when they feel the biological clock is ticking."

"Hmm. Well we always planned to start a family some day but it might be tough if we are sailing around the world. And that is the plan. At least it has been the plan. I guess I'll just have to wait and see what she has to say. Now let's take a look at your boat."

The luau that night was as good as any that they had ever been to. They spent as much time as they could, visiting with all their friends in the village and the night just flew by.

Later when Kent and Teddi crawled into bed, exhausted from a very long and busy day Teddi sleepily asked "Honey, how long do you think we'll be sailing?"

Kent answered "Oh I don't know. I didn't want to put a time limit on it. I just thought we'd play it by ear. Why do you want to know?"

"No reason, sweetie, just kind of wondering. Good night and sweet dreams."

Two days later they left the island en route to their destination of Fort Lauderdale where a beautiful Cabo Rico sailboat was waiting to be commissioned.

PART TWO

Chapter Twenty Five

ON ISLA DE LA TORTUGA GRANDE

She woke up gasping and hyperventilating, with a sheen of perspiration across her lip. She gazed about, trying to remember where she was and how she got there. Everything was a blur and so confusing. Her forehead was bathed in a cold sweat, her heart hammered in her chest and a formless panic gnawed hungrily at her innards, she had a splitting headache.

The room was small and stark and little else but a platform bed. Where is Ron? What is that hospital smell? Anesthesia? Am I in a hospital? I have a hospital gown on. But wait—my arms are tied to the bed rails. What's going on? Where am I?

"Hello! Is anyone there? Please help me." She called.

The door opened slowly. Two men dressed in scrubs entered with a nurse slightly behind. The tall one said "Hello Sandra. We're glad to see that you are finally awake, and I'm sure you are very eager to find out why you are here. I'm Dr. Tobias and this is Dr. Syed. Nurse Tallett will be taking care of your every day needs and administering the meds that you will occasionally need."

"Where am I? How did I get here? Where's Ron?"

"One thing at a time, Sandra. First of all you are in a special kind of a hospital on Isla de la Tortuga Grande. You were chosen to be here because of your very desirable anatomical characteristics and exceptional good health. You will be pleased to know that you will be a part of an experiment to benefit future mankind. You are confused because part of your memory has been expunged and now we must find out what has been retained so we can make adjustments on you and others. We have some questions."

"I don't want to be an experiment. Why am I tied down? Where is my husband, Ron?"

"That answers the first question, she remembers his name. Can you describe him?"

"Certainly, he's—he's. Oh I'm so confused, I can't remember what he looks like."

"Hmm, some progress on this one with a partial expunge" said Syed

"Yes we must be careful and not go too far. Adjusting the gain on the equipment helps. Sandra, can you tell us what you remember about the trip here to the island?" said Tobias.

"I—I remember being on a ship. So sleepy, and so sick, I couldn't see anything. My eyes were covered and I was lying in a bunk. Then I woke up in this room."

"We must be careful Amad. Remember what happened to the others with too much gain. Destroying the mind renders the specimen useless" said Syed.

"Do you remember being on St. Martin or the La Samana Hotel?" asked Tobias.

"No. Please, I have a bad headache."

"Do you remember the dinner party on the ship and meeting me and Dr. Syed?"

"No. Please, no more questions. Can you give me some aspirin—my head—I feel sick."

"I think we've learned enough to make further adjustments, Farouk" said Tobias. "We must erase all memory of her husband so there will be no investigation in the future. Nurse, prepare her for further treatment in the Reality Room for tomorrow morning and then move her to a more suitable room. We want her in a tranquil state when her fertile period starts in a week or so.

"What do you mean? Sandra screamed "I want out of here. I want to see Ron."

"Give her a sedative nurse. I want her relaxed in the morning."

After the doctors left, the nurse injected medication into the shunt in Sandra's arm and she drifted into oblivion.

The next morning Sandra woke in a fog but completely relaxed. She was in a bright, sunny room with pleasant pastel walls and she was lying in a very comfortable hospital bed. Shortly after she awoke, an orderly brought in a breakfast tray with fresh fruit, cereal, a delicious Danish and fresh coffee. She was famished and she wolfed it all down.

Soon the nurse arrived with two burly men, transferred her to a gurney and wheeled her down the hall. They entered a room through a set of automatic double doors that silently swung open as they approached and closed after they passed through. The room was dimly lit and it took a few minutes for her eyes to adjust to the low indirect lighting.

She gazed around. She could see screens, electronics and speakers on every wall. A cabinet with glass doors and filled with medications hung on one wall. Centrally located was a large, plush, reclining chair with many adjustable segments.

Hanging over the chair were cables with electrodes attached. The cables led to an enclosed mechanism on the ceiling.

Sandra saw Tobias and asked "What is this place?"

"This is the Reality Room, Sandra" he answered "and is set up to create and implant situations that never really happened. Don't be frightened. You will feel much better when we are finished. You will have no anxiety or pressures because we will wipe them away and put new ones in your memory banks. We hope to eliminate that headache and otherwise you will feel no pain. Now you will go into a deep sleep."

Dr. Syed entered the room and Dr. Tobias said "Alright Farouk, do your magic on her and let's try to get it right. I don't want to lose this one. She's got potential and we found that her fertile period is soon. I want to fertilize her with the new batch of semen which is supposed to be better than the last. Remember only do what you must at this point. When we fertilize, we can program her to believe that she has been made pregnant by her husband and it will make her more at peace with her pregnancy. Not like the last few that we lost. I think we are getting closer to achieving a super race for cloning."

"Yes Amad. If you can give me the perfect physical specimen, I can achieve the mental programming needed to satisfy our benefactors. We will be heroes."

"I know Farouk, very rich heroes. But there are a few small adjustments to be made, eliminating the head trauma for one. And I'm still looking for the one female with all the requisites I feel we need."

Sandra was gently moved from the gurney to the chair. Motors whirred as adjustments were made. Electrodes were attached to her head and on her body. She was in a deep sleep and strangely at peace.

Soon she was dreaming. Soothing music was playing and a subtle perfume wafted through the air. She was in a beautiful garden and felt free as a bird. She had such a feeling of contentment. Soon she would see Ron.

Chapter Twenty Six

The flight from their remote Pacific island to Fort Lauderdale, Florida was long and very tiring. After several layovers, too short to get a room and too long to be comfortable, tempers were getting very ragged. Both Kent and Teddi had several encounters with uncooperative airport employees upon reaching Fort Lauderdale and when they began harping at each other over some inconsequential disagreement, they both looked at each other and burst out laughing. They decided that the next stop was going to be a hotel bed and some well needed rest.

They loaded their luggage into a cab and Kent instructed the driver to take them to the nearest good hotel.

When they got to their room at noon, they hit the bed and slept until 10:00 that night. Both were famished so they ordered room service and dined on ham sandwiches, potato salad and beer followed up with peach cobbler and ice cream. It was delicious. Feeling satisfied they went back to bed and slept straight through until 7:00 A.M. when they awoke fully rested and ready to journey to Cabo Rico Yachts on 17th Street for the first look at their new boat.

After they arrived and completed all the necessary paperwork at the office and received the Documentation Certificate as well as Warranties, etc. they were greeted by several neatly dressed dock hands along with a well tanned young man who said, "Welcome to Cabo Rico Yachts. My name is Mark and I'd like to show you around the boat. If you'd like we can take her out for a shake down cruise this afternoon to help you get the feel of her."

"That'd be great" said Kent "this is my wife Teddi, and I'm Kent Allison."

"I'm pleased to meet you both. She's ready to sail except for the personal touches that I'm sure you will want to add before you start your cruise."

Teddi asked "How long can we keep her here? We need to provision her before we get underway."

"Take as long as you need. The slip is yours while you provision her and test her. You may want to stay in your hotel for a few days before you live aboard and can load all your gear. We are storing several boxes that you shipped from your trawler. I'll have them delivered to your boat. By the way, we took the liberty of having Sea Rose II painted on the transom and a long stem rose painted next to the name. I hope its okay."

"We noticed and it's beautiful" said Teddi.

"Okay then let's go sailing."

They boarded the boat and went below first, at Teddi's insistence. She was not disappointed. It had elegant and comfortable living accommodations surrounded with hand finished, solid teak grown on plantations in Costa Rica. Teddi could readily see that she was designed to carry all the provisions and equipment needed for long distance sailing.

The design included two double cabins, full galley, private heads and separate shower stalls and even a small work room. But the real plus was a third cabin which they had customized into a laundry/office. She had 165 gallons of fresh water storage and 72 gallons of fuel storage. They were very happy that they decided to go with the 42 foot design.

Kent's main interest was topside. She has a cutter rig which means she carries 3 sails, the main, the jib or genoa and a stay sail. She has self tailing winches, a roller furling mainsail and genoa, and all lines running back to the cockpit. She looks fast and will be comfortable underway, safe and easy to sail. Mark advised that she's balanced beautifully in light or heavy air with hands off tracking ability combining with a fine turn of speed.

They got underway, motoring out through the harbor with the 75 H.P. Yanmar engine purring like a kitten. After they passed through the break wall with the mainsail already unfurled, they turned off the engine, flew the genny, and the staysail, and turned to sail on a beam reach. They heeled over to12 degrees in a 15 knot wind. It was exhilarating. The Sea Rose II squatted and set sail. She was free from man made hindrances. The only noise was the surf rushing under the bow. Kent looked at Teddi and both, with wide grins, had tears in their eyes. He embraced her, their tears intermingled and stained their cheeks. This was sailing as it was meant to be. They were going to be very happy on this beautiful, beautiful sail boat.

The happy couple spent the next two weeks preparing for their cruise. The boat had all the latest electronic equipment installed but it all needed checkout and programming before they could trust it on an extended cruise and Kent assumed this responsibility. Teddi not only saw to the provisioning and buying all the necessary equipment to make them self sufficient while at sea but she also started a herb garden which would greatly enhance her meals during those long lonely times between ports of call. Much of her time was spent away from the boat on shopping sprees.

Time flew by and soon it was time to take the first leg of their journey. They left Fort Lauderdale, entered the Straits of Florida which is the body of water between Florida and the Bahamas and is commonly considered to be the Atlantic Ocean. It is a part of the ocean but in reality the Atlantic Ocean is east of the Bahamas.

The Gulf Stream flows within these straits. The Stream is a 40 to 50 mile wide current that flows northeast. The speed of this current averages about 2 or 3 knots but can range up to 6 knots on occasion. It is 4 to 6 degrees warmer than surrounding waters and this warmth plays a big part in the weather conditions of Bermuda and also England.

The current also must be considered when crossing the straits en route to the Bahamas especially in a slow moving sailboat. When Kent made a float plan and charted the course from Fort Lauderdale, he chose going to West End on Grand Bahama Island because it was northeast and the current would aid him by pushing him north while steering east.

The first day was one of adjusting to sailing conditions but the weather was perfect and everything was working well. Sea life abounded and dolphins playfully swam about them both following closely on their stern quarter and swimming in front of their bow, two of them doing flip flops while staying just barely in front of the bow stem.

Sea turtles were on the surface and swimming towards the Florida beaches to lay their eggs. Flying fish soared off into the distance. "Something must be chasing them." said Teddi as she went below to prepare some lunch.

They quietly rested after lunch, the steering vane was keeping them on course and Kent was lounging in the salon while Teddi washed the dishes. They were quite content with the way the cruise was going. The weather was great with a gentle 10 knot breeze, making just enough headway for a relaxing sail and time to have enjoyed their lunch. It will be a great evening to sit topside with a glass of wine and watch the sunset.

Suddenly the stillness was shattered with a loud whooshing roar. Kent quickly jumped to his feet and bounded topside. He jumped on deck just in time to see a whale, perhaps 40 to 50 feet in length, about 50 yards away from the boat.

It submerged and swam under the stern, surfacing a short distance away. He yelled below for Teddi to come topside. This was not one of those gentle creatures that they had encountered while on the dinghy. Kent had heard of accounts, rather dubiously, of whales attacking boats, but the possibility existed and he wanted Teddi up here so she'd know the situation and not be trapped below in an emergency.

The whale made two more passes. The first seemed to be one of scoping out the prey and the second one appeared very threatening. The attack stories were gaining more credibility.

The huge black animal swam rapidly on the surface straight at the cockpit, where Kent and Teddi stood anxiously watching this spectacular performance. The monster neared the boat and Teddi screamed "he's going to ram us." At the last second the black behemoth dove, plunging under the surface.

They hung over the lifelines staring at the slowly rising head. The whale hesitated with its head close to the surface, then it submerged again, surfacing on the other side and turned to stare at them. It then flipped its tail and disappeared from view.

Apparently it just wanted to establish its superiority over this man made device, just to make sure these frail human beings understood what kind of consequences Mother Nature could dish out.

It never returned. Kent and Teddi had a new respect for sea creatures. The rest of the afternoon passed peacefully, and that evening Teddi prepared one of her gourmet meals.

Kent was relaxing in the cockpit preparing to watch what looked like a glorious setting sun when Teddi brought up a bottle of wine and one glass.

He said "Well what with that wonderful meal and one of our best bottles of wine I have a feeling you're about to ask for something. But why only one glass?"

"It's more of a celebration than a request honey. I have some news that I've been waiting for the right time to tell you. While we were in Fort Lauderdale I visited a gynecologist for my check up and he did some tests to confirm my suspicions. The tests were positive honey. I'm pregnant."

Kent's jaw dropped and he got a silly grin on his face before he let out loud "Oh my God".

"Oh honey, I hope you're not disappointed. We will probably need to alter our plans. The doctor said I should plan to be off the boat 2 months before delivery."

"Honey, we've got the rest of our lives to sail around the world. Let's celebrate this wonderful news and plan the rest of the trip later. Now I understand why you brought only one glass."

Chapter Twenty Seven

The distance from Fort Lauderdale to West End is 83 nautical miles, more than they could make in one day so they had their first over night sail with both of them standing a four hour helm watch.

"Ya know, Kent, we're in the Bermuda Triangle so sleep lightly in case I need you. There have been some strange happenings in this area. I remember the story about Chuck Muir, his wife and another couple who left West End in their sail boat to get back to Jupiter on a stormy day. They never arrived and what's strange is that nothing was ever found of their boat or of them, for that matter." said Teddi.

"I know honey. And, of course that's only one of several strange stories about the Bermuda Triangle. If we want to sail the Bahamas we can't bypass the Triangle. We'll be out of it once we're south of Puerto Rico and into the Leeward Islands. Don't worry. I'll sleep with one eye and one ear open listening for your call."

Later, in the early evening, Kent became aware of a distant drone of an engine. He scanned the horizon and saw a small power boat closing on them from the south and watched with growing uneasiness as the boat drew nearer.

Warnings issued by the U. S. Coast Guard were explicit about the dangers of yacht hijackings in the Caribbean and joining waters and counseled extreme caution. After their encounter with the hijacking in the South Pacific, a power boat coming directly at them was causing him great anxiety.

He called Teddi to come topside and bring his rifle with a box of ammo. He said "we don't want to end up a blood spattered derelict boat drifting off the Bahamas, with the crew unaccounted for. I think we should assume the worst and hope for the best."

"But honey, what if they're in distress and need some help" said Teddi.

"I somehow don't think so" answered Kent "but I'll hail them on channel 16. If they need help, they'll answer."

Kent spoke into the radio microphone "This is Sea Rose II calling the power boat on our stern, do you need assistance. Over." He repeated the call two more times and received nothing but static each time. It was now within 200 yards.

The boat approached closer and three men were visible with one waving and motioning to heave to. The second man appeared to be holding a gun of some sort. Kent turned into the waves on a close reach, causing an uncomfortable pitch, but it also caused the smaller boat even more discomfort riding the crest and troughs of the waves. Kent raised the rifle and pointed directly at the man at the helm but the power boat continued its course.

The boat was now close enough for Kent to get a good view of the men. They were definitely not your everyday Sunday boaters out for a little cruise. "I'm assuming the worst" he said to himself.

He was able to steady himself on the gunwale and draw a bead on the driver. He aimed about two feet over his head and squeezed off a shot that buzzed right over his head. The driver panicked and pulled the wheel hard to the right and the boat came close to broaching, sending the other two men sprawling and close to falling overboard. There was much yelling and hand waving by both of them directed at the helmsman. He turned and yelled back at both of them in obvious disagreement but the boat continued on a course away from the Sea Rose II. Kent breathed a sigh of relief, kept them in sight for awhile and then came back on course. He kept a nervous eye on the horizon and neither one slept very soundly that night but the "would be" pirates never returned.

The next morning they entered Old Bahama Bay Marina at West

End. After docking, Kent raised the Q flag which means they are quarantined until cleared by customs. Clearing customs at West End is an easy task and soon they were relaxing in the sun.

The next day they got underway for the Abacos which is known for their great cruising grounds for sailors. After leaving West End they entered Little Bahama Bank which has an average depth of 15 feet of crystal clear water. It's best to keep to established routes here because of numerous shoals and it's best to find an anchorage by last light and travel only by daylight to keep from going aground. So the next stop would be Great Sale Cay, an uninhabited island and a favorite anchorage for visiting sailors.

It was a bright morning with a high clear sky into which towered soft columns of clouds of blinding white. They were threading a fine course through clear green water where reefs lurked below the surface but soon they were out of the shoal area off of West End.

It was a great day of sailing and they made Great Sale Cay by late that afternoon. They had a wonderful evening and met several other sailors who helped them celebrate their new found expectancy.

That night they discussed a new cruising plan. Ultimately they wanted to be back in Hawaii when the baby was born. This meant cutting the Caribbean a little short and heading south to the Panama Canal for transit to the Pacific Ocean.

"We can work our way up the coast to Acapulco, head west to Islas Revillagigedo which would take us a week or so and then the big jump to Hawaii which will take about 3 weeks. Then when the baby's ready to travel, we'll decide what we'll do as far as getting home to Tortola. Does that sound like a plan?"

"Yes, honey it does" said Teddi "but I feel bad about not continuing as we originally planned."

Kent took her in his arms and said "Darling you've made me the happiest man in the world. I wouldn't have it any other way. Please don't feel that you've spoiled anything. This baby is our number one priority and will only add to an already perfect marriage."

"Thank you Kent. I should have known that you'd feel that way. I'm very happy. And I'm so looking forward to the baby. Should we pick out a name?"

Kent chuckled "Let's think about that for a while hon, we have plenty of time."

"Yea, you're right. What a beautiful evening. It's so relaxing here sitting under a moonlit sky." She said.

"That is a beautiful moon. It's now on the wane." He said.

"Can you tell that just by looking? Or have you been keeping track?" she asked.

"Let me show you hon" he said "extend your right arm out towards the moon. Put the round part of your open hand, that's between your thumb and your forefinger, so that it's beside the moon. If the round part of your hand meets the round part of the moon, it's on the wane. If the round part of the moon is on the other side it's waxing."

"You're so smart. I sure hope the baby inherits your intelligence." She said.

"And your good looks" he said.

The sailing en route to Great Abaco Island was as good as you could get. Marsh Harbour is the main town and the harbor itself is crowded with cruising boats. Kent opted to anchor at Little Harbor which is close to town but not as congested. They wanted to see some of the smaller cays but would stop here to pick up a few provisions and some ice.

Hope Town was close by so they anchored there next, launched the dinghy and had lunch at a fantastic island restaurant. After lunch they hopped over to Tahiti Beach anchored and swam at the deserted beach. They decided to spend the night at this anchorage. It was beautiful and tranquil.

The next morning Kent found that the electric anchor windlass was not working and couldn't locate the problem. Not being all that familiar with the boat yet he decided to radio the marina in Little Harbor to see if he could get some assistance. They advised him that the electrician was out, but would return shortly and he would radio Kent back.

Kent decided to wait for the call before leaving when the radio cackled and a voice said "Sea Rose II, Sea Rose II this is Semper Avante. Come in please."

Kent answered "Semper Avante, this is Sea Rose II. Did you call me?"

"This is Semper Avante. Captain, I'm the trawler anchored just east of you here at Tahiti Beach. I heard your call and I understand that you have an electrical problem, I'm an electrician. Can I be of help?"

"That's correct sir and yes, I'd appreciate the help. It's a new boat so it can't be major."

"If you can come over and pick me up in your dinghy I'll see what I can do."

"I'll be right there" said Kent.

Kent motored over to the trawler and came along side at the swim platform on the stern. A pleasant looking lady with a Swedish accent met him and said "hello, I'm Inga. Dave will be right with you."

"Thank you Inga. My name is Kent."

"My pleasure Kent. Here's Dave now."

"Hi Kent. I'll be right down, just hold her into the swim platform."

Kent was amazed to see that Dave had no legs. They had both been amputated above the knee. But before he could react to help, Dave was already clamoring over the swim platform and onto the dinghy. He was aghast.

Dave looked at Kent and laughed "It's amazing how people get speechless the first time they see me. Let me explain because I know you're dying to know. When I was a young man I was a lineman for New England Electric. While working on high tension wires I had an unfortunate accident, was electrocuted and burned over 75% of my body. After years of surgery and with the support of my wife and kids I survived but lost my legs. I've got prosthesis for each leg but found that on a boat I get around much better without them. It's amazing how well you can learn to scoot on your butt. I still understand electricity and have a deep respect for it, so possibly I can help."

"Sounds good to me Dave. Let's take a look."

They made their way back to the Sea Rose II and Kent explained the problem. Dave asked Kent for the schematics which were included with the manuals.

He studied them for a moment and then asked if Kent tripped the circuit breaker.

Kent answered "No because there wasn't one on the main panel and he could not locate a fuse."

Dave answered "that's because the breaker is on the sub panel where the on/off switch for the anchor windlass is located. The reason it's there is because it's so easy to trip the switch if your anchor gets fouled and you can conveniently reset it and then continue lifting the anchor. That's the way it's designed."

"Well—I feel pretty stupid" said Kent "I was looking right at it but it didn't register as being an overload switch."

Dave laughed and said "I'd much rather tell you this than say you had a real problem, Kent."

Teddi walked in and Kent introduced her and explained about Dave.

Dave said "Would you like to come over and meet my wife, Teddi?"

"Yes, it will be great talking to a woman. In fact I have some questions to ask her."

They motored over to the trawler and before long they felt like they were old friends. Teddi announced that she was pregnant and Inga hovered over her like a mother hen.

Teddi asked if Inga would come topside with her. She had questions about her pregnancy and felt a little privacy would be in order.

CHAPTER TWENTY EIGHT

The next day they got underway and island hopped for the day. They sailed north to Green Turtle Cay, a favorite spot for sailors, and walked through the quaint town. The next stop was Man of War Cay where they visited an ancient cemetery with nostalgic epitaphs on the tombstones of sailors that had lived and died here in the Abacos.

Their last stop would be at the Hole in the Wall on the southern tip of Great Abaco. They hated to leave a place with so many wonderful memories.

After they were sailing on blue water Teddi said "What a wonderful couple were the folks from the "Semper Avante". To think of the tragedy that hit them so early in their married life, and then to go on to recover, have children, raise a family and finally retire to live their dream on their boat. Just to name it "Forever Forward" tells you so much about them and their outlook on life. I'm so happy that we met them. It makes you realize how lucky we are to have each other and the life that we have."

"I wouldn't have had it any other way honey. And it will only get better now that we will have started a family."

The next port of call would be San Salvador which is the island commonly thought to be the first spot that Christopher Columbus landed. Many now dispute this attribution but long established official endorsement has earned it issuance of a set of Bahamian Quin centennial Postage Stamps.

That was good enough for Kent. He wanted to see the spot of the first landing by Columbus in 1492. It's a small island measuring 12 by 6 nm and it is tightly bound by reefs except in the north. There is an absence of natural harbors and only one small marina. Kent chose to dock at the marina and not anchor because of surge from the ocean surf.

They ventured a trip into Cockburn Town and found it to be a bit rundown and not the happy, vibrant place they found the Abacos to be. Although they found the surrounding water was famous for diving and Kent enjoyed this since he had not had the opportunity to dive since they left Tortola.

There were incredible drop offs a very short distance from the island. In fact not more than five nm out, the depth was 24,000 feet. But a day and a night here was enough so they got underway with the next major lay over in the Turks and Caicos Islands easily a three day sail.

Grand Turk Island was just one of the several other islands that claimed being the first landfall of Christopher Columbus. Others were Cat Island, Conception Island, Mayaguana and Semana Cay and others.

Kent said "I guess we'll never know for sure but for myself, I saw enough of San Salvador. Our next stop will be Providenciales in the Caicos Islands. The locals there call the city Provo. That's a lot easier to pronounce. We'll be in blue water all the way and the weather forecast looks good with a fresh breeze so we should have good sailing most of the way. I'll take the watch the bulk of the time but I'll need some relief later on."

"No problem honey, it's pretty easy in this kind of weather and especially with the steering vane working so well. It sure pays to have a quality boat like this one. I'm glad we spent the extra money" said Teddi.

"The main thing is to watch out for other vessels since we're pretty much in the shipping lanes and the big ones have radar and look out watches so we're pretty safe."

The day passed uneventful and all was well. They had their evening meal in the cockpit since weather was so cooperative. Kent was enjoying a glass of after dinner wine and Teddi cleared away the dishes and went below to wash them and stow them away.

She called up to Kent "I'm going to take a nap. I'm bushed. When I get rested up I'll relieve you so you can catch forty winks."

"Okay dear. Get a good rest because I'm not a bit tired and I'll work on a float plan until it gets dark."

Time passed quickly and it was close to midnight when Teddi stuck her head up through the hatch and said "I'm awake dear. I'll get a cup of coffee and be right up to relieve you."

A few minutes later she appeared with a cup in her hand and said "Okay skipper, go sack out. I feel all rested now."

"Sounds good. I was getting sleepy. The course is 132 degrees and we're holding steady on it but the wind has lessened so we're not making as many knots as we were earlier. You shouldn't have a problem. Yell if you do."

He went below and stretched out in the quarter berth so he'd have quick access to topside if he was needed. It wasn't long before he was sound asleep and having pleasant dreams. After a few hours of sound sleep he became half awake and heard a snap above his head caused by a flap of the mainsail.

He wondered if it wasn't just an errant puff as happened earlier. But the sail flapped again and soon filled out as he felt the boat heel to leeward. The mast creaked and they were making way again slowly picking up speed.

He thought he was dreaming again but no that was Teddi's voice "Kent are you awake? I see lights."

Kent suddenly became fully awake and he scrambled out of the bunk and climbed up to the cockpit.

"What have you got dear?"

Teddi pointed. A ship was approaching from the north. Its port running light was intermittently visible and her range lights were open a few degrees indicating that they were a few points on her port bow.

They watched the distance close for about fifteen minutes without any noticeable change in relative bearing. By all rules of seamanship this meant they were on a collision course.

Kent grabbed the VHF radio and called on channel 16 trying to contact the huge ship. No response. The Sea Rose II was lit up like a

Christmas tree and easily visible on this clear night. Apparently the lookout had not seen them or if he had he was not about to change course or speed.

Kent started the engine, shifted into reverse and gave it half throttle to halt all forward motion and let the blind behemoth pass in front of them. Suddenly when the huge ship was less than a quarter mile away it made a panic turn to port heeling sharply as it did. For a few horrifying seconds they were dead in her path looking down the barrel of her aligned range lights and both red and green running lights.

He jammed the gear shift forward and gave her full throttle. It was panic time, it seemed like an eternity before they started moving forward again and then another eternity before they gained any headway at all. Suddenly Sea Rose II was running for her life. They could hear the throb of the ships engines as she passed by close to their stern and her great bulk blotting out the sky.

The Sea Rose II pitched wildly as the huge bow wake lifted her and then dropped her into a deep trough like a cork and then buried her bow. As soon as she righted herself the stern wake caught up to them and rocked them violently from side to side. Kent steered straight through the huge boiling wake, taking green water over the bow, crested and then down again into another trough, mast vibrating from the turbulence and then into the relative calm sea directly to the stern of the huge ship. He fought the hidden turbulence caused by the huge twin screws until it finally subsided. The adrenalin was still pumping as the Sea Rose II settled down. The freighter continued on unconcerned.

He shut down the engine, pointed her into the wind and sat down until the trembling stopped. He felt weak and had a sick feeling in his stomach.

Teddi said "I was so scared. You saved us honey. They would have run us down."

"Thank God that we have a seaworthy boat here" said Kent breathlessly.

CHAPTER TWENTY NINE

The next day they were in sight of Mayaguana and by the end of the day it was almost out of sight. They thought about stopping but were sailing so well on a fresh breeze they decided to continue on to Provo, a very desirable port of call. Provo offered just about everything on their contingency list.

Since the Turks and Caicos are part of the British Admiralty, another customs clearance would not be needed. There are two groups of islands, the greater part, the Caicos, forming a crescent around the northern edge of the Caicos Bank. The Turks are outlying islands and are separated by deep water from the Caicos.

Provo was the city of choice for its shore side facilities and shelter. Turtle Cove Marina was highly recommended and that's the spot Kent would aim for. Due to the protective reef which lines the north side of the island and the narrow poorly marked channel going into the marina Kent would need all the help he could get from Teddi. But this was the place for appearance, facilities, and the feel of a U.S. type marina. With Teddi's delicate condition he thought it best.

The first part was easy. He went to Providenciales north waypoint, steered 137degrees and traveled 8.5 nm over deep water to Sellers Cut waypoint. After negotiating the cut it was a matter of following the red and green day markers in the channel for 2.1 nm using the old seaman's guide of red-right-returning. The charts showed 5.5 ft. at mean low water and since his draft was 5.25 feet and it was approaching low tide he would be close. The channel markers were 6 foot floating posts and it was evident that several were missing.

The chart showed nine legs before you enter the final 180 degree curve which then takes you to the marina entrance. After they had cleared the cut and entered the channel the biggest danger was to be swept sideways by wind or wave and end up on the rocks but they were in luck since it was a calm day.

On in the channel there were mud banks on each side latticed with mangroves and evidence of fishing traps. They groped blindly for the deep part of the channel and could find no day markers. Kent slowed and told Teddi to keep a close eye on the depth gauge. It was now dead low tide and spots in the center of the channel were showing less than seven feet. He radioed the marina to advise that they were arriving soon and to get a dock assignment and to advise his predicament in the channel. They advised that it would get deeper as he approached the marina.

As he signed off, the depth gauge showed 8 feet and climbing, so he kicked up the RPM's and day markers appeared again.

"I think we're home free" said Kent.

Suddenly a shift in current and a gust of wind pushed the boat to starboard. Teddi screamed "Kent the depth is 8—7—6—5—4!! BACK DOWN—BACK DOWN!! Oh my God we're aground."

The boat ran hard upon sticky mud, its bow dipping down as she came to a hard halt. Kent reversed the engines and she didn't budge. He didn't want to run the engine too long in this shallow water because of the danger of clogging the filters or of pulling sand into the engine.

He broke out the spare anchor, put on a bathing suit and walked it to the other side of the channel. He then wound the anchor line around a winch and tried to winch the boat off of the shoal to no avail. It was then he opted to call the marina again.

"Turtle Cove Marina, this is Sea Rose II, can you send a tow? We've run aground just past English Channel."

"Our regular tow boat is out for the day on a job but we can send a local fisherman named Bones. He can help and if he can't get you off you'll have to wait for high tide."

"Thank you Turtle Cove. When will he be here?"

"He's on his way and should arrive within 15 minutes."

It wasn't long before they heard the put-put of an outboard motor and around the bend a fishing boat appeared. Sitting in the stern, steering towards them, was a black man with snow white hair and full beard and a huge grin on his face.

He called out "don't worry skipper, Bones is here and we'll have that beautiful sailboat floatin' again in no time at all."

He pulled along side. "Hello skipper. This spot has seen sailboats before. The deep water is off to the left and if the marker that was blown away in the last storm was still here you would have seen that. Right in the middle is a big mud flat and just sucks you right in. Secure a line to your stern and we'll try to pull you back and get some water under you."

"Okay Bones. My name is Kent Allison and this is my wife Teddi."

Kent tied a line to a cleat and threw the bitter end to Bones who made it fast to his boat.

"I'm going to rock you from side to side before we pull straight back to break the suction in the mud and when we pull back, gun your engine in reverse and give 'er hell."

"Okay" said Kent. "Let's give it a try.

After a few minutes of worrying the sailboat back and forth, Bones put a strain on the tow line and yelled "Okay skipper now give 'er hell."

Both engines screamed with full power. The sailboat didn't move. Kent and Teddi moved from one side of the cockpit to the other trying to rock the boat. The outboard was smoking and Kent was sure it would overheat and seize up. There was a slight rumble from under the keel and a tremble from the deck under their feet. Suddenly they lurched astern and they were free of the slimy mud bottom. They were floating again. What a wonderful feeling.

Thunderous laughter and whooping came from the fishing boat. Bones yelled "See I told you so skipper. Here's your line and now just follow me to the marina. I'll make sure you don't get into any more trouble. I'll show you which dock you'll be using. The office folks have already gone home. You can see them in the morning."

Both boats meandered up the channel and on into the marina. After they tied up Kent yelled "Hey Bones I'm ready for a cold one. How about you?"

"Give me a minute to secure my boat and I'll be right with you skipper."

Bones tied up at a nearby dock and came aboard. Kent asked him "What do I owe you for the tow Bones?"

"No charge skipper. I have an arrangement with the marina where I help them and they give me free dockage. I make my money taking people fishing. My specialty is bonefish fishing. That's how I got my name."

"Wow! That sounds like fun. I'd like to go sometime while we're here if you've got an opening. I haven't been bonefish fishing for years."

"I'm open tomorrow morning. If you're up by 6 or 6:30 just meet me at my boat and we'll go out."

"I'll be there Bones."

They drank their beer, told some sea stories and became fast friends in no time at all, the way seafaring men seem to bond.

Kent asked "Do you know of a place here in Provo called Suzi's Raw Bar & Grill? A friend of ours, Roger McNulty recommended it. He said to look it up and mention his name."

"Yes, it's a good spot and run by good folks. You'll find it" he called back as he shuffled off.

Later Kent walked to a car rental agency right outside the marina entrance and picked up a rental car. They thought they'd treat themselves to a restaurant dinner tonight and cruise around the island.

Kent said "While I'm out fishing with Bones tomorrow you can start replenishing our provisions. We'll locate some stores tonight so you'll know where to go in the morning."

"I think I can find some things right on the property. Looks like a very well run marina."

"One of these times when we're exploring I want to look around for Suzi's Raw Bar & Grill."

They headed west and made note of the shopping areas for Teddi. Soon they came to a cove on the west side of the island where several ships were anchored. Kent checked his map and saw that this was called

Tiki Huts Anchorage. It was not well protected from the open water and he could note some surge.

"This is obviously an anchorage for mega yachts and larger ships. With any kind of weather a small boat like ours would beat itself to death. Turtle Cove Marina is the right spot for us. Even though it was hard to get into." said Kent.

"Oh look Kent at that beautiful yacht anchored in close. It's so dazzling white it almost hurts your eyes. How big do you think it is?"

"That one's well over 200 feet. It either belongs to a corporation or to a multi-multi billionaire. I can't quite make out the name. It looks like – yes - it looks like "Shangrila". Wow - there's even a small swimming pool amidships—big bucks."

"Well I've had enough looking for today. It's almost sunset and I'm starving. I keep reminding you that I'm eating for two now." She said.

Kent chuckled "Okay let's go. I'm hungry too."

They drove back towards the business district and took a shorter route. As they rounded a bend they came upon a hand painted sign that said:

Suzi's Raw Bar & Grill
2 ½ miles ahead

"Well I'll be darned" said Kent "Bones was right. Let's give it a try."

They drove on and sure enough came upon Suzi's. It was an open air Tiki bar type place and it looked like a popular spot. They found a parking spot down the road and hiked back to the restaurant.

When they got there a pretty young waitress directed them to the only open table at the edge of the patio while she was delivering a serving of fried green tomatoes.

After they sat down the same girl brought a hand written menu and took their drink order. "The fish of the day is yellow tail and it was swimming this morning. I'll be back" she said.

"I have a feeling that this is a great place hon" said Kent "Roger said the conch chowder is to die for."

"Some chowder and the yellow tail sounds great to me" she said.

The waitress returned with Kent's Dewars and a lemonade for Teddi. "What'll it be folks?"

"We'd like a couple of bowls of conch chowder and we'll try the yellow tail and what ever comes with it."

"Good choice. A.D. will be out with the chowder in a few minutes. Just relax with your drinks for awhile. We're a little behind."

They sat and savored the island atmosphere all around them when they were approached by a dark complexioned man with a mid eastern look about him.

"Pardon me" he said, with a strange accent "my name is Dr. Amad Tobias. You look like new arrivals to Provo and I wish to welcome you."

"Thank you Dr. Tobias. My name is Kent Allison and this is my wife Teddi. Are you part of the local welcoming committee?" said Kent.

"Oh no, I am also visiting. My ship is anchored at Tiki Huts Anchorage. I happened to observe you looking at my ship awhile ago. I was waiting to come ashore and saw you with binoculars. Did you like my ship?"

"Yes, it's beautiful."

"Please, I would like to invite you and the beautiful Mrs. Allison to come aboard. Are you staying at the hotel? I can send a car for you."

Kent felt a kick to the shins under the table.

"No. We sailed in today in our boat. Thank you for the invitation but we're pretty tired and need some rest tonight."

"Of course, I understand. Maybe you could join our Bon Voyage Party tomorrow evening. We will be leaving the following day."

"Probably not, doctor. We'll also be leaving and it's a long sail to St. Martin."

"Very well then maybe we'll see you in St. Martin. That is one of several stops we will make." He bowed and left the table.

"Kent, that guy gives me the creeps" said Teddi.

"I know what you mean. It's almost like he exudes evil."

As they finished their drinks, a smiling gentlemen approached their table with a tray loaded down with two bowls of chowder. In a delightful southern accent he said "I'm so sorry for the wait folks. Seems like everyone wants to eat at once. I see that you're a Dewars man. Can I get you another one?"

"You sure can. You must be A.D. A mutual friend, Roger McNulty, told us to stop and say hello."

"Yes I'm A.D. How is old Roger?"

"He's doing well." Kent gave him a shortened version of the circumstances under which they met.

"That's quite a story. I'd like to hear more in detail and I know Suzi would like to talk to you. Would it be possible to come back tomorrow when we're not so busy?"

"We'd love to. Can we come for a late lunch after the rush is over?"

"By all means—your meals are coming now, please enjoy and we'll see you tomorrow."

After they finished a delightful fish dinner, they made there way back to the boat and relaxed after a very busy day.

Kent was enjoying a glass of wine and said to Teddi "I think I'll check around for a local to act as a pilot for us until we clear the Caicos Bank. I'd hate to run aground again and there's a lot of shoal in this area."

"Good thinking honey. We were lucky today. Let's go to bed. We've got a busy day tomorrow."

CHAPTER THIRTY

The next morning Kent was up before sunrise. He put on a pot of coffee and dressed in his fishing clothes. After pouring a cup of coffee he filled a thermos with the rest and trudged off to the slip where Bones had his fishing boat tied up.

When he arrived Bones was already there, hustling and bustling around preparing for a morning on the water. "Come on skipper. The fish are bitin'. I can hear them callin' my name." And he laughed in his way that seemed like it was coming from deep in his belly.

His voice was the timber of an old creaking cuttysark, as if his vocal cords had sucked in too much salt air over his many years on the water.

Kent threw off the dock lines as Bones pulled the lanyard to start the outboard motor. It sprang into life and they were free of the dock and on there way through the mist heading to Bones' special place to catch bonefish.

Soon it was sunrise and the sun was weak in the pale gray sky. The light was bleak and cool. The gloomy dawn found them under a swollen bruised sky that pressed down upon them.

"It's best that we do our fishing in the morning today. When that sun starts blazing down later and with all this humidity we'd melt away and get eaten alive by those pesky black flies. And besides, the fish

- 152 -

always bite better in the mornin' when it's a little cooler. We'll be at my secret spot in about an hour."

As promised, they arrived at the fishing hole in a secluded cove well hidden both from the water or the shore. The sun was higher now and had burned away the mist and high fog and it started getting warmer. And as promised the fish were biting. They both had close to their limit in a few hours and Kent's arms ached from constantly pulling them in. As he pulled another one into the boat, Bones chortled "that's a grunt skipper. Throw him back, we want bonefish today" and again the deep laugh echoed across the cove.

"Let's take a break, Bones" said Kent "I've got a thermos of coffee and some cinnamon bread that Teddy baked the other day. I could use some about now."

"Good idea" said Bones as he secured the rods, "we've about got our limit anyhow."

As they were drinking their coffee Kent asked Bones "How long have you been here on Provo?"

"Too many years to count, skipper. Before here, I lived in the Bahamas and before that, in the Islas Los Testigos, where I was born. I met my wife in Nassau. We had a son, who still lives there. He's a doctor and his daughter is a nurse. His son works as an orderly while he studies Hospital Management. I'm very proud of my son and my grandchildren."

"And rightly so, I imagine your wife is too."

"Yes she was. But I lost my wife a little over a year ago. She passed away here in Provo from breast cancer."

"I'm sorry to hear that, Bones."

"Skip' we had a good life and most of it here. We were lashed to this place together, me and her, like riggin' and sail, but the sail gone now and it's not the same place—can't be the same place without her. I guess that's why I'm moving back to Islas Los Testigos. Provo's like a sunken ship for me skipper. This place is in the past, but the wind keeps blowing and pushing me along on a beam reach. That's the way she would have wanted it skipper, for me to keep sailin' so I'm goin' home to live out my days. Next I got to figure out how I'm going to get there. I'm pretty lonesome here and I still have some family there."

"Tell me about these islands. I'm not at all familiar."

"I don't doubt that skipper. My islands are about 45 miles northeast of Isla Margarita which is about 100 miles east northeast of Caracas. We are a possession of Venezuela but they pretty much leave us alone. The islands are very remote and off the beaten track. They are inhabited by a handful of interconnected fishing families who jealously protect the rich bounty of these islands caused by the Orinoco flow. The only government interference is from an outpost manned by so called coast guard who are supposed to administer the rules for fishing. The island chiefs really run the islands. I have heard that a new officer is now at the station and he's not popular with the islanders. They are beautiful islands with huge sand dunes, gorgeous beaches and lots of fish and the families want to keep it from encroachment. There are no ferries or airport so the only way in is by boat and there are no commercial harbors."

"Sounds like a great place to kick back and relax. Would they mind an occasional sailboat stopping by?"

"No. In fact boats like yours are about the only ones that stop because we don't offer the things that cruise ships are looking for like shopping and fancy restaurants."

"Hmmm! Bones would you be interested in crewing on my boat? We planned our next stop to be St. Martin and then proceeding southwest towards the Panama Canal. It would be very easy to detour a little south to your islands. I'd love to see them, especially if I had someone to introduce me to your island chiefs. I'd be very happy to trade your passage for your knowledge of the Bank and help with the sailing."

"Skipper, you're the answer to my prayers. My sweet darlin' must have sent you to old Bones. She's probably lookin' down and smilin' and sayin' "go home Bones, go home" Oh Lordy. Can you give me two or three days to wind up my affairs? I've already got a buyer for my little boat and other than that I'm about ready."

"Take what time you need" replied Kent "And I know Teddi will be very happy to hear that her sailing duties will be curtailed for the time being."

They shook hands on their arrangement and Kent briefed him on what was to be done before they could get underway. Bones was beside himself with happiness and was practically glowing. His exuberance spilled over and Kent was laughing out loud.

Two very happy men made their way back to Turtle Cove Marina. On the way they passed the white mega yacht anchored at Tiki Huts Anchorage. Bones gave a little shudder as they passed by and said "there's evil aboard that ship skipper. I'll be happy when it leaves."

After they filleted their catch, Kent took enough back to the boat for a couple of meals. The rest went with Bones with the biggest part to go to Suzi's Raw Bar for the catch of the day.

"Well honey" said Kent "Not only did I have a great day fishing but I made a deal with Bones to crew for us for the next couple of weeks."

"Oh,that's great. That solves your problem of getting through the banks and solves my problem of standing helm watches, at least for a while. Tell me all about it."

Kent gave her the low down on the islands that they'd be seeing and about Bones' family.

After taking a little nap through the noon hour they hopped into their car and made their way to Suzi's Raw Bar and Grill for a late lunch.

When they arrived, the lunch crowd had thinned out and there were only a few tables occupied. A.D. saw them coming and said "Sit over hear. This is the best spot in the house with a cool breeze to keep away some of the heat. Have you had lunch?"

"No we haven't A.D. And I'll bet the catch of the day is bonefish."

A.D. chuckled and said "Bones already told me that you caught most of these. Lunch is on the house. I'll tell Suzi to grill them for you and then come on out to meet you two."

A.D. left and headed for the kitchen. When he came back he had two cold beers and a frosty glass of lemonade. He said "Suzi gave me the rest of the afternoon off and told me to sit with you until she comes out. She doesn't want you to get away."

"I'm curious A.D. How did you and Suzi happen to open a Tiki Bar here in Provo?"

"It's a long story. The shortened version is this. I'm a retired FBI agent and part of the job was to be assigned to various cities so Suzi and I seemed to be constantly on the move our whole married life. Suzi has been a wife and mother our whole marriage and now and then worked at a few office jobs. We came here after retirement and liked it so much we decided to stay a while. We got acquainted with the folks that owned this place but they weren't doing so well health wise. So we decided to give them a hand. It got so they were too sick to run it so the next thing I knew we were restaurant owners."

"Well you sure look like your doing well."

The waitress came with a tray of food. Kent and Teddi wasted no time in digging in.

After a few minutes a pretty little blonde lady walked up to the table and in a delightful southern accent said "Hi!! How are you all doing here? Is the fish okay?"

"It's great" said Kent "you must be Suzi."

"I sure am. Now tell me how you know Roger."

Kent went through the whole scenario of the hijacking and Tortolo and how they arrived here. This took several hours and meant several beers and lemonades. They became fast friends by the time he was finished.

A.D. then said "I don't want to put a damper on this happy gathering but I wanted to caution you folks about a certain situation here on Provo."

"What's that A.D.?"

"Yesterday I noticed a man talking to you and I couldn't help but overhear him inviting you to tour his ship. He's not a good person and I want to caution you about going there."

"We don't intend to" said Kent "but tell me about him. What's his nationality?"

"He's from Iraq. And the rumor is that his ship is the former yacht of Saddam Hussein.

During the last time he was in port, a young tourist couple, who had been invited aboard for a party, strangely disappeared. Several other islands have reported similar incidents. The ships captain was notified, this morning, to leave the island and they're not welcome anywhere in the British Commonwealth in the future."

"I just know they kidnapped those people" said Suzi "A.D. tell them what you found out."

"I contacted an old buddy who is still with the FBI and asked him to check up on Amad Tobias and the other doctor Farouk Syed.

The report that I got showed that both of these men were born in Iraq but got their education in various institutions in the U.S. and in Europe. They then worked in a research hospital in Iraq and, directly under orders from Hussein, conducted some outrageous experiments, mostly with pregnant women. When Hussein was overthrown they disappeared for a while and then showed up in Iran, again working in a research hospital with a reputation for secret experiments. No great amount of detail was available. Again, they seemed to drop off of the face of the earth and then reappeared here in the Caribbean. They supposedly are heading up a hospital on some island near Venezuela, but it's all very hush, hush."

"Wow. That's some story" said Kent "you can be assured we won't be attending any parties aboard that ship."

"Please steer clear of these nasty people" Suzi said in a quavering voice "it just makes me shiver when I think of what happened to that young couple."

"Tell me A.D. is anything being done about stopping these people and finding the abducted couple?"

"One of the problems here in these islands is the many, many different jurisdictions and some of these island governments are fraught with puppet governors placed there by dishonest people. Some are very good and have forthright police protection. But getting everyone on the same page is very difficult and sometimes can be frustrating. This is one of those times."

Teddi shuddered "I never want to see that man again. I just knew the minute that I saw him that he was evil. I'm so glad we steered clear of him."

CHAPTER THIRTY ONE

The next four days in Provo passed without further incident. Bones came aboard and settled in nicely. They got underway and made it through the Banks with no problem. Conditions were perfect with both men standing watch at the helm, and Teddi providing them with meals and taking care of all the domestic duties.

On the fifth day they spotted the mountains of St. Martin. Kent charted a course for the northwest side of the 33 square mile island, where he could anchor in Marigot harbor and check in with customs.

"How long will we stay in Marigot, skipper?" asked Bones.

"We'll let Teddi decide on that Bones, but I'd say at least 4 or 5 days. As you know, it's quite a unique island. In spite of its small size it's been divided between two countries for 350 years now. The French side which is St. Martin and the Dutch side, which is Ste. Maarten, provides two distinct cultures. We'll anchor in Marigot, the capital of the French side but I know that Teddi wants to visit Philipsburg on the Dutch side for some duty free shopping. Also Grand Case, north of Marigot has some fine dining that would be nice to try. Once we check in with customs, we can travel both sides of the island without any further document disclosure by agreement with the two countries."

"I have two cousins that live here on the French side skipper. I haven't seen them for a good many years. I'd like to visit them if I could get some personal time."

"By all means Bones, your time here is your own. Just touch base with us after a few days and we'll set a departure time. No need to rush—I'd like to get some beach time. These white sand beaches are about as good as you can get."

They soon entered beautiful Marigot harbor and motored to the mooring buoys where they made fast to a vacant one.

"Hoist the Q flag, Bones, while I get the dinghy ready to launch. I want to check in before they close shop for the day."

After the dinghy was in the water and the outboard running smoothly, Kent motored into the city dock where he tied up in an area with several other docked dinghies. He then walked to the Customs office with his documentation and all the passports.

Checking in at a foreign port can be very pleasant or it can be very trying. In some cases, where the officer is very territorial and feels that his position is one of extreme authority, it can be a rough go and time consuming. Fortunately St. Martin is very receptive to tourists and visiting sailors.

The government offices were in an old fort with long cannon ranged on the entrance of the channel. In the courtyard were two wings. One wing for customs and other government offices and one wing for police headquarters. The customs office was pleasant and neat. Kent was greeted very politely, but in French, by a young receptionist. When Kent responded in English, she switched to English and asked if she could help.

"We arrived today and are moored at a mooring buoy in the harbor. I have my papers with me and would like to check in" said Kent.

"Of course, please be seated and I will tell Monsieur Boudreau that you are waiting."

After a few minutes he was ushered into Monsieur Boudreau's office and was met by a dapper looking Frenchman in dress khakis who scanned his documents. He asked if all crew members passports were here, nodded at the affirmative answer, stamped them and welcomed Kent to the island. What a nice welcome it and just set the tone for a very pleasant port of call (or at least up to this point).

He made his way back to the dinghy and motored back to the boat where Bones and Teddi had already rigged a bimini, over the cockpit, to shade it from the blazing sun and provide a cool place to relax.

"Okay crew, it's time to kick back a bit before we go ashore. We're all checked in and I could use an adult beverage to take the edge off—how about you Bones?"

"A cold beer would taste good about now skipper and I'm sure that Miss Teddi could use some of that lemonade I saw her mixing up a few minutes ago."

"Okay you guys relax and I'll bring up a tray of drinks and then let's make a plan—I'm anxious to feel some solid ground under my feet—and soon" said Teddi.

After they relaxed with their drinks, the plan was for Kent to take Bones in to shore, so he could look up his cousins, and then Kent would rent a car so he and Teddi could tour the island. He told Teddi to get herself ready and he would take her to dinner as a reward for all the good meals she had prepared on the trip.

He found a small puddle jumper to rent and drove it back to the parking area by the dinghy. When he got back to the boat, Teddi was ready to go. He quickly showered and they made their way to the restaurant in the La Samana Hotel which came highly recommended by a local bystander who said 'That's where Jackie Kennedy used to stay".

The hotel was located high up on a hill overlooking the ocean and a beautiful white sandy beach. What a gorgeous spot. No wonder Jackie stayed here.

The restaurant was very French and priced accordingly. Kent said, "Enjoy this, hon, we won't be dining like this very often—unless I hit the lottery" as he scanned the menu.

Teddi giggled, wiggled in her chair and continued reading the menu without looking up.

This was a place to dine—and dine they did. The waiter treated them like royalty and Kent responded by ordering the best on the menu including a bottle of champagne. Teddi agreed to have one small glass but just one time only.

As they were finishing desert they felt someone approaching their table and when he got closer they were startled to see that it was the strange doctor that had approached them at Suzi's place in Provo. It seemed like an evil cloud descended around them as he stopped.

"Well I believe it is Captain and Mrs. Allison, how are you? It is I, Dr. Tobias. We met in Provo" he said with an oily greeting.

"Yes doctor, we remember you. I didn't see your ship in the harbor." answered Kent.

"Marigot harbor is a little bit tight for us so we are in Phillipsburg. It has dockage for larger ships. In fact all the cruise ships tie up there. If you get to Philipsburg you must come aboard to visit. Perhaps stay for lunch or even dinner. We have a wonderful chef."

"Thank you but I doubt if we'll have time. We'll see a few beaches and then be on our way" Kent said in a very emphatic tone.

"What a pity. We'd very much like to entertain Mrs. Allison. I'm sure such a beautiful woman likes some of the finer things in life." He said with a leer that sent shivers up Teddi's spine. "Well I must join my associates. Goodbye for now."

After he walked away Teddi said "Oh Kent I'm truly afraid of that man—look, my hand is trembling. He just upsets me something terrible."

"Just relax sweetheart. Don't let him spoil a perfect evening. I wouldn't let him harm a hair on your head. Let's forget we even saw him—we'll probably never see him again."

Teddi sighed, smiled at Kent and said, "Thank you darling. I know that you'd protect me with your life. I'll try to forget that beast—thank you for a wonderful evening."

They finished desert, paid the check and drove back to the harbor where they parked the car. They didn't notice the van parked in the alley with three men inside intently watching them. It pulled away right after they motored out to the boat in their dinghy.

They were happy and secure on their boat and slept peacefully that night looking forward to the next day for some relaxing beach time. Kent had mentioned going to a spot called Orient Beach here on the French side. Teddi couldn't wait—she needed some time to just kick back and relax—and so did Kent.

The next day they got into their little puddle jumper, wearing their bathing suits under a cover up and carrying a cooler and picnic basket loaded with food and drinks. It will be a full day of fun and relaxation on the beautiful white beaches of St. Martin. They drove around and took in the sights until the sun took its toll on them driving with no air conditioning. Teddi finally said "I've had enough. Let's go swimming, I'm sweltering."

They soon arrived at a remote spot where their map showed a remote, rustic parking area with access to Orient Beach. They parked, unloaded the cooler and picnic basket and trudged through an opening in the very thick over grown rain forest. It led them to a winding trail, through the dense growth, which would end at the beach.

Shortly after they entered the dense forest they heard someone approaching from around the bend ahead of them. Soon a tall, statuesque, young blonde came into view and as she walked past she smilingly said "Bon jour" and continued on.

Teddi gasped, glared at Kent and said, "Oh my God, Kent, she was naked."

Kent chuckled and said, "Yes—I did noticed that" and he chuckled again.

They continued walking with Teddi muttering quietly to herself. Kent just smiled.

When they got to the beach, they chose a spot away from the few sunbathers that were relaxing on the sand. Teddi mentioned that most of them had scooped out a depression in the sand and had spread their towels in the shallow hole.

Suddenly she realized that none of the sunbathers had bathing suits on. She glared at Kent and said "Alright mister, did you know that this was a nude beach?"

Kent burst out laughing. "Come on now Teddi, we've been to many Pacific islands that have topless beaches. These are just happy people enjoying nature."

"Well, topless is one thing but complete nudity is something else. So don't get any ideas mister, my suit stays on. It MUST stay on."

"No, I didn't expect you to join the crowd but I'm going to take a swim in the altogether. And you know what? I'll bet no one will even notice."

Teddi just laughed and said "You never cease to amaze me Captain Allison and I guess that's why I love you so much."

They spent a lovely day at Orient Beach and enjoyed a cool lunch.

It was very private and no one even stopped by to pass the time of day. By late afternoon they had enough sun and decided to head to the car and do some more exploring around this beautiful island.

As they walked through the trail leading back to the car, a group of three, fully dressed, dark complexioned men approached them. The men stopped and one looked at Kent and asked "Pardon me sir, can you tell us what is the name of this place?"

"Why yes, it's called Orient Beach" said Kent as one of the men slipped past and behind him.

"Thank you, Captain."

Suddenly, without warning, Kent felt a blinding sharp pain at the back of his head. The world was reeling and as he slumped to his knees. Through the foggy haze, he saw a huge bald man grab a struggling and screaming Teddi. Another sharp pain blasted his temple and all went black. That was the last thing he remembered.

The huge bald man had grabbed Teddi and jammed a medicinal smelling cloth over her nose and mouth. She struggled and held her breath, the man was extremely strong and she tried to strike out but he had her arms pinned to her body. His forearms were as thick as logs and he had strength beyond what a normal man could muster. She wanted to scream again but the cloth was tight against her mouth and she couldn't. Finally she could hold her breath no longer and breathed deeply through her nose. It smelled terrible, tears rolled down her cheeks and she felt sick. The trees started spinning and then the darkness came like a curtain being drawn closed. She collapsed into the arms of her assailant and was in complete oblivion. Potpoo, the bald giant, turned his cannonball head on his thick neck and stared at her limp body. His eyes were deep in heavy folds of flesh.

He lifted her easily and held her in his thick arms while awaiting his henchmen.

While the other two dragged Kent's trussed up body into the brush, Potpoo carried Teddi to the awaiting van. After placing her gently inside, he injected a sedative in her arm. She was in a deep sleep in minutes.

Hours later, Kent awoke with a splitting headache and bound hand and foot with plastic ties and duck tape. He had been dragged into the thick brush along side of the path. He tried to yell but his mouth was sealed shut with duck tape. How long had he been unconscious? Where was Teddi? Can he work himself free? Maybe if he scooted back to the trail someone might help him. He wormed his way to the trail. It was difficult and exhausting but he must find Teddi. He shuddered when he thought what may have happened to her. The thorns on the jungle growth grabbed at his body as he tried to make his way. They ripped his shirt and scratched the tender skin on his torso.

When he finally made his way to the trail, it was deserted and it was getting dark. He was in pain from insect bites. His abrasions were burning from sweat and his head was throbbing. He'd try to make it to the car and maybe he could find something sharp to cut his bonds. It was slow going but he was making headway. Only a little further, he thought after what seemed like an eternity of wriggling like a snake. It was dark but the car was in sight. He was all alone. The only sounds were from some night creature's eerie calls.

As he entered the parking area, he spied a glass bottle glittering in the moonlight. He made his way to it and tried to break it but the sand was too soft to cause it to shatter. He pushed the bottle to the edge of the parking lot where the pavement began and slammed the bottle down with his bound up hands. It was difficult because he couldn't get much movement with both hands and arms bound. After several tries the bottle shattered. He grasped the broken off neck, of the bottle, and sawed at the plastic ties with the sharp edge. After he freed his hands he worked on the duck tape which had his arms pinned to his body and then freed his legs. Lastly he pulled the tape from his mouth which ripped the hair from his head and beard and caused even more pain.

After he was finally free he searched the area in vain for Teddi. He now realized that she had been abducted and he'd better get some help. He recalled seeing police headquarters next to the Customs Office in Marigot. That seemed to be the best place to report this and get some help. He reached in his pocket for the keys and yes they were still there. And strangely enough all his money and credit cards were also there. THIS WAS NOT A ROBBERY. He jumped in the car, started it and squealed out onto the road.

On the drive to Marigot he broke all speed records and when he laid on his horn to pass a slow pick up truck he was greeted with a torrent of French obscenities and hand gestures. But he didn't care—he raced on—he had to get help to find Teddi.

He replayed the incident over and over in his mind. Why didn't they rob him? And how did they know to call him Captain? He wore no clothing to indicate this. And most importantly, where did they take Teddi? He prayed that she was safe and unharmed.

Chapter Thirty Two

Kent screeched to a halt in front of the Marigot police station and ran inside. He staggered as he approached the front desk.

The young patrolman at the desk rose up and yelled at him to stop. Even though the order was in French, Kent understood the urgency and came up short of the desk.

"Please you must help me. My wife and I were attacked and she has been abducted. Can you help me find her?"

The patrolman switched to English. "Monsieur you are injured, please sit and try to contain yourself. I will get the Lieutenant to hear your complaint."

A voice came from the open door of an adjoining office, "I hear the commotion, send him in."

Kent was ushered into the office and the officer said, "I am Lieutenant Cousineau. Who are you and what is the problem?"

Kent introduced himself and told of their recent arrival in Marigot harbor and then quickly told him about the encounter with the three men at Orient Beach.

"Can you describe these men, Monsieur?"

"As much as I can remember, two of them were of average height and weight, swarthy complexion, dark hair and both had beards. The other one was a huge man, bald and clean shaven. He looked like a cross of mid east and maybe oriental."

"Hmmm. One moment please Monsieur." He then called out to the front desk "Patrolman, is Officer Beth Laurent still on duty?"

"She is just going off duty, Lieutenant. She is back in the break room now."

"Please ask her to come to my office."

"Oui Lieutenant."

"I have sent for a doctor to dress your wounds, Captain and we may have a lead on your abductors."

A female police officer entered the room and the lieutenant asked "Beth, please tell us again about the three men at the waterfront today."

"Oui, Lieutenant" said Beth " while patrolling the parking area by the pier, where the dinghies are docked, I noticed three men in a group talking and gesturing while looking out at the mooring buoy area. They were speaking in a language that I'm not familiar with but I asked if I could be of assistance. They responded that they needed no help and then hurriedly left the area in a large van. I thought that they acted suspicious so I included them in my report."

"Can you describe the van?"

"Oui. It was white and of American manufacture. Probably a rental from Philipsburg since our local auto rental agency has only small European cars."

"Thank you Beth. You've been very helpful. That will be all."

"Captain Allison, I will make an inquiry at police headquarters in Phillipsburg. While I do so, go with the doctor who has arrived and let him dress your wounds."

Kent returned to the front where the doctor awaited and went with him to a treatment room. The doctor first examined his eyes and determined that he suffered a concussion but felt a fracture was not evident. However an x-ray may be needed. He stitched up the cut on his head and then applied disinfectant to the scratches and abrasions on his body.

"Very well Monsieur, you should recover nicely from these wounds, however I recommend bed rest for the rest of the day and have someone watch that you do not lapse into a coma from the head wound."

Kent said "Thank you doctor but bed rest is out of the question. I must find my wife—I will find my wife. Please tell me what I owe you and I'll get on with my search."

"I understand, but you must try to curtail your physical activities. You owe me nothing. The town of Marigot pays me a retainer for these treatments. Good luck."

The Lieutenant entered the room and said "we might be in luck. The duty officer in Phillipsburg received a report—just hours ago—that early yesterday evening a group of men from a ship called Shangrila were transferring a patient in a wheelchair out to their ship."

"The officer noticed that the patient was a young woman, who was in a semi conscious state, and appeared to be anxious and at times agitated. When queried, the attending physician said that the woman was a passenger who had eaten some tainted food while ashore and he was returning her to the ship for treatment. She was incoherent, very ill and under the care of a physician and also en route to get treatment so there was no reason to detain them any further.

"There were three men with the doctor—whose name was Tobias—and the men fit the description that you gave me."

"That's her! That's her—and that doctor is the creep that approached us in Provo. They must get her off of that ship—she's in danger" said Kent

"Now I must give you the bad news, Captain. The Shangrila left Philipsburg harbor before sunrise today—an unusual departure time—she is already at sea and left no float plan with the harbormaster. We don't know where she's headed."

"Oh my God" said Kent as he slumped into a chair, "can't we do anything?"

"I'm afraid all we can do at this point is make a report to the Coast Guard, but even they are limited and of course the ship is en route to anywhere in the world. We have heard of many strange stories about that ship and it is not very welcome in many ports. It is said that its home port is at the hospital in Islas Los Testigos. This might be a good place to start, monsieur."

Kent's eyes lit up "that's where Bones is from. Lieutenant, my crew member is named St. John and is called Bones. He was going to look up his cousins here in Marigot who own a fishing boat. I think their name is also St. John. Would you have any idea where I might find them?"

"Hmm. I'm not familiar with the name but the fishing fleet is located just north of town before you get to Concordia. You might inquire at the marina office there. And, by the way, you might want to change clothes. Yours are pretty ragged. You may find better cooperation if you look more presentable and I'm sure you'll feel better.

"Thank you for all of your help Lieutenant. I'll do as you say. Please radio my boat if you hear any thing further," he said as they shook hands.

Kent scrambled out to the car with renewed energy and headed first to the Sea Rose II for a change of clothes and then to the road leading north out of town. It was now midmorning and he must not waste any time. He must find Bones.

After he left town, he soon spotted a sign that said 'Fishing Fleet—One Kilometer ahead'. He soon came to a narrow road which led to the boat docks and saw a building with "Marina" painted on the door.

He pulled up in front of the building, parked his car and entered. A young "island looking" man said "Hey mon, you want to go fishin'?"

"Not today" Kent answered "but maybe you can help me. I'm looking for two men who own a boat here and I think their name is St. John. I need to contact my crew member who is their cousin. It's important."

"Oh. You must be looking for Bones. Yes he's here. The three of them are at the end of B dock filleting the fish they caught early this morning. It's only a short walk. It's the second dock that you'll come to."

Kent followed the directions and sure enough there was Bones with his two cousins.

"Bones! Bones—thank God I found you. I need your help."

"Skipper, what is it? You look terrible. Do we have a problem? Did someone rob you?"

"Bones, its Teddi—they took Teddi—we've got to find her." He was frantic.

"Wait a minute skipper—slow down—you'd better explain. First of all these are my cousins Pierre and Jean Paul St John. Now let's go to the boat and tell me what's going on here. I'm all confused."

They walked to the boat tied up on B dock and Kent settled down long enough to tell the story of the abduction and the information that he got from the police department.

All three listened attentively. When Kent finished Pierre said "this is not good skipper, those men are very bad. We left our island to come here because of them. We moved here with our families and bought this boat because of some strange circumstances going on. That hospital was built on one of the out islands much to the objection of all the fishing families that live there."

Jean Paul added "Our islands are owned by the Venezuelan government and for the last century they have pretty much left us to run things as we saw fit and didn't bother us. But as of late the corruption of those in authority has run rampant. They have placed a tyrant in the government office on the main island. He now has absolute control. Two years ago construction started on the hospital without any notification to the island chiefs. When they objected they were beaten and sent back to their island homes."

"What goes on at the hospital is suspicious and obscure since only a few domestic workers from our islands are allowed there, and only in the day light hours. Our sister, Lolita, is one of those. She told us that it is a research hospital and the few patients that are there are all women who are pregnant. Everything is kept very secretive."

"The hospital staff never comes to the other islands but Lolita tells us that they all seem to be of Mid East descent. They bring in supplies and travel to the main land by ship. We don't see them and as long as we leave them alone they don't bother us. But the tyrant on our island rules with an iron fist. It is no longer pleasant to live there."

Kent was very quiet and stared off into space. His eyes clouded up and he said "Teddi's pregnant."

Bones sighed deeply and all was very quiet. Soon he said "Skipper what do you want us to do? My cousins and I are with you all the way—we must find Miss Teddi."

"At least I know she's alive" said Kent "and I'm going to go get her. I don't care where she is or who's got her—I'm going to get her—or die trying. I can use all the help I can get but if any of you would rather not go with me I understand. I'd like to leave on the Sea Rose II tonight."

"I'm with you skipper" said Bones.

"We are too" said Pierre and Jean Paul at the same time. "Maybe we can get our islands back at the same time. We know others that feel the same as we do."

Kent and Bones hopped in the car and made their way to get the Sea Rose II ready for a three or four day sail. Jean Paul and Pierre went home to explain to their wives what was about to take place. They knew that the wives wouldn't be happy but they were sure that they'd understand and support them, it was their home too.

When Kent had his boat provisioned and crew aboard he made ready to get underway. He eased the engine forward taking up the mooring line. As soon as Bones yelled that he was free he called to pile on the canvas, sail after sail bursting out in quick successive explosions of brilliant white and the Sea Rose II tore eagerly out of the bay.

The night, under the full moon, was easily enough light to leave Marigot harbor and the Sea Rose II sailed out to sea. The helm watch will be broken up into four hour watches which will make for an easy sail. They will have plenty of crew to take advantage of every bit of wind and make good time.

The wind is in their favor tonight and they were making a good seven knots on a due south course.

CHAPTER THIRTY THREE

Potpoo gently lifted her out of the wheel chair and placed her on the stretcher that had been carried down the gangway by two orderlies.

Dr Tobias instructed the orderlies, "take her to one of the cabins on the main deck and place her on the bed. Nurse Tallett would take over from there."

The local policemen had seemed satisfied with his explanation—for now—but he better not waste any time leaving this port. He achieved his purpose and now must make haste.

He then called the captain from the quarterdeck phone and instructed him to prepare to leave Phillipsburg before dawn and chart a course for Islas Los Testigos. He then retired to his cabin where Dr. Syed sat awaiting him.

"Well Amad I see you were finally successful in obtaining the new specimen that you so eagerly desired. Your obsession was such that I wonder how much of your desire was to achieve a successful research project or how much was your own carnal lust." said Syed.

"It is no concern of yours Farouk," he answered sharply. "This specimen is of the highest quality and I'm sure she will go a long way in helping us obtain the perfect off-spring that will be a very possible fore runner for cloning. Your expertise is limited to the virtual reality equipment and that's where you should concentrate your efforts. My personal life is my own."

"Oh no," he snickered "it seems I have touched a nerve. My apologies if I have disturbed you doctor" he said, dripping with sarcasm.

"Just keep your opinions to yourself, Farouk," he said while glaring at the little man.

"Were you able to make contact in Philipsburg for the new batch of semen?"

"Yes, it's in the cryogenics lab. It's guaranteed to be of the parameters that we set previously. I made certain that they understand if another batch is as poor as the last there will be serious consequences. It was a waste to destroy specimens, as we had to last month. I think only three or four are worth carrying to fruition," answered Syed.

Tobias mused "with the Allison woman and the other three we were able to collect we should have enough to create some interesting experiments. Our benefactors are getting anxious."

"Ah yes, our benefactors. I only hope that we haven't promised more than we can deliver. They have been very generous but they soon are going to want to see results."

"Don't worry Farouk, we are very close. Now I must see to my latest specimen."

As he was walking to Teddi's cabin Dr. Tobias was stopped by a lumbering Potpoo who haltingly said "Dr. Tobias, may I ask you something?"

"What is it Potpoo?"

"Doctor I am in need."

"Okay Potpoo. What is it?" he said in agitation.

"Sometimes the experiments turn out badly" he stammered "and you have me destroy both woman and baby" he hesitated and looked off. "If this should happen with that Allison woman could I keep her for myself instead of destroying her? She is oh, so beautiful and I like her very, very much. Please, please may I?" he rambled on.

"Well Potpoo, that's a request I can't answer at this time. Let's wait and see how it goes."

"Oh. Oh. Well, thank you doctor. Okay I will wait," said Potpoo with a sad look.

Tobias continued on to Teddi's cabin muttering to himself, cursing the stupid giant and shaking his head. He entered the room. "Have you got her settled in, nurse?"

Nurse Tallett answered "yes doctor. I gave her another sedative just now so she's resting peacefully. She was getting very irritated and anxious. This one seems to have some spirit and she's very beautiful. Maybe this will be the one to give us the alpha male we're looking for."

'Yes. We'll be underway soon. Keep her sedated for another day. I would like to interview her before we arrive and before she goes through virtual reality. Keep me apprised of any changes or problems. How are the other specimens?"

"They are all in a twilight state now. Not as deeply as the Allison woman since we've had them aboard for the last week. But none are presenting a problem. I want to make sure they get nourishment and they can't get it if they're too far under. When will we reach the hospital?"

"We should arrive in two days or so depending on weather. Keep them healthy. Sick women don't carry babies well."

Tobias went back to Teddi's cabin and sat next to her bed and stared at her, possessively, for a long while. He finally whispered into her ear "Don't worry my darling I would never give you to that monster—you are mine and we'll make beautiful music together."

Chapter Thirty Four

The winds continued to be favorable deep into the night. If only they continued at this speed and direction Sea Rose II could make it to the Islas Los Testigos in four days.

A beautiful phenomenon was taking place on this perfect night. The sea was a glowing phosphorescent body of matter wherever it was disturbed. Great masses of ocean plankton glowed green and spread in the wake like lace on a woman's gown. Bones arrived to relieve Kent at the wheel and stared aft at the glowing wake. He remarked "It looks just like a peacock's tail."

They continued to make good speed and now that they had some time, Kent tried to hatch a plan. He queried Pierre and Jean Paul to give him as much they could about the geography of the islands and the surrounding waters that they could remember. They knew very little about the hospital on Isla de la Tortuga Grande because very few islanders were allowed on the island. But they felt that once they arrived their sister could fill them in since she was one of the few domestics that traveled to the island each day. As far as the idiosyncrasies of the islands themselves, the two boys were very helpful.

Pierre felt that they could sneak onto the island at night by swimming from Little Turtle which is a ridge of limestone, with a lagoon and reef lying about a mile and a half from Tortuga Grande. They can get to

Little Turtle on the dinghy which they can launch from the sail boat anchored in a cove at Isla Rajada, the island closest to Tortuga Grande (Big Turtle). When they get the layout, scout the island and find out where they are keeping Teddi, then they can plan further.

Initially they will find out if they can count on any help from the Venezuelan authorities at the coast guard office. This was doubtful. Next they will check with the council of the island chiefs which will be more likely to get some cooperation. But they may be limited because of the recent tightening of security.

Then they will get as much information from Lolita and other domestics as they can. Everything must be done as secretly as possible because the one advantage that they have is surprise. It is rumored that the authorities have intimidated certain islanders and have forced them to be observant of any wrong doing and to report to them under threat to their families.

The wind continued to be favorable and as they had hoped, they arrived at the big island, Testigo Grande, late in the evening of the fourth day. Kent decided to dock at Playa Real which was closer to the small village where the coast guard station was located. Pierre was acquainted with the harbor master and since it was after dark they were able to quietly slip in, unnoticed, and tie up at the fuel dock. The marina was closed but Pierre walked to the harbor masters cottage and, after explaining, secured a slip to tie up.

After discussing the whole situation with the harbor master and since they were able to enter the harbor under cover of darkness they decided not to check in with the authorities as yet. The three crew members all had close relatives here on the island and they wanted to talk to them to fully explain and see if they had any suggestions.

The first stop was at the two boy's mother's house. When their mother came to the door and saw who was waking her at this hour, there was hugging and kissing and tears of joy with all three. And then Lolita appeared. She was a big, strong woman and she grabbed both boys at the same time and hugged them until they were gasping for breath.

After the formalities were done they retired to the kitchen where the food and drink appeared in abundance. All the family news was brought up to date on both sides and then the mother went on to tell how the islands were not like they used to be. She told about the new man in charge of the coast guard station which now was more like a police station. And how the authorities from the mainland were now more strict with the rules of fishing. She told how the island chiefs wanted to send a representative to Caracas to complain about conditions and how this had been discouraged by force. So now they were very secretive about how to proceed next.

She said that since the hospital was built on Big Turtle it has only gotten worse. When they were first told that a hospital was being built they thought it would benefit them but not one patient has come from the islands. And during construction no islanders were used to build it. "We don't know what is done there but Lolita says that there are very strange experiments and all patients are young women. They come by boat and all seem to be pregnant or at least become pregnant. She thinks they are inseminated and then they stay awhile and most leave or at least seem to disappear. Lolita is frightened."

"If papa was still living I'm sure he would find out what is going on. The other island chiefs seem to be a little lost without him. Since you two boys are back maybe we can get them together and have a council meeting to formulate a contingent to go to Caracas."

Pierre spoke up. He said "First of all we must help Kent. His wife was abducted by those animals, that call themselves doctors, and some other beasts from the island hospital. She is pregnant and being held against her will. We must move quickly before we are discovered. Lolita what can you tell us about the layout of the hospital?"

"Yes, of course, I can draw a rough map for you. The largest building is the main laboratory where the technicians work and they take patients in for what I've heard is programming. No one is allowed in there but the doctors and the technicians. Next is the research facility which houses the offices and a series of small laboratories. One lab houses cryogenics. I think semen is kept there. We are able to enter this building and clean but always closely guarded. Sleeping quarters are also in this building.

About fifty yards north is a small but well equipped hospital. There are 20 patients rooms but only about 4 are in use right now. Quite a few women have disappeared lately. It's so strange."

"The equipment is all state of the art. They have several birthing suites, incubators, mass spectrometers, an electronic microscope but strangely enough right now there is not one baby in the hospital. A group of pregnant women were discharged before birth. They just disappeared over a weekend when none of us were working. They were just gone when we got back and the little doctor told us to clean the rooms."

"Thank you Lolita" said Kent "if you can give us a rough map it will be very helpful."

"Please be careful" said the mother "these people are evil."

"We will mother" said Jean Paul "but right now we need some rest."

"You're right Jean Paul" said Kent "I think we should get back to the boat and catch forty winks while it's light so we won't be seen. I want to slip out tonight and go ahead with the plan to scout the hospital so we can get Teddi out of there. I think it's going to take a couple of tries before we're successful. Lolita please get whatever information you feel that will help us but don't put yourself in jeopardy."

"The ship came in yesterday with several ladies and one seemed to be very special to Dr Tobias. She is very beautiful. Could this be your wife?"

"It's very possible. Would it be possible for you to talk to her?"

"I'm scheduled to clean rooms in the hospital tomorrow. I don't know if hers will be one of mine or not but I will try. Sometimes we trade rooms with the other girls. What should I say?"

"Just tell her that Kent is near and he will come and get you. Tell her to keep alert and don't let them sedate you. But Lolita, don't let anyone see or hear you talking to her"

"I will do my best Senor Kent."

Kent and Bones went back to the boat to get some rest but Pierre and Jean Paul stayed at their mother's house to rest and catch up on family news.

As they passed the marina office, the Harbor Master called out to them "Captain Allison, please come in to my office."

As they walked through the door Kent said "What is it? You look worried."

"Maybe I gave you bad advice when I told you to hold off checking in with the coast guard. They came by asking who is in the sailboat and where is the Q flag."

"We should have flown the Q flag and checked in this morning. It's not too late. Bones go down to the boat and raise the quarantine flag. I've got the papers with me. I'll go to the office and make some excuse as to why I'm a little late."

Kent walked to the center of the little business district. There wasn't much to choose from. The people here are very poor. It would seem they survive on fishing. There is no agriculture to speak of and the land is quite dry and barren. The locals do have a few goats and chickens and there are many wild iguanas. There are no gas stations, no telephones, no newspapers or even shops except for a small grocery store and the coast guard/police station.

It was a single story cinder block and glass structure half the size of the average McDonalds. The officer at the front desk rattled something in Spanish. After Kent asked him to speak a little slower, he referred him to an elaborately uniformed officer seated at a desk in the rear of the room. Kent approached him, papers in hand.

The officer was short, at least forty pounds over weight, with a pencil thin mustache and a cold smile. His English was serviceable, though broken and heavily accented but Kent decided against telling him that his Spanish was probably better. The name plate on his desk said Commander Lopez.

"So, Senor, you are the boat that pulled in during the night and neglected to check in this morning. Are you not aware that you are under quarantine until you are cleared?"

Kent answered "I'm very sorry Captain Lopez. My passengers, the St. John brothers, were so anxious to see their mother and it was very late, so late that I knew your office would not be open until this morning. Time just got away from me. I have all my papers here with me now and my mate raised the Q flag which he neglected to do when we docked."

"I am merely a Commander not a Captain Senor. Hand me your papers and let's see what I can do for you. Ah yes. This may be serious enough to require a substantial fine in order for you to clear customs. We don't get many visitors here and we must be very careful about smugglers here in the Caribbean."

Kent narrowed his eyes but kept silent and waited for Lopez to finish scanning the papers.

He slapped the documents down on the desk. "I can give you a three day clearance, Senor, if you are willing to pay $100.00 per day in U.S. currency. Otherwise I must ask you to clear this port within the hour." in a rough, authoritative voice.

"I understand Commander" said Kent in a respectful tone and keeping his temper in check. "I assume you want this in cash?"

"Yes, of course. And these two passengers, the St. John brothers, are they coming back to live or are they just visiting?"

"They're just visiting family and will be leaving when I do. They live on St. Martin."

"Very well, tell them to stop by and I must stamp their passports since they are no longer residents."

"Thank you Commander. I'll make sure they stop by." said Kent as he handed over three $100.00 bills. He collected his documentation papers, turned on his heel and walked out past the smirking officer at the front desk who sarcastically said "Adios, Senor—gringo."

Kent grimaced as he heard boisterous laughter from inside and knew that he was the butt of their joke. They were number two on his priority list.

When he got back to the boat Bones was already very nervous and agitated. When Kent told him of his encounter with the Commander, Bones became livid and it took a while before Kent could calm him down.

"Please Bones, my purpose here is to find Teddi and if it takes a little grease on a palm, I'll do it even if I don't like it. Don't make any waves until I achieve my purpose."

"It didn't used to be like this skipper. This was a nice laid back place to live before. I'm not sure I want to stay. After I help you find Miss Teddi, I've got a decision to make."

"Okay Bones. But for now, please go tell the boys that they must stop by the Commanders office and take their passports. And tell them to cool it, at least for now."

"Don't worry skipper, we won't do anything to screw up the mission. But when this is done we may come back and straighten things out. This is our home."

CHAPTER THIRTY FIVE

Kent and Bones turned in since they were up most of last night and tonight would be another without rest. They awoke early in the evening when Pierre and Jean Paul came aboard. Pierre had a rough map of the island and hospital location furnished by Lolita.

Kent studied it and formulated a plan. He said to the others "there's a new moon tonight so it will be very dark which works to our advantage. We'll wait until all is quiet here in the harbor and steal out under the mains'le only. There's a light wind and that way we'll be without noise to arouse any suspicion. When we clear the harbor we can sail or motor, whichever is best, and make way to Rajada where we'll anchor in the small cove on the east side of the island. Bones I want you to stay with the sailboat. If anything goes wrong and we don't make it back, I want you to high-tail it back to Testigo Grande and tie up at the dock. At that point you can decide the best way to help us or to somehow get the Venezuelan government involved. The three of us will take the dinghy to Little Turtle where Jean Paul will stay with the dinghy. If Pierre and I don't make it back, you can hotfoot it back and help Bones. Pierre, you and I will swim to the island and scout it out for our rescue mission tomorrow night. Let's look over the map. It's a very small island with a well protected bay to dock their ship.

"It appears that the Main Laboratory where most of the

programming, and what ever else is done, is located at the south end of the island. I imagine that it is well guarded so we'll stay clear. The labs and living quarters are just north and centrally located on the island—also a place to use caution—especially at night when it will be occupied"

"Next are the huge generators, the heart of their system, since it's their only source of power—and I imagine they use a lot of power—this may be critical on our rescue night."

"Pierre is there a possibility that we can have access to a few sticks of dynamite?"

Pierre smiled "There is a possibility skipper, but I must make sure after we get back on Testigo Grande" he said as he stared at Bones with questioning eyes.

"Good. And last, but not least, is our target. The hospital is located at the north end of the island. Little Turtle is located on the northeast side so it should be an easy swim directly to the north side of the island. There's a good beach to land on and should be an easy access to the hospital. This beach is used by the patients, as well as some of the technicians for relaxation. It should be deserted at that time of night."

"Well boys, what do you think? Any suggestions? And just in case any of you feel apprehensive about this and would rather not participate, I will understand. Now is the time to let me know so I can adjust the plan."

Kent sensed the ill ease as the three crew members silently looked at each other and finally Pierre said "tell him Bones, tell him what the old man told us."

Bones took a deep breath and said "Skipper, we had a meeting with the oldest island chief and he encouraged us to go ahead and make a plan to rescue Miss Teddi and whoever else we can help in that hospital. It seems that the chiefs have all been very unhappy with the conditions here on our islands. He has sent two of the chiefs to Caracas to officially complain about the circumstances here. One of them has a brother-in-law in politics on the mainland and he has promised to accompany them to the government offices in Caracas. As with all politics it may take longer—than what you would like—to officially take action, so he said to go ahead—but be discreet— try not to harm life or limb to ourselves or others—or to destroy property, so as not to hinder the mission to Caracas. But to answer your question, we are with you all the way—we are willing to do what ever it takes to help get our home free from this oppression and we'll do whatever we have to do to get Miss Teddi free.

"Thanks guys. You don't know how much this means to me and after this rescue is over and I get Teddi safely out of here, I promise to return and help to get rid of these monsters. Let's make preparations to get underway."

The night was calm and dark with no moon. The boat was safely anchored at Rajada with Bones aboard standing watch, the dinghy beached on Little Turtle and Jean Paul observing the surroundings with the night binoculars. All was going according to plan, Kent and Pierre swam to the north end of Big Turtle. They landed on the sandy beach and scurried into the rain forest to keep from being discovered.

As they rested from the long swim they observed the surrounding area. A well worn path led to a building, which according to their map, was the hospital. It was likely the confining residence for Teddi and the other patients. There was a windowless double door on the beach side of the building. A large padlock was very evident on the outside of the door. There would be no access here without a key or bolt cutters.

They silently stole around to the front of the building and observed the main entrance. Posted by the doorway was a security guard, well over six feet tall, broad-shouldered, and quite imposing in his starched khakis. Through the glass doors they could see, seated at a desk in the lobby, a large, formidable woman in a nurse's uniform.

The dirt and stone path leading away from the hospital was weakly illuminated by ground level lighting, and wound its way through the lush jungle growth, past the phalanx of mammoth generators and ended at the living quarters and labs. They made their way along the path but ducked into the bushes whenever they had the chance. So far they encountered no other guards or any other islander.

They skirted around the labs and living quarters, no guards were evident here—but they were not needed since these buildings were for resident personnel.

The largest building housed the main laboratory. It was obviously the heart of the system and the most impressive of the three buildings—a state of the art structure. The importance was evident by the two guards posted at the one and only entrance. The only windows in the building were at the entrance lobby emphasizing how secret the experiments must be in this evil looking building.

As they were making their way back to the beach they heard voices approaching. They ducked into the heavy jungle growth and lay quietly until two guards passed by on the path. They quickly rose up and hurriedly trotted down the path. Suddenly a shout from the direction of the hospital echoed "Hey, whose there?"

They stopped and dove into the brush and lay still. Pounding footsteps ran by on the path as the two guards, that had passed them, ran by. One of them called out "Martinez, what's the problem?"

"I heard footsteps like someone running, Sergeant."

"Are you sure? We didn't see anyone. Was it this way?"

"Yes sir, it was."

"Okay, we'll take a look. You get back to your post at the door."

Kent and Pierre lay very quietly and when the two guards made their way on the other side of the path, they crawled through the brush as silently as they could towards the beach. It was dirty, tedious work but finally they were at the edge of the rain forest and had just the expanse of the beach to cross.

They waited until they couldn't hear the guards beating through the brush and then they made a mad dash for the surf.

About half way there they heard a shout "Halt. Stop where you are or I'll shoot."

They ducked their heads and kept on running and as they hit the water, a shot rang out, but they were already in the foaming surf. They both swam as fast and as hard as they could. Several more shots rang out and Kent saw a splash close by. He had lost track of Pierre but he had seen him hit the water ahead of him, and Pierre was a strong swimmer, so he was certain he would be out of range soon. However the guard had a good bead on Kent and a few shots splashed close by—too close for comfort.

Suddenly the water seemed to boil all around him and a pod of bottle nosed dolphins came flashing in to meet him, their tall fins cutting the surface as they steeple chased over the swells. They circled him, whistling and snorting with their huge mouths in that silly dolphin grin, gamboling and squeaking while they looked him over.

One big old bull nuzzled against Kent which allowed him to grab the dorsal fin. The old boy was offering him a tow. Kent hung on as the old bull took off and Kent surfed along for about a half mile in what seemed no time at all. He was safely away from the beach and had even passed up Pierre. As happened once before, dolphins had come to his rescue. He, thankfully, watched in wonderment as they swam on out to sea.

Pierre swam up to his side and said with a hearty laugh

"Skipper, I couldn't believe my eyes when I saw you flash by. That old bull was having a ball. It was awesome"

"I couldn't believe it myself. What a thrill! I can't help but wonder about the intelligence of those creatures. They seem to sense when trouble is brewing. How can you explain it? They're magnificent..... But let's get back to the dinghy. We've got to get back before daylight."

ON THE ISLAND

"Where did they go Sergeant?"

"They went into the surf. I'm not sure what happened—maybe sharks got them. There was a lot of splashing and I may have winged one of them. I think they were just kids from Rajada satisfying their curiosity. Let's check and see if anything was disturbed and make a report to the Captain."

LATER—IN THE SECURITY OFFICE

"We checked the whole island thoroughly Captain. Everything was in place. Nothing had been disturbed. There was no boat. We feel certain that it was teenagers out for a lark. We've had this happen before. Just kids"

"Very well, make out a report so I can give it to the doctors. You know how touchy they can get."

CHAPTER THIRTY SIX

Teddi thrashed violently in a troubled sleep. It was so dark and she was searching for Kent. She had to find him, but she was all alone and she was in a dank, dismal swamp. What was that noise? Something or some ONE was chasing her. She could hear loud splashing in the swamp behind her. I've got to run but my legs are so heavy, I've got to save my baby—

HELP—HELP ME—KEEENNT. HELLLLLP MEEEE!!!!

Suddenly she was rudely awakened by a nurse. "Be quiet, you'll wake up the other patients. Just relax, you were dreaming, you'll be fine. Just go back to sleep. The doctor wants you to be alert in the morning"

"Where am I? What patients? Oh that awful man was hurting me. Is Kent okay? Why did they attack us? Where is Kent?"

"I said, go back to sleep. The doctor will be in to talk to you in a few hours and he'll explain everything." said the nurse as she left the room.

Teddi lay there trying to put things together. She was still woozy from the sedative and still shaken from the very realistic nightmare, and then she realized that she was strapped to the bed. No wonder she dreamt that she couldn't run. Her legs and arms are tied down and she had very little movement. She could move her head and she was oh so thirsty!

She then dozed off and when she awoke with a start she looked around. "Oh good" she thought "it's getting light out. I can barely see out of the window. It looks like some trees outside. I must be on the ground floor or not very high because I can't see the treetops. If only I could rise up, maybe I could see where I am."

The door swung open and a young Hispanic man wheeled in a breakfast cart. "I will leave this for you Senorita but only Nurse Tallet can free your arms. She'll be here soon."

As he was leaving the same nurse that she saw earlier entered the room. "Alright dear, I'll free up your arms so you can eat and if you're a good girl we'll leave them free but if you get wild again we must restrain you."

"What do you mean, wild again?" said Teddi "Where am I? Where's Kent?"

"Never mind, just be a good girl. The doctor will be in after breakfast."

"I need to use the bathroom" said Teddi.

"Okay I'll take off the leg restraints. I know that the doctor wants you to be comfortable. But remember, be good, don't do anything foolish and you can remain unrestrained."

After the nurse left, Teddi examined her arms and could see bruises, shaped like huge fingers. Her shoulders and thighs also hurt and what she could see also was bruised. But she was famished so she dug into her breakfast. It was delicious. At least this hospital had good food.

As Teddi lay there, still confused as to where she was, the door slowly opened and two doctors walked in. As she looked up she was startled to see Dr. Tobias and she put her hand to her mouth and suppressed a surprised whimper.

She stared at him as he said "Now, now, my dearest Mrs. Allison don't be frightened, no one here will harm you in any way. You are under my exclusive care. I want you to try to relax while I explain why you are here. We will see to it that you will come to be very happy to be here. But first we need some information."

"What did you do to Kent? Who were those men? Where am I?"

"Don't worry about Kent, he's okay. He's probably off somewhere sailing on his boat. I'm sorry that those men were over exuberant, they have been reprimanded. You are in a special kind of private hospital on an island off the coast of Venezuela. We do research here and you will be a part of an experiment that will do you no harm and it could benefit all of mankind some day. Just lay back, my dear, and relax. This is Dr. Syed, he'll ask you some questions."

"I don't want to be an experiment. Please let me go. I don't want my baby to be hurt."

"What did you say??" nervously questioned Tobias as he glanced at a startled Syed, who was wide eyed, with mouth agape.

"I'm pregnant" cried Teddi in a firm but frightened voice.

The two doctors stood up staring at each other with puzzled looks on their faces.

Syed muttered "Doctor, I think we should have a consultation" as he turned and left the room.

"My dear, are you sure? How far along are you?"

"Of course I'm sure. I'm still in the first trimester."

Tobias turned and left the room after giving Teddi two capsules and a glass of water.

Dr. Syed was waiting in the hall for Tobias. His tone was brusque "Okay Amad what great plan do you have now? This special patient is turning out to be one big problem. I think this one should be terminated before we get ourselves into one big mess. That husband of hers is still loose and he looked like the type that doesn't give up easily. Especially now."

"I will admit it isn't going as we planned but maybe we can salvage something out of this. She's still a very desirable specimen. Let's not do anything rash as yet. I'm going to my office to think and sort this out." He no longer had the authoritative demeanor.

Dr. Syed left the hospital and walked briskly past the generators towards the living quarters building. He had a bottle of scotch squirreled away in his room and although it was early in the day, he felt badly in need of a good belt. He got to his room and poured out a healthy drink and gulped it down. As he sat staring out the window the scotch started to relaxed him so he poured another one and sipped it while his courage increased with each sip.

As he looked out, and he saw the giant Potpoo lumbering towards him on the path, an idea struck him. He thought to himself. "Why does Tobias think he can call all the shots? I have as much authority as he does and he fantasizes over that woman. He just wants her for his own pleasure and it's going to jeopardize the whole operation. I'm going to take matters into my own hands. I'll show him."

"Potpoo, come into my room" he called through his open window.

The giant lifted his cannonball head when he heard Syed's call and grunted to himself. He entered the building and shuffled down the hall to Syed's room, knocked on the door and entered when the door swung open.

"Come in Potpoo, I have an assignment for you."

Popoo grimaced and rubbed his hands together, in anticipation, while he listened intently.

Syed continued "There is a specimen that needs to be terminated. She's in room number four. This must be done tonight after all is quiet and done discretely while Dr. Tobias is sleeping. It's the Allison woman and...."

Potpoo bellowed "Noooooo! She's mine. You can't hurt her. I want her for mine."

"You fool! Do as I say, you imbecile! I want her dead and the body disposed of by daylight tomorrow. Is that clear?" He said in agitation.

Those were the doctor's last words on this earth. Potpoo grabbed his neck in one giant paw, squeezed with all his massive strength and all life oozed out of the little man's body in seconds. His head was still attached but only by flesh and it flopped to the side as Potpoo released him.

The huge assassin stood beside the body and blubbered "I told you, she's mine, she's mine." He locked the door with the doctor's keys as he was leaving and lumbered down the path, sobbing and muttering to himself. "I told him. I told him. He shouldn't have told me to hurt her. I've got to find the other doctor and tell him. I want her for me. I must have her."

CHAPTER THIRTY SEVEN

After the doctors left, Teddi felt very drowsy and soon dozed off. She slept comfortably until lunch time and awoke when a food tray was wheeled into her room. This time it was brought in by a heavy set Hispanic woman who greeted her pleasantly, as she entered the room.

"Good afternoon Senora Allison my name is Lolita and I have brought your lunch."

Lolita nervously glanced around and then silently closed the door. She hovered over Teddi's bed and whispered "Senora, I have a message from Kent."

"Kent? Is he okay? Where is he?" Her heart was beating like a trip hammer.

"Shhh. Please Senora, I am not supposed to be here. I bribed the orderly to allow me to bring your food. Captain Kent told me to tell you to stay alert and that he was coming for you as soon as he could, maybe even tonight."

"How will he do it? When will he come? Please tell me."

"I don't know any details, but he knows where you are being held. My brothers and I will help all that we can. That's all I know, Senora, now I must go before they get suspicious."

She left the room and Teddi felt renewed just knowing that Kent was okay and trying to come to her. She must play along with these people to make it as easy for Kent as she could. As she ate her lunch she thought "I must keep up my strength, I must, no telling what I may have to do to escape this place.

Later that afternoon, the nurse came in accompanied by an orderly, pushing a wheelchair. She said "We're going to wheel you out to the patio for some fresh air and later Dr. Tobias wants to talk to you further about your treatment. It seems that you've given him reason to alter the original schedule that was planned for you."

The orderly wheeled her outside to a pleasant fenced-in patio. He turned to leave and said "I must leave you for a moment Senora to bring another lady out and then I will stay and assist both of you for your needs."

As she sat there alone, she sensed someone staring at her. She turned to look over the fence and was startled to see the bald giant that had abducted her. He had a strange look on his face, almost angelic and his slanted eyes were filled with tears. He took a step towards the patio and appeared to be ready to scale the fence when he suddenly stopped and ducked into the bushes. She breathed a sigh of relief but found she was trembling.

Just then the orderly came through the door pushing another wheelchair with a pleasant looking, pregnant young girl sitting in it. He said "Okay ladies you can visit with each other. This is Sandra and this is Teddi. I'm going to sit in the corner and relax with a smoke. I'll stay away from you so it shouldn't bother you at all, this is the only place we're allowed to do that."

"Hello Sandra. How far along are you?"

"I'm about five months, but I miss Ron so much. I don't know why he doesn't come to see me more often. It seems like he only comes after I'm in the Reality Room. This place so strange and, oh I get so confused. I just can't remember things.

"What is this place, Sandra? I've only been here since yesterday. At least that's all I remember."

"Remembering is the most confusing thing Teddi. Have you been to the Reality Room yet?"

"No, the only place I've been is right here. I think I was going to go somewhere but when I told them I was pregnant they got all excited and now that strange Dr. Tobias wants to talk to me about treatment. I don't want to be treated by him. I'm getting out of here."

"Getting out of here might be very difficult. They have guards all over the place and every time I start saying that I want to go home, they send me in for another treatment. I think that my memory is getting better and I'm less confused, but that other strange doctor, the little one, said something about turning up the gain next time. He really gives me the creeps. I think they are giving me a treatment tomorrow."

Teddi leaned over and whispered "Sandra, do you really want to get out of here?"

"Oh yes, Teddi. But how could you do it?"

"I can't give you any details but be ready tonight. What room are you in?"

I'm in Room # 1, the very first one in the hallway. I think I've been here longer than anyone. The other girls just disappeared. I'm really worried, they're here one day and gone the next. I think there are only a few of us here now and they are new. They seem to be under sedation, at least they all remain in their rooms. It's so strange"

"If they give you any sleeping pills tonight try not to swallow them. Stay alert and try to stay awake. Shhh, be quiet. Here comes Tobias."

As Tobias entered the patio he said "Take Sandra back to her room Pedro, I want to speak to Mrs. Allison privately."

Pedro wheeled Sandra into the hospital and Tobias turned to face Teddi.

"Well Teddi, you've certainly thrown a monkey wrench into our schedule and treatment plan for you, but we can adjust. I wanted to consult with Dr. Syed about a schedule for the Virtual Reality Room. He seems to have wandered off somewhere, but that's not a problem. We'll set up a time tomorrow or even the next day since we are not so busy right now."

"I don't understand why I'm going into this special treatment room doctor. What is it and how will it affect me and my baby?"

"It will not harm either you or the fetus, so don't concern yourself, just get plenty of rest tonight and let me take care of the rest."

He turned and walked back into the hospital, called the orderly and said "Pedro, take her back to her room and tomorrow morning prepare her for a transfer to the Main Lab for a treatment. I'll instruct nurse Tallett to get the meds for her. Have you seen Dr. Syed?"

"I'll have her ready doctor and no I haven't seen Dr. Syed since earlier this morning."

Tobias left and walked towards the living quarters. He approached Syed's room and knocked. When he got no response he tried to open the door and found that it was locked. He muttered to himself "That man is becoming irresponsible and I'm sure he's hitting the bottle. I'm going to speak to our benefactors about replacing him. Soon"

As he left the building and was walking on the path, Potpoo suddenly loomed up in front of a very startled Dr. Tobias, grabbed him by the shoulders and lifting him clear of the ground and growled "You promised she would be mine if you didn't want her. Why are you going to dispose of her?"

"Potpoo put me down and step back" he screamed, bug eyed." What is the matter with you? You look out of your mind and are not making sense. What are you talking about?"

"Dr. Syed told me to terminate Mrs. Allison. BUT I WONT DO IT" yelled the giant.

"WHAT? Where is that little weasel? I gave no such order. Just calm yourself Potpoo. Go to your room and relax while I get this matter straightened out."

Potpoo lowered Tobias, tears flowed. He turned and lumbered off mumbling and sobbing, flexing his huge paws as he made his way to the living quarters. He was oblivious as to what he had done to Syed and his encounter with Tobias, all this caused by his grief for Teddi.

Tobias stared at Potpoo's back, sensing how close he had come to an encounter that, in no way, could he have survived. His whole body trembled. He thought to himself "this is not over. That imbecile is overwrought and very dangerous. Hmm, I wonder if that is why Syed is not available. I'm going to have to search further and find him. He's hiding somewhere. Probably drunk."

CHAPTER THIRTY EIGHT

The rescue plan was prepared when the four men got back on Testigo Grande. Basically the four would sail to Little Turtle tonight, where Bones would stay aboard the boat, the three younger men would launch two dinghies and quietly row them to the island, landing at the same beach as before.

Pierre will create a diversion at the main lab which is the farthest away from the hospital to draw the security men to that part of the island. Jean Paul will plant a dynamite charge at the generators to destroy the panel board which will kill all power. Kent will wait at the hospital entrance until the commotion starts and subdue the guard and the nurse at the front desk and rescue Teddi. If all goes well they will launch the two dinghies, use the motors and power out to the sail boat.

"Okay men, let's get some rest. It's going to be a long, tedious night. All the equipment is aboard so all we have to do is shove off when all is quiet."

BACK ON TORTUGA GRANDE

Tobias and the two bearded henchmen searched the island for Dr.

Syed with no luck. They decided to search his quarters to try to find a clue as to his whereabouts.

Tobias used a master key to open the door to Syed's suite. He slowly swung the door open and the three entered the room. The stench of death was in the air.

"Here he is, doctor on the floor behind the bed. Oh my God, he's dead. Look at his throat, it's been crushed."

"Now we know what that brute is capable of" whispered Tobias.

"Potpoo has snapped and I for one don't want him to be mad at me" said the tall one.

"We've got to do something" said Tobias "I sent him to his room. I'm sure he trusts the two of you so both of you go and tell him that I want to see him in my office at the main lab. Tell him I have good news for him about Mrs. Allison. When we get him there I'll give him a drink which will quickly tranquilize him and then we'll decide what to do with him. I'll get security to remove this body and take it to the morgue in the hospital."

After the two bearded men left, Tobias retired to his room to think and try to sort out the recent problems that have cropped up. It was getting very complicated what with the sudden change of Syed's attitude and Potpoo going off the deep end. Maybe it all was caused by the addition of the Allison woman. It would be silly to let his carnal desires jeopardize the whole operation. Hmmm. I think it might be a good idea to enjoy her for a while and then let Potpoo take over. It would settle him down and we can replace Syed. After all she wouldn't last long under the passion of the huge monster. And then she'd be gone and forgotten.

Later, Dr. Tobias was relaxing with his decision when his door burst open and the tall one rushed in and said "we can't find him, Doctor, he's not in his room. One of the guards said he thought he saw him going towards the hospital but we searched and could not find him."

"We've got to find him. He's very dangerous in his present state of mind. He has an obsession for that Allison woman and in his little pea brain that's the only thing that's important to him. Go get security and search for him, you must find him."

****

Potpoo lay on his bed trying to sort things out but it was always so hard for him when things were not structured and he was not given direction. He scrunched up his face and clinched his hands. What should he do? He knew it was wrong to do what he did to Dr. Syed and he would be punished but they promised him he would have the pretty lady as his own.

"I still want her" he said and his own voice startled him. "I must have her and take her back to Bandar Abbas. The ship is leaving tomorrow. I'll go with them. I can sneak aboard tonight with the lady and they will not know until we are far out to sea, too late to bring me back. I'll go down to the ship now and talk to my friends in the crew."

He left his room and shuffled down to the dock where the ship was tied up. He went aboard and found the deck hands that always were friendly to him.

"Hi Potpoo. Why haven't you been down here to see us lately?"

"The doctors give me a lot of things to keep me busy. When is the ship leaving for Bandar Abbas?"

"We leave tomorrow morning before daylight. Why? Are you getting homesick?"

"Yes, I want to go home."

"You better talk to the doctors about that first, big fella. See you later, we have to prepare to get underway."

Potpoo walked around looking for a place to stow away. The crew was used to seeing him wander around and knew he was slow, and didn't cause any problems, so they thought nothing more about it. He found an empty stateroom that was used when they found women to take to the island. The key was on the table so he took it and locked the door as he was leaving.

When he left the ship he walked towards the hospital along the waters edge to keep out of sight. Suddenly he heard a shout "Hold it Potpoo. Stay where you are. The doctor wants to see you."

Potpoo turned and saw a guard with his pistol trained on him. The guard approached him and said "I don't want to hurt you Potpoo so don't try anything funny. Let's go back to the main lab."

Potpoo raised his hands and stared at the guard.

In his little pea brain he saw this guard only as a deterrent to his plan to take Teddi to Iran. He calmly said "I don't want to go" and as quick as a cat he jumped at the guard and swung a huge fist to the head. The guard raised his pistol and fired a shot. The bullet tore into Potpoo's body but didn't even phase him. The punch was a glancing blow to the side of the guard's head, but enough to knock him off his feet and stun him momentarily.

Even though wounded, Potpoo still had the strength of a bull. He leaped on top of the guard, ripped the pistol from his hand and tossed it aside. He wrapped his massive arms around his torso and squeezed the kicking, squirming guard until he could feel the crunch of his ribs. The sharp jagged ends of the ribs tore into his lungs and they collapsed, the air was trapped in the chest cavity and the lungs no longer were able to give breath. He stopped kicking and became limp. As Potpoo released his hold, the lifeless body gave a massive shudder and lay silent.

Potpoo stood over the body and stared. He reached for his side where the bullet had entered, and now lay buried in his abdomen. He felt the round hole where blood oozed out and stained his shirt. It wasn't bad, he thought, because he didn't feel much pain. That's good, because he had to get to his woman and take her to the ship.

He staggered down the path. It was now dark and he had to hide until he could get her and take her to the ship. He remembered a little work shed by the hospital where he could hole up until it was late enough to steal her and sneak aboard.

He lay in the shed watching the path leading to the hospital. Hours slowly passed, once in a while a security man would walk by. He thought they were probably looking for him. He was not feeling very good, a little nauseated and kind of dizzy. It couldn't be the wound because it hardly was bleeding now. His little pea brain just didn't know that the bleeding was all internal. Suddenly he became aware of a familiar figure walking on the path towards the hospital. It was Dr. Tobias. Where was he going? Could it be to the Allison woman's room? He must find out.

As Tobias entered the hospital, Potpoo slipped out of the shed and made his way around the hospital to the patio. The double door was not padlocked until nightfall. Maybe it was still open and he could sneak in. But it was getting late.

As he got to the patio he saw the orderly just ready to secure the door for the night. He said "Pedro, I want to get in before you lock up."

"Wait a minute Potpoo, I think Dr. Tobias wants you. You better come with me."

Potpoo walked slowly towards Pedro and with one swoop of his massive arm knocked him head over heels. Pedro landed very hard, striking his head, on the patio deck. He lay very still and Potpoo dragged him off to the side into some thick undergrowth. He then threw the padlock into the brush and silently entered the hospital.

He crept down the hall carefully avoiding meeting with anyone until he was outside of Room # 4. He peered inside the room. Yes, there was Dr. Tobias talking to a very agitated Mrs. Allison. He had a hypo in his hand and it looked like he wanted to inject her with something but she was resisting and struggled to get away from him. "May be it was something to hurt her or maybe even kill her" he mumbled to himself.

"I won't let him hurt you" he screamed as he lunged at a startled Dr. Tobias, grabbed the hypo and jammed it into Tobias's eye. Tobias screamed and tore the hypo out of his eye. "You fool" he yelled and pulled a gun from his holster. He squeezed off two shots, both hitting the charging Potpoo, who staggered but kept coming. He grabbed the doctor in a bear hug, the gun was now facing the doctor's chest and it went off. The doctor slumped to the floor, a baffled, wide eyed look on his face as he was falling. Potpoo stood over him and suddenly dropped to one knee. He was weak from the internal blood loss and the room was spinning.

Teddi ran from the room, when the men were grappling, and burst into Sandra's room. Sandra was startled and screamed "Teddi what's going on? What's all that noise?"

"Shhh. Keep quiet, I'll explain."

They huddled together as they listened to the guard running past to investigate what the shots and yelling were all about.

The guard exploded into the room and saw Potpoo kneeling next to Tobias' hemorrhaging body. The sight unnerved him and he was paralyzed with fear when Potpoo stood, loomed over the body with an agonized look on his face and dripping blood from the last two wounds. He turned towards the panic stricken guard and before the guard could react, Potpoo charged, and using all his draining strength, he barreled into him, knocking him through the open door and into the hall, where he went sprawling.

Dizzy and disoriented from the impact of the 360 lb. giant, the guard tried to draw his gun but Potpoo rose up from the floor and pancaked on top of him before he could extract it from the holster. As they struggled, two more guards ran into the hall with drawn AK 47's. The prone guard yelled "Shoot him, shoot him or he'll kill me.'

A fusillade of shots rang out from the two automatic weapons, the most rounds striking a convulsing Potpoo. The giant rose up, flailing his arms and roaring like an enraged bull. He was still huge and formidable even in his final moments. He took two staggering steps towards the two guards, blood pouring from many wounds, and then fell forward in a final desperate lunge. He fell to the floor and landed like a huge redwood tree felled from a lumber jack's axe. A violent spasm came as he gasped his final breath.

The guards carefully approached Potpoo's sprawled out body and one nudged him with his foot. "He's gone" he said. And they both pulled him off of the prostrate guard who was now silent. When he was free from under the giant's body, they found the guard with staring, open eyes and a bullet hole in the center of his forehead.

"Don't turn the lights on, Sandra, let's get over in the corner and squat down low, maybe they won't see us if they come in" whispered Teddi.

"I hear running—there's more of them, They're yelling now and—oh my God, they're shooting automatic weapons—oh Teddi, I'm so scared" said a trembling Sandra.

"Come and sit with me, honey. Let's hope Kent gets here and gets us out of this. Oh I just hope he's okay and they're not shooting at him."

The two pregnant women huddled in the corner, in the darkened room, waiting and silently praying for rescue.

As the two guards stood over the body of their fallen comrade the floor nurse ran into the hall with the Colonel in charge of the Guards and two more men.

She said "let me help with the wounded."

One of the guards said "they are all dead, Colonel, except for Dr. Tobias, he's in Room # 4. It looks like he was shot while struggling with Potpoo, he's unconscious, but breathing. We killed Potpoo and an errant shot killed Lopez. We also found a body in the brush near the patio, we think it's the orderly, Potpoo probably killed him, too."

"What about the patients" asked the Colonel.

"We only have four at this time and two are under deep sedation. The Allison woman was in #4 and Sandra, our only long term one is in #1. I'll check on them." answered the nurse as she walked towards #4.

"Okay, both of you men get a couple of gurneys so we can get these bodies down to the morgue. With one doctor dead, one unconscious and the ship leaving in a few hours, it looks like I'm in charge. I've got to get in touch with the owners and find out what to do next."

"Colonel, Colonel" called the nurse "the Allison woman is gone, she probably got frightened when Potpoo and the doctor were struggling and ran off. I'll check on Sandra."

"She can't go far, we'll find her." said the Colonel.

The nurse opened the door to Room #1 and peered in. It was dark and quiet. She started to turn on the light but hesitated, thinking to herself "why wake her and cause more problems. I better find Ms. Tallett to tell her Allison is missing and get some direction."

The nurse scurried off to the living quarters to awaken nurse Tallett. The Captain and two guards returned to the security office in the main lab building and the two remaining guards started moving bodies to the morgue and Tobias to a hospital bed where an intern examined him.

Tobias stirred and the intern told him "Just relax doctor. The bullet passed clear through and it appears it didn't hit anything vital. I'm not sure about your eye, it looks like it's losing some fluid. I'm getting some help and we'll move you to the ship. I can work on you there and we'll be underway as soon as I get you aboard. I have a feeling we don't want to be here on the island for awhile." Tobias nodded and closed his eyes.

CHAPTER THIRTY NINE

Down at the beach, on the north end of the island, two rubber dinghies, with the three men aboard, silently rowed in from the sea. They beached the boats and dragged them up to the tree line where they covered them with palm fronds. Two of them had side arms and one had an automatic rifle along with a knapsack of equipment.

"Okay men let's get up to the hospital where I'll wait for the explosion and Pierre's diversion at the main lab" said Kent.

They crawled through the underbrush and were soon in sight of the rear of the hospital. Kent intended to cut the lock with bolt cutters, when Pierre caused the diversion at the lab, but for now he'd stay hidden.

Suddenly the doors flew open and two security guards came out pushing a gurney. One of them said "He's right over here in the bushes, let's get him loaded."

They lifted the dead body on to the gurney, pushed it through the open doors and then closed the doors after them.

Kent said "hold it guys, something's going on here. They didn't lock the door. Maybe we should look around first. This might be easier than we thought. Or maybe security is even tighter, making it much harder than we thought. Could go either way."

The three of them waited until the activity on the other side of the door stopped. Then Kent quietly stole up to the door and carefully opened it just a crack so he could peer inside. The hall was empty and it appeared that the front desk was empty. "Hmm. Strange" thought Kent.

He could see that the door to #4 was open. That's Teddi's room. Not a good sign, but he couldn't see inside. He turned to his two companions and said "Jean Paul, go to the generators and set the charge. Come back here and we'll use the remote to blow it if we need to. Pierre you can wait here for me. I don't think we'll need the diversion at the main lab. Keep me covered with the automatic rifle."

He opened the rear door wide enough to slip through and left it ajar, so Pierre could watch. He silently stole to the open door of #4 and peered in. The light was out but, lights from the hall were enough to illuminate the room. He could see that it was empty but also that it was all in disarray. "Not good" he thought to himself "Lolita said that room #1 had a girl named Sandra in it, who may have befriended Teddi. That's my only choice."

He slinked down the hall. #1 was adjacent to the lobby so he had to be careful. He crouched in front of the closed door and listened intently. All was quiet, she probably was sleeping. He put his hand on the handle and turned it. Good, it wasn't locked. He hesitated, he heard a whisper from inside and what sounded like a shooshing sound. He slowly pushed the door open and entered the room.

A tiny little voice said "it's Kent—Oh my God, it's Kent." The next sound was the patter of bare feet and Kent caught a charging Teddi in his arms. Tears flowed and Kent showered her with kisses. He swung the door closed and in the darkness he said "my darling I was so scared that you were gone for good. Thank God I found you. Now, let's get out of here."

"Can we take Sandra? Oh Kent, please. She's five months pregnant and wants to see her husband so bad. She's scared that they'll do more terrible things to her. Please let's take her with us."

"Sure we can honey. Wait—be very quiet—I hear someone coming. Sandra, get back in bed and cover up. Teddi, you and I can get in that corner where you were hiding before. Quietly now" whispered Kent.

As the Colonel in charge and the floor nurse entered the hospital, she said "I'm sure Allison wasn't in her room and I looked in all the rest of the rooms, except for Sandra's. She could be hiding in there but I'm sure Sandra is sleeping. I don't want to wake her.

"Listen nurse, the way things happened here tonight, I'm not sure what the status will be for all these women. I'm waiting for a return radio message from the chief of security in Iran, as soon as he contacts the owners of this operation, he'll get back to me. They may need to contact some authority in the government. This was a hush, hush research project and it goes up pretty high. Can you imagine the investment here?"

"Okay, I'll look in on her and check out the room. Here we are. This is #1."

She opened the door and switched on the light as they entered.

The sudden brightness blinded Kent for an instant, but he was ready and had his pistol drawn. In a loud, firm voice he yelled "FREEZE!! Keep your hands where I can see them, soldier. Get in here—both of you and move against the wall."

"You won't get away with this" said the Colonel "my men know that I came here and are on the alert."

"Just relax and no one will get hurt. First of all remove your pistol with two fingers of your right hand, grab the barrel with the left hand and hand it to me."

The Colonel did as he was told.

"Teddi, take Sandra and go to the patio entrance where you'll see one of my men. His name is Pierre. Wait there with him and I'll be along after I detain the Colonel."

Suddenly Pierre excitedly burst into the room and cried "Skipper, I hear shooting and yelling at the generator area. I'm afraid Jean Paul has been discovered."

"Take the women to the dinghies, launch one and take them to the boat. Use the motor, there's no need to be silent now. HURRY!! I'm going to help Jean Paul."

"No, Kent. They'll kill you. Stay with me" shrieked Teddi.

"GO WITH PIERRE TEDDI" Kent ordered in a loud, firm voice.

As Kent was distracted by Teddi, the Colonel charged him, knocked him askew and off balance. As he groped for Kent's gun, Pierre rushed him from behind, swung the butt of the automatic rifle, striking him on the temple, and opened an inch long gash. The Colonel slumped to the floor and lay there unconscious.

"Get moving, Pierre. I'll lock up these two in here. Jean Paul and I will follow in the other dinghy. Give me the rifle, I'll need it more than you will. MOVE IT!! Get these women on the sailboat and wait for us."

Pierre and the two women hustled down the hall to the patio door. Kent cautiously ran the other way, after locking the nurse and Colonel in the room. There was no longer a guard at the entrance so he burst through the doors and hurriedly made his way to the generators.

As he rounded a corner on the path he saw several guards standing over a prone figure. He was sure it was Jean Paul. As he watched, one of the guards kicked Jean Paul in the belly. A grunt and then a slow moan came from the prone body.

Kent could wait no longer. He screamed "FREEZE!! I've got you covered" from his hiding place in the brush.

One of the guards dropped to a knee and fired a burst from his AK-47 in Kent's direction but it was wide of the mark. Kent drew a bead on the culprit and fired his automatic rifle. The soldier flew back and landed hard from the force of the bullets. He didn't move—blood flowed freely from two chest wounds.

"Drop your weapons and put your hands behind your heads or my men will open fire on all of you" said Kent, trying a bluff.

Two of the guards complied and dropped their guns but the third ran a few steps and dove for the bushes firing his gun as he did. Before he could hide himself deeper in the brush, Kent cut him down with a long burst from his automatic rifle.

"Jean Paul, can you get up?"

"Si skipper—I'm just a little sore" as he pushed himself to his knees and then stood up.

As he walked past the two remaining guards Jean Paul swung a round house right to the jaw of the guard that had kicked him earlier. The guard went sprawling on his face and then slowly raised himself to his knees, spitting blood and what looked like part of a tooth.

Jean Paul uttered some Spanish, or maybe it was French, at the battered soldier. Kent did not understand it, but he knew that it wasn't complementary

"Okay Jean Paul, put these tie ties on them, hands and feet, and let's get out of here."

"I was able to set the charge in the panel skipper. We can blow it at any time with the remote."

"Not yet—we may need it later—let's go."

As they were running down the path, a siren wailed from the main lab.

"There goes the alarm—probably a call to the lab people and other technicians to go to a secure station. I'm sure all the guards have all been called to general quarters before this. We've got to move fast."

As soon as he said that, he heard movement and voices on the path ahead of them.

"Hide in the brush, Jean Paul." He whispered.

As they lay down in the heavy undergrowth, four heavily armed guards ran by in double time.

After they passed Kent said "They may be going to their stations. Hopefully they'll all be at some other part of the island. Let's go."

They passed the hospital and entered the rain forest, which paralleled the beach. They moved as quietly as they could through this very thick jungle. When they reached the beach Kent pulled Jean Paul back and whispered "Guards. Stay down."

Two uniformed guards were in the prone position behind a dune with rifles trained on the remaining dinghy. They were partly hidden by the dune and did not present a clear shot. Kent and Jean Paul were at their backs and could only get an occasional glimpse and a reflection off of their rifles.

"Okay, now is the time to use the remote and blow the dynamite at the generator. When they hear the blast they may head back in that direction. If not they may, at least, rise up enough to give us a clear shot or it may just create enough confusion for us to reach the boat."

Jean Paul actuated the remote and in seconds, a bright orange fire ball lit up the sky, followed a few seconds later by a loud rumble. As hoped, the two guards stood up and jabbered in Spanish. Kent and Jean Paul trained their rifles on them but didn't fire because the guards suddenly took off in a sprint towards the jungle and soon disappeared.

"Wow! That was some blast" said Kent "did you use all the dynamite?"

Jean Paul just chuckled and sheepishly looked away.

The two waited until they heard no more running and crashing through the brush, then they ran to the beached dinghy. They launched it and Kent pulled the starter lanyard. It kicked over on the second pull and they were on their way at full speed.

Kent and Jean Paul reached the sail boat just before dawn. The first dinghy was tied up on the swim ladder of the Sea Rose II. Teddi was safe. When she heard the approaching outboard motor Teddi ran topside. She hopefully looked for Kent.

"Oh thank God" she exclaimed as they came into view "I was so scared that something bad had happened when we saw the flash in the sky and then heard the explosion, but Pierre told us that, probably, it was set off by Jean Paul as a diversion for escape, or at least that was the plan."

"Yes honey and it worked exactly like that. But I think Jean Paul used a little bit more dynamite than we planned. It was a bit more of an explosion than I anticipated.

Jean Paul laughed and said "It got everyone's attention".

Bones came topside and said "One more thing, skipper, just after the explosion, the ship sailed away from the island and they were really pouring the coals to her. Suddenly she turned around and went back and then she headed out again, flank speed. She was heading east."

"No telling what the repercussions are going to be, after this. I saw quite a few dead bodies other than the ones we did in, along with a destroyed electrical system, and general turmoil on the whole island. Depending on their attitude we could be in trouble" said Kent.

"Let's get underway. I want to make La Asuncion on Isla Margarita before nightfall. We've got to get the Venezuelan authorities involved in this. They can't all be corrupt. Someone has to take responsibility" he continued.

They pulled the dinghies aboard, weighed anchor and got underway for Isla Margarita.

Isla Margarita was 45 miles west of their position, so with a fresh breeze out of the south east they made good time. The island is well populated with Venezuelans and has an established governmental authority present.

Kent radioed ahead and asked to speak directly to the head of Customs and Immigration and was told to stand by for a return call in a short while. When the call came in, it was from Senor Jose V. Martinez, Chief Officer of Customs headquartered in Caracas.

Kent introduced himself to Martinez and said "Senor Martinez, I would like to meet with the authorities at Isla Margarita to discuss a very sensitive situation at Islas La Testigos. Can you arrange that?"

"Martinez replied "Captain Allison, we are very aware of the situation and are most anxious to talk to you. Some representatives from the Testigos met with me and my staff late yesterday afternoon. As we speak, a Venezuelan Coast Guard Frigate manned with Customs and Immigration officials is en route to Tortuga Grande for a full blown investigation. We also are investigating the local authorities and those in charge at the Testigos to find out why these conditions were allowed to start and to continue without notification here at headquarters. When you reach La Asuncion on Isla Margarita, proceed to the quarantine anchorage where a harbor patrol boat will be awaiting you. Please bring all of your papers and also all of your crew and passengers and board the patrol boat. They will deliver you to the local authorities where you can make a full report and we can then decide the next step. Please be aware that the government of Venezuela is investigating this thoroughly and expect your full cooperation in solving the problem. Do you have any questions?"

"No questions, Senor. Our E.T.A. at Isla Margarita is 1600 hours today. Sea Rose II out"

Kent turned to his crew and passengers and said "I think we've created a bit of a stir."

As they were entering the harbor at La Asuncion on Isla Margarita, a Coast Guard helicopter flew over the boat, on its way in to the island, where it landed in the vicinity of the harbor. Kent noticed curious passengers looking down at their boat as it passed over.

"Yes" he thought to himself "we seem to have created some attention from the authorities."

His crew doused the sails and he kicked over the engine. He steered the boat towards the anchorage and sure enough a harbor patrol boat was waiting for them. They pulled within hailing distance and a voice from a bullhorn called out "Please follow me, Captain, we have a spot for you to drop anchor."

"Well" said Bones "we're getting special attention. I hope its friendly attention."

"I somehow think that it is, Bones. Make ready to drop the anchor."

The Patrol Boat slowed and waved to drop anchor here.

Kent put the bow into the wind, slowed to idle, shifted gears to neutral and yelled "Okay Bones drop it here". When he felt the hook hit bottom he put it in reverse until he felt the anchor take hold.

When the anchor chain was made fast, the sails stowed away and fenders hung over the side, the patrol boat pulled along side and rafted off.

When they were securely tied on, the young skipper, dressed in neatly pressed khakis and a gold braid trimmed hat called "Permission to come aboard Captain Allison?"

"Permission granted" answered Kent and the Coast Guardsman clamored into the cockpit.

"Welcome to Isla Margarita, Captain. I am Lieutenant Alverez. I have been assigned to assist you and will remain with you as long as you are here on our island. If you will please gather all your documents and advise your crew and passengers to bring their passports and board my boat, we will make haste and get underway. I understand that Senor Jose V. Martinez has made a special trip by helicopter to be here for the interview. I'm not aware of all the details of this operation but you must be pretty important if Senor Martinez has made a special trip to hear your report. He reports directly to the Minister of the Interior."

"Well I'm very happy to hear that your government has responded like they have, although I'm sure that the Testigo Chiefs that met with him yesterday have explained the urgency of the problem. However, much has happened in the last 24 hours and I hope they understand why we had to do what we did. Let's get aboard, my crew is ready" responded Kent.

CHAPTER FORTY

As the Venezuelan Coast Guard frigate came within sight of Tortuga Grande, they spied a sleek mega yacht leaving the harbor at a high rate of speed. They veered away from the island and gave chase at flank speed. The Coast Guard Captain instructed the radio operator to try to establish contact and instruct them to heave to.

The frigate was slowly gaining on them as the officer of the deck reported that no response was coming from the yacht. The Captain instructed to keep trying and if no response came, the forward battery was to fire a shoot across their bow as soon as they were within range.

No response came. As the forward battery swung about to prepare to fire, the yacht slowed and a call came over the radio.

"This is the motor yacht Shangrila. We are a documented vessel with our home port in Bandar Abbas, Iran. May we ask why you are hailing us?"

The Captain said "Tell them that they are in Venezuelan waters and we want to inspect their vessel due to a report of a smuggling operation in this area. Stand by for a boarding party." The radioman passed on the message.

After a slight delay the yacht answered "We will heave to and stand by for your boarding party."

The frigate launched two motor whale boats, one with six armed guards and one with two Customs Inspectors along with four more armed guards. They came along side the yacht, tied off while the men off loaded and then cast off, standing by, clear of the vessel. The frigate continued training the 3 inch forward battery on the yacht to discourage any thought of resistance.

Aboard the yacht, the chief inspector was greeted by the captain and was handed the necessary documents and manifests. The inspector scanned them and said "These seem to be in order, captain. May we inspect your cabins and cargo holds."

"Of course. We have nothing to hide. May I ask what type of contraband you are looking for?"

"Aside from the usual drugs and firearms, we also have word of this ship being involved in a kidnapping and transporting of women. Our officials in Caracas have uncovered an elaborate plan aided by several corrupt government officials to use the island, which you just departed from, as a clinic for unlawful experiments on women. We are certain that it has resulted in the death of innocent victims."

"I know nothing of such experiments sir. My crew and I are restricted from leaving the ship while docked at Tortuga Grande. My orders come directly from my government in Iran. We have now been instructed to return to Bandar Abbas for reassignment. Our transporting of patients under the direction of Dr. Tobias is no longer in effect. In fact Dr. Tobias is on board and has been recalled to Iran."

"I see" said the inspector "do you have any other passengers aboard?"

"Only an intern who is attending Dr. Tobias —the doctor was wounded by an employee who went berserk and shot him. Also the Colonel, several security men and the head nurse came aboard at the last moment. There was an accident of some kind which caused an explosion and we received word from Iran to get underway immediately."

"You have no other women patients aboard?"

"No sir."

"We will conduct a search and I will await orders from Caracas after we report our findings. Now may I see this Dr. Tobias? I'm curious to find out why someone hasn't shot him sooner than this. Please take me to him and then remain on the bridge until I receive word on the next step."

The inspector instructed further "Ensign take a squad and gather the passengers. Disarm the security men and place the whole group under guard on the fantail. Signal the frigate to launch the tender to use as transport to ferry these people to our ship where they should be kept under guard. The rest of your men can accompany my assistant and conduct a thorough search. I want to know anything that seems out of order."

The captain escorted the inspector and two of the Coast Guardsmen to the sick bay where Tobias was being attended.

The Chief Inspector entered sick bay and observed the intern administering aid to a Mideast appearing man.

The inspector calmly said "Stand aside young man. I wish to question this man."

The intern bristled and sternly said "This man is my patient and is in no condition for interrogation."

"I said—STAND ASIDE!" said the inspector, now glaring at the intern and no longer in a calm voice. I have questions for this piece of inhuman filth."

The intern slowly slinked away.

Tobias opened his eyes and stared at this very official looking Hispanic gentleman who was glaring at the intern and now shifted that glare to him. He shuddered and closed his eyes trying to escape from this obvious threat.

"Open your eyes Tobias. I will not address you as 'Doctor' since you are a disgrace to the profession."

Tobias opened his eyes and said "What do you want?"

"Are you Amad Tobias, Administrator of the Clinic on Tortuga Grande?"

"Yes. Of course I am."

"Does this clinic operate as a research hospital under the direction of the Republic of Iran?"

"Yes it does."

"And are these experiments conducted on human females and involve enforced pregnancy as well as brain washing experiments?"

"I refuse to answer any more questions. I am under the protection of the government of Iran and I will see to it that you will answer to them for this interrogation."

The inspector broke into a wry grin and said "You will be asked much more when I deliver you to the authorities in Caracas and don't be surprised at the lack of support from the government of Iran as well as the Venezuelan authorities that you had met in the past."

"Get him ready to board the tender for transfer to our ship. This intern is to accompany him. Make it fast. I hear the tender approaching now."

When the tender arrived, a packet was given to the inspector who opened it and read the orders inside. When he was finished he went to the bridge and told the ships captain "I have received my orders. Our two governments have reached an agreement. You are to release all passengers to the Venezuelan Coast Guard for transport to Caracas for trial. You are then to immediately leave Venezuelan waters. You and your crew along with your ship will not be detained as long as you do not attempt to return to the island or any port under Venezuelan jurisdiction. If you do, your ship will be seized and you, as well as your crew, will be detained as smugglers. I suggest that you make all haste as soon as we depart from your ship."

"You have my word to do so, Inspector" said the Iranian captain, breathing a sigh of relief.

CHAPTER FORTY ONE

Kent, Teddi along with Bones, Pierre, Jean Paul and Sandra all boarded the Harbor Patrol boat for transfer to the City Dock where a van awaited them to take them to City hall. A meeting with the Venezuelan authorities was to commence as soon as they arrived.

On the way in to the dock, Kent noticed the trawler Semper Avante anchored a short distance from them. As they passed close by, both Inga and Dave were standing on the stern by the transom waving and calling their name. It was a pleasant surprise and when time allowed they will contact them and get together to bring them up to date.

They tied up at the City Dock, disembarked and boarded the van where they were then bussed to City Hall. Upon arrival they were ushered into a meeting room where a huge conference table, surrounded by padded chairs, was the center piece. Their guide motioned for them to be seated and announced in broken English that the others would join them shortly. He offered water or coffee, took their orders and left the room.

In a very short time the door opened and a group of Hispanic gentlemen entered. Kent and the other men in his group all rose to their feet and gazed towards the group which consisted of three men neatly dressed in conservative, trim business suits and three more dressed in high ranking military uniforms with a maritime theme, probably Navy or Coast Guard officers.

After the new group had chosen seats, the obvious leader of the group, who had chosen the seat at the head of the conference table, announced "Please be seated gentlemen" in very well modulated English and a hint of command in his voice.

He remained standing, ramrod straight, and continued in an authoritative voice "My name is Senor Jose V. Martinez. I am Chief Officer of Customs and Inspection stationed at the Customs Office in Caracas. With me today is the Mayor of La Asuncion, our host for this assemblage, and also attending is the lead prosecutor for the city of Caracas. Our military contingent includes the Commanders for this district for both the Venezuelan Navy and Coast Guard."

He took his seat and his demeanor seemed to soften. He turned towards Kent and said "Captain Allison and Mrs. Allison, my government welcomes you to Venezuela. Even though at this particular time, there are some issues of contention by those in both governments, and even if we cooperate with Iran on oil issues we do not condone inhuman acts. We recognize the service you have given and regret the inconvenience caused by some undesirable men who were allowed to perform inhuman acts by some greedy, dishonest officials. Please accept our apologies on behalf of our government."

"Thank you Senor Martinez. We accept your apology and are very impressed with the response to this difficult dilemma created by evildoers from a country noted for its terrorism" said Kent.

Martinez acknowledged with a nod of his head and then continued "now will you please introduce your companions and what is their connection? After which I will tell you the action that has already taken place and what further action is planned."

"Certainly senor" answered Kent. "This, of course is my wife Teddi who was kidnapped by Tobias and held in the hospital on Tortuga Grande. This other lady is Sandra Smith, also kidnapped about six months ago and was inseminated by Tobias and his group. She has many horror stories to relate. The older gentleman is Bones St. John, a crew member and future resident of Islas Testigos and also Pierre and Jean Paul St. John ex residents of Islas Testigos, currently residents of St Martin. Without their help I never would have been able to rescue my wife and Mrs. Smith. They put themselves in jeopardy to help me and to rid their homeland of the scum on that island."

"Yes, I have a short report of the property damage at the hospital. I'm anxious to hear the whole story. Very well, let me review what has taken place and is now ongoing."

Martinez continued "I told you by radio that a Coast Guard frigate was en route to Tortuga Grande. When it arrived, a mega yacht was observed leaving the island hurriedly. It was intercepted and boarded. A number of personnel from the island were aboard making an exit and bound for Iran. We detained all but the ships crew and returned the hospital personnel to the island. The ship and its crew were released with the orders not to return to Venezuelan waters under threat of confiscation and prison. Dr. Tobias, although wounded, was among those returned to the island. Any questions?"

Kent asked "How bad are Tobias' wounds and what about the other doctor?"

"He appears to have a flesh wound and is in no danger. Dr. Syed was found dead when our men searched the morgue along with the giant assassin and several others who all appeared to die from violent means of one type or another. The bodies are being removed and will be brought here for disposal if no one claims them. All personnel from the island except those brought in from Islas Testigos, will be transported to Caracas where they will be questioned and processed. We will indict those who deserve punishment. A thorough investigation is now in process in our own ranks. Those guilty of allowing this to take place and those who participated will be severely punished. The Minister of the Interior himself has ordered that this be cleared up with all possible haste. I have been given Carte Blanche to do anything necessary to get it done and put to bed. It is a very distasteful situation. The two women patients were revived from heavy sedation and have been transported by boat to Caracas where they are hospitalized and are being administered to by the finest gynecologists in Caracas. Their prognosis appears positive at this point but further study as to their condition is yet to be determined. They have both agreed to give a deposition when strong enough to do so. We are attempting to contact their families as we speak."

Martinez continued "The next subject will require some input from you Captain Allison and from Mrs. Smith. First of all Mrs. Smith, we have located your husband and he is now en route to Caracas. We can arrange a telephone hook up when he arrives there. We would like you and your husband to testify at the trials of this rabble. We will provide medical care for you, and your husband, as well as living quarters, all as guests of Dept. of the Interior. Please discuss this with your husband. He will be briefed before he calls."

"Now we must discuss the disposition of the hospital and the Islas de la Tortuga Grande. We have had some discussions at length with the island chiefs. First of all, the two Coast Guardsmen stationed at Islas Testigos have been removed and are en route to the base on Isla Margarita under guard. They will face a Summary Court Martial for conduct unbecoming a line officer and non commissioned officer. You have met Lieutenant Alvarez. He is being reassigned to Islas Testigos to reestablish the more desirable conditions that had been enjoyed in years past and deteriorated by the previous crew. Lieutenant Alvarez is an upstanding young officer and is expected to advance far in the service of his country. He will remain on Islas Testigos until order has been restored and train a replacement for permanent duty. He then will move on to his next assignment which I'm sure will include a promotion."

He continued "On the island which houses the hospital, there has been some property damage to the electrical system. The generators seem to be intact but the control panel was destroyed by some unknown means."

A quiet descended upon the meeting room. Martinez hesitated with a dramatic pause. He looked around the room at each person. Jean Paul glanced at Kent with a worried look on his face and a sheen of perspiration on his upper lip.

Martinez said "We don't understand why the felons wanted to destroy the equipment but in doing so they also caused a destructive surge which completely wiped out the software in the so called Virtual Reality Equipment. Perhaps they were trying to cover their tracks and didn't have time to destroy more of that horrible machinery. It is being dismantled and will be destroyed although it is of no use without proper software."

Jean Paul relaxed.

"The island chiefs have requested that we leave the rest of the hospital intact. They have agreed to rebuild the electrical system at their expense and to staff the hospital with medical personnel and a maintenance staff. They would like to maintain the hospital for use by the residents of their islands, as well as any surrounding islands in need of medical service. We have agreed to do so, with the understanding that the hospital is to be used as a non profit organization and be properly staffed and efficiently run, or the government of Venezuela will reclaim it and make an evaluation of the next appropriate action."

"Captain Allison, you and your wife are free to do as you please. You are under no restrictions and can leave or sail these waters as you chose. Have you and your crew discussed your itinerary?" asked Martinez.

"Yes, Senor Martinez. Pierre and Jean Paul would like to return to their families in Marigot. I have agreed to pay their airfare home in exchange for the fine assistance they gave me. They will then discuss their future with their wives. I have agreed to take Bones back to Los Testigos where he will retire and spend the rest of his days fishing for the fun of fishing. Teddi and I will spend some time on those tranquil islands and just unwind before we continue our cruise. Ms. Smith is under your care as you indicated before."

"Very well Captain. Lieutenant Alvarez will take the five of you back to your boat and after your two crew members collect their gear, he will take them to the airport. If you leave an address we will forward to you the disposition of the prisoners. Good bye and have a pleasant voyage." He said as he stood and shook hands with Kent.

They all left the building and rode the van back to the dock where they boarded the Harbor Patrol Boat and were ferried back to Sea Rose II. After all the appropriate good byes and hugging, Pierre and Jean Paul left for the airport with Alvarez. Bones and Kent were relaxing with a beer when the radio crackled and a call came in from Semper Avante.

When Kent responded, Dave said "Hey skipper, there's all kinds of scuttlebutt flying around about your meeting with all the customs people. If Inga and I motor over can you fill us in? We're dying of curiosity."

"Sure—come on over Dave. I have something else to discuss with you anyway."

CHAPTER FORTY TWO

The next morning Kent was checking out the rigging and making sure everything was shipshape, while Teddi and Bones motored in to shore to buy the provisions for the next leg of the cruise. He heard a small boat approaching and looked up to see Dave and Inga coming towards him.

Dave called out "Ahoy Sea Rose, can we come aboard?"

Kent smiled and called back "Come around to the stern and throw me a line, I'll make it fast and you can come aboard."

After their small boat was made secure, Dave and Inga clamored aboard. There were hand shakes and hugs and assurances that everyone was healthy and happy.

Inga said "Kent we've been so worried about Teddi. Is she okay? Was she really abducted like the rumors say?"

"She's fine Inga. She will be seeing a gynecologist later today but every thing seems okay at this point. She's doing some shopping with a friend right now and should be back within the hour. Sit down and I'll fill you guys in on the whole sordid mess."

For the next 30 or 40 minutes Kent told the story and answered their questions. Just then Teddi and Bones pulled along side and Teddi called "Hey, I see we've got company."

Teddi climbed aboard and Inga grabbed her and squeezed her,

jabbering all the time with questions like "How did she feel?" and stroking her like a mother hen.

Teddi laughed and said "I'm okay Inga. Please don't worry. I'm going to see a doctor today just to make sure."

"Thank God" said Inga "we were so worried."

After Kent and Bones unloaded the dinghy they all relaxed for a pleasant visit.

Kent asked "what are your plans Dave? Where are you heading next?"

Dave answered "It looks like we're going to wind up cruising for a while. Our savings account is getting low and my pension isn't quite enough to make it alone so we're heading back to Florida where I'll pick up some work and replenish our nest egg. Then we'll resume our cruising."

"What kind of work will you look for?"

"Well during my rehab after the accident I attended Boston College and got my degree in Electrical Engineering so I'll look for a project where I can hire on either as a consultant or possibly as a temporary employee."

"Dave I have a suggestion for you that you may or may not be interested in. You'll remember I told you about the destruction of the electrical system at the island hospital."

"Yes. And I'll bet there's more damage down stream due to the surge.'

"You're probably correct. But anyway, the government has turned over the hospital to the Islas Testigos people, and it's their responsibility to repair the damage. They don't have the local talent so they'll need to go outside to get the job done. I also know that they don't have a lot of resources to pay a large contractor to do the job. Would this be something you'd be interested in talking to them about?"

"Gosh Kent, I'd be happy to talk to them but I'm not sure I'm qualified and I certainly would need help on the labor end. We can stop there, it's on our way, so I wouldn't lose any time. Yes! Yes! If they want to talk to me, I'll be very happy to stop and give it a look see."

"Okay then. Teddi, Bones and I are leaving in the morning and should make Testigo Grande by afternoon. We plan on meeting with the island chiefs the next day. I'll tell them about you and get an idea of their plan, if they even have a plan at this stage of the game. Then when I have an idea of what's going on I'll radio you and we'll take it from there."

Early the next morning, the Sea Rose II got under way and when she reached blue water, the sailing conditions were perfect. Almost as if God said "Okay guys you've earned it, I'm giving you the best that I have."

The three of them sat back in the cockpit and enjoyed Gods best.

Bones mused "I had a conversation with Dave before we left and I told him that I'd be happy to round up a crew of island people to help if he decided to do the job. And I also had a thought about the hospital staff so I called my son in Nassau and told him about the hospital. He's scheduling a trip to look it over and talk to the chiefs. Both he and my grandchildren have been contemplating a move sometime in the near future and this could fit into their plans very well. As you know they all have medical backgrounds."

"That sounds great, Bones. Wouldn't it be wonderful if all of you could come home and turn this into a wonderful asset to your islands? I hate to say this but it's almost déjà vu."

"It would be an answer to my dreams" said Bones

It was later that day when they were anchored at Testigo Grande that Kent and Teddi were finally by themselves and could reflect on the events of the recent past. Bones had left to stay with the St. John relatives until he could reestablish himself on the island.

'Teddi I was so despondent when you were gone, I thought I'd lose my mind. I knew that I loved you but I didn't know that there wasn't anything that I wouldn't do to get you back safely. I'm so happy now and I don't ever want us to be apart."

"I don't ever want us to be separated again either my darling" said Teddi "but when I was in that hospital I somehow knew that you would be there to rescue me. I knew neither hell nor high water would stop you."

"You got that right sweetheart, no one would have stopped me. But you know, now that it's over and I've got you back, revenge is far from being sweet, it is entirely tasteless."

"I know what you mean hon and I really regret the loss of life, too. I know it's on your mind, but it was through no fault of yours. In the long run you probably saved the lives of many women and even more unborn babies. Those men and women were devils."

"Thank you sweetheart but I can't help but think about it. I guess it's time to get on with the rest of our lives."

The next week went by quickly. The island people were so appreciative of the way Kent and Teddi helped rid them of a very distasteful situation, they treated them like kings.

Bones was looked upon as a leader and was treated with great respect by all. He advised the island chiefs to look favorably at using Dave as an electrical consultant and the chiefs agreed to interview him after he looked over the situation at the hospital.

Bones' son had flown in to the mainland and hired a boat to bring him to Testigos Grande to talk to the chiefs. He was now at the hospital and it looked very favorable for him and his family to take it over after all repairs were made.

Kent and Teddi were now rested and ready to resume their cruise. It looked like everything was back to normal here in Islas los Testigos and they were getting anxious to be underway again. It was about 800 miles to the Panama Canal and with many islands along the way, for about 425 miles along the coast of Venezuela, it should be an easy leg. Then southwest for about 375 miles to the canal over open water. Kent felt that they could take a week to 10 or 12 days depending on weather and some stops at a few choice islands on the way.

The following day they motored into the dock to say their goodbyes to Bones, the St. Johns family and the other friends they had met here on the island.

When they told Bones that they were getting underway the next morning he became quite emotional. Between sobs he said "I just wish my wife was still alive so she could meet you two wonderful people. You have given us our island back and we will never forget you. I will have all of my family with me in my last remaining days and we will be at peace. Thank you—thank you both."

"Bones it was a pleasure and a privilege to have you as a friend. If not for your help I'm not sure I would have gotten Teddi back from the hell she was in. It's my turn to thank you, my good friend."

"Good sailing skipper."

They all hugged and Bones shuffled off with stooped shoulders.

Kent and Teddi made their way back to the dinghy and motored back to the anchored Sea Rose II. Kent had some gear to stow and the dinghy to haul aboard so they could make a good start in the morning, hopefully at first light.

While he was working topside and Teddi was below making sure all was stowed and ready for sea, the Semper Avante steamed into the harbor and anchored close by. Dave called out "Hello Kent. Can I come over and talk to you?"

"Come on over Dave. We're just battening down so we can pull out in the morning."

Later when Dave and Inga arrived he said "Gosh skipper we're sorry to see you go. It looks like Inga and I are going to spend some time here. I surveyed the damage and it looks like something I'd like to tackle. I met the chiefs at the hospital and they offered me a modest weekly salary, living quarters, groceries and a bonus when it was finished depending on what I could save them in the way of cost. This is a great place to relax and enjoy life. We're going to accept the offer and we may stay awhile when we're done."

"That sounds wonderful Dave. I'm so glad that I could put you together with them."

"Well it sure provided us with an answer of how to extend our cruising days. We are eternally grateful." Said Dave "and it sounds like our two spouses are down below jabbering away. I'm sure Inga is giving her motherly advice on what to do and what not to do while pregnant. We'd really appreciate an announcement when the baby is born. I'll give you our son's address and he can forward it to us wherever we may be."

"Rest assured that we will do that Dave. Let's somehow keep in touch. I'll give you some addresses of several spots where we can be reached before you leave."

Chapter Forty Three

They awoke before sunrise the next day anxious to get underway. Before the sun came over the horizon, as light was reflected into the eastern sky, they set sail. No matter how many times this part of the trip was repeated it was always a thrill to surge ahead at full sail into the open blue water.

They sailed due west and would try for the Netherland Antilles, with possibly one stop for an overnight stay at La Orchila, and that should put them at Bonaire in 3 or 4 days. Along with Curacao and Aruba, it should be a fun place to be with great facilities.

Everything went according to plan and they left Aruba skirting the Peninsula de Guajira in Columbia on a direct course to Colon at the Atlantic side of the Panama Canal. It was probably going to be three days over open water but the weather forecast was good and no problems were anticipated.

In the afternoon of the third day Kent used the VHF radio to call the Panama Canal Yacht Club in Colon to secure a slip and make transit arrangements. The radio operator advised in perfect English to anchor in Bahia Limon where they could clear customs and then enter the Yacht Club the next morning where the arrangements could be made with the services of an agent. This would simplify matters in obtaining a Transit Advisor (pilot), line handlers, fenders and payment of transit costs.

As they approached Colon they entered a turning area for ships heading to and from the canal. Traffic was heavy with huge container ships heading in both directions with speeds up to 26 knots. Kent had to keep on his toes to dodge these behemoths and several times was within a mile of ships on either side going in opposite directions. All went well but the mass of ships at the head of the huge bay resembled a nest of spiders. He threaded his way through the congestion of anchored vessels, finally found an open spot and dropped anchor. He radioed customs and was told that a launch would visit him shortly.

The creation of the Panama Canal was through great physical exertion, expense and engineering genius to bring into existence. It was done through the culmination of the efforts of so many people, from the rank and file laborers toiling in the humid tropical heat to the indomitable American spirit of accomplishment.

The digging of a channel across the isthmus was first tried by the French in 1881 and turned out to be a disastrous failure. It was restarted in 1906 by the United States and completed in 1914, with the loss of 25,000 lives. There were those that felt it would be wiser to use the San Juan River on the Nicaragua/Costa Rica border along with the huge Lake de Nicaragua as a more likely choice but the Isthmus of Panama won out.

Kent and Teddi slept soundly that night after a tension filled day entering the canal area.

They awoke the next day to a busy, clamoring harbor. Nothing like the slow, peaceful island harbors they had experienced in the last few months. After a quick breakfast they weighed anchor and motored to their assigned dock where transiting arrangements could be made. After they tied up an official from the ACP—Panama Canal Authority—came aboard. She measured the length of the boat and filled out a questionnaire.

The official advised, since Kent was going to handle one of the lines and Teddi was acting as helmsman, they would need to hire only three line handlers and one Transit Advisor who would act as pilot. And since they had no lines of 125 ft. length, they must rent them, as well as heavy duty fenders. "I can recommend several agents who can handle making all the arrangements if you choose" she said.

"Yes, of course, we would prefer an agent. When do you think we will be able to make transit?" answered Kent.

She answered "It will be several days at best. We are not so busy right now. At most it could be a week or so."

"Wow" said Teddi.

The lady glanced up and said "I've seen waits up to 6 or 8 weeks for pleasure boats during very busy times with the transit of huge commercial vessels. We must lock through several small pleasure vessels at a time. Fees are based on tonnage and to give you an idea of the difference, your fee will be $19.42 U S. The fee for the Queen Elizabeth in 1980 was $89,154.62. We cannot possibly get enough pleasure boats in the locks to come close to the fee of a large commercial liner that has a schedule to meet. I'm sure that you understand."

"We understand" said Kent, not wanting to antagonize the lady and cause more delays.

"We typically do 40 transits every 24 hours, so it shouldn't be an extreme wait. I'll send an agent over when I get to my office" she said as she jumped onto the dock.

After she left Teddi said "well hon, we might as well take it easy for awhile, it may be a long day when we go through those huge locks."

On the third afternoon a dapper gentleman approached the boat and called "hello Captain Allison, my name is Pete Stevens and I'll be your agent on the transit. Let's go over everything and if we agree on all charges I will make arrangements for you to join a group of smaller boats and enter the first lock in the morning."

"Come aboard Pete. I was briefed on the approximate charges so I'm sure we won't have a problem" said a very relieved Captain Allison.

Very early the next morning, even before first light, the crew came aboard. The pilot instructed them on how to use the lines and other details on what to expect and they soon were underway.

The Gatun Locks are first—a set of three locks to raise the boats to Gatun Lake which is a man made lake 85 feet above sea level. The locks are 1000 ft. long and 110 ft. wide. The average time for a lock to fill is seven minutes. They entered the first lock.

Gatun Lake was excavated to supply water to the locks, which is fed by gravity through a system of huge culverts. From these culverts, the water passes into 20 smaller tubes under the chamber and distributes this water through 100 inlets that measure four and one half feet in diameter. The surge is awesome.

Men high above on the lock walls toss heaving lines to them which they bend on to their heavier lines. They were warned to be alert when the heaving lines were tossed since on the end is a 'monkey fist' which is a ball of line about as big as a fist, wrapped around a hunk of lead. If you're not paying attention you could get beaned and knocked cold by an errant toss.

Port and starboard bow lines were led up their respected sides and secured to bollards on the lock wall. They then reeved the lines through the blocks and then to the winches where they were able to take up the slack as the water level rose. The stern lines were done in the same manner.

Kent handled a bow line so he could observe what was happening and follow instructions from the pilot.

As water rushed in Sea Rose II surged at her lines as the powerful flood of water buffeted her. This showed the wisdom of assigning a man to each mooring line. Proper line handling maintained the central position of the boat in the lock. The same procedure followed in the next two locks.

Gatun Lake is 31 miles across and speed is of the essence, according to the pilot, so Sea Rose motored at full speed. He suggested a short cut a small boat could take called Banana Channel. It was narrow but well marked and showed what the early pioneers were faced with.

Next is Pedro Miguel Lock which lowers 31 ft. to Miraflores Lake, on which they motor one mile to Miraflores Lock. It descends 54 ft. to sea level—the Pacific Ocean.

Teddi was right—it was a busy, busy day. The agent had pre-arranged a berth at Flamenco Marina. It was large and well equipped and a good place to plan their next course.

Kent studied the charts to establish a float plan and noticed a curious anomaly of their course through the canal. The Isthmus of Panama is shaped like an S tilted to the northwest. The canal is cut through the middle part of the S and follows a northwesterly to southeasterly direction. Therefore a vessel traveling west from the Atlantic to the

Pacific follows a course southeast through the canal even though, in general, the Pacific Ocean is west of the Atlantic.

Nevertheless they will now follow the coast northwest to Acapulco stopping every three or four days at coastal cities to rest and replenish stores as well as some sightseeing in Costa Rica, Nicaragua, El Salvador, Guatemala and Mexico. When they reach Acapulco they'll head west northwest to Islas Revillagigedo, an archipelago of islands owned by Mexico which is about 800 miles over open water. The islands are spread out for about 350 miles and when they depart from the farthest west island they begin the longest part of their journey over open water, about 2400 miles which will take them close to a month to navigate.

The next few months passed quickly with Teddi progressing very well in her pregnancy and both enjoying fine sailing conditions and very interesting ports of call. They met many other cruising sailors from countries around the world, some of which were traveling the same course as they and the friendly encounters were exciting and enjoyable.

They were able to join a group of sailors traveling from Acapulco to the Revillagigedo archipelago which made the journey seem to go quicker and more safely, traveling in a convoy of sail boats.

But soon it was time to make that final leg of their cruise to Oahu. This part will be on their own but both were very capable sailors and had no apprehension about the trek.

They left the farthest west island, prepared for a month long sail.

The Sea Rose II was a very seaworthy boat and could most likely handle any situation, except for the most extreme conditions. Kent was also one and the same and the first half of their sail presented conditions of very light winds, winds of 25 knots and anything in between, all of which presented no problems and nothing extremely uncomfortable.

During their third week on the water, the Sea Rose clawed her way westward with the flying fish sailing ahead of her, close on the wind until she broke free and charged her way into a nor'easter. She leaped forward as if she was being pursued by some unseen force of nature. She dove into the waves and was all but buried under the frothing green seas.

The gale-force wind took very little time to build the seas to the point where Kent was very concerned. This was due to the current and the wind being in opposite directions which made for very steep waves. On their present course there was a real danger of burying the leeward rail, broaching and resulting in a roll over.

He yelled for Teddi to don foul weather gear, her life jacket and safety harness and come topside. He already had his gear on and the safety harness attached to a hand rail. Heaving to or lying ahull presented some unacceptable risks like a roll over. This left skudding or running off with the waves as the only acceptable solution and with this kind of sea it was still not a sure thing.

He started the engine and headed downwind, taking the seas about 15 degrees on the port quarter. This seemed about right as the boat heeled slightly, presenting her rounded hull to the seas and gave sufficient helm response to keep her from broaching and cause a roll over.

The risk of running off, in these severe conditions, was too much boat speed with this heavy, following sea. The danger it presents is to plane down the face of a wave, burying the bow and having the following sea lift the stern and pitchpole the boat end over end, seldom ending in an upright position.

This is too horrible to even think about. All too few boats and crews have survived this type of calamity and the consequences are dire and the survival is minimal. The wind was howling and the Sea Rose was gaining too much speed too quickly.

Kent responded just as quickly and yelled for Teddi to take the wheel and keep the wind on the port quarter. "Don't let the surf push the stern around or we'll broach" he yelled.

She had a look of panic on her face as she grasped the wheel and she froze. Kent stood on the forward side of the wheel, placing his hands on hers and steered. Her hands had a death grip on the wheel and he calmly said "Teddi, you can do this. One of us has to steer and one of us has to decrease the boat speed with a drogue. Which do you want to do."

"Stay with me for a few seconds while I settle myself, Kent. I'll do it, honey." She said.

Kent smiled at her and slowly released his hands from hers. She had grasped the situation and took command of the wheel now, with a determined look on her face. She was now in charge of her emotions.

Kent rushed to the lazarette, opened it and retrieved a rubber tire, a left over fender from the canal, and kept aboard for this exact situation. He groped down further and pulled out a coil of ½ inch line. He took the bitter end and cleated it off on a stern cleat, passed the coil of line through the center opening of the tire and wrapped a bight of line three turns around a self tailing winch. He lowered the tire over the transom and fed the line out from the self tailing winch.

The boat slowed immediately from this increased drag and when the speed decreased by a couple of knots or so, he made the line fast. He didn't want to decrease the speed too much to hamper steering and cause the boat to broach. If it did slow too much he could pull line in with the self tailing winch which would decrease the drag to increase the speed.

He hugged Teddi and relieved her on the wheel. They could ride out the storm now in relative safety.

"Go below and relax awhile hon" said Kent.

"I think I want to stay topside for awhile, in case you need me" she smiled uneasily.

The storm eased off during the night and by the next morning Kent was able to retrieve the drogue and fly a reefed in mains'le a storm sail and make 7 knots. Teddi brewed some coffee and came topside with a thermos full. It was delicious.

Soon enough conditions became normal again and Kent was able to catch a good sized grouper which Teddi turned into a gourmets delight. They opened their last bottle of wine which Kent nursed along until it was empty. He was whipped and was looking forward to some rest.

Boredom was beginning to set in when one afternoon they spied an albatross winging its way westward along with them. It followed them for 3 days and then was gone much to Teddi's disappointment. This soon changed when a few days later more birds were seen following them and Kent told her "Those birds are an indication that land is not too far ahead dear. According to the GPS we're about 200 miles from the big island of Hawaii."

"It will be good to be back" she said "I'm starting to find it a little difficult to get around. My belly keeps getting in the way"

"I guess it's time to reflect about the last 6 months or so" he said "any thoughts come to mind?"

She pondered for a minute, gazed at Kent and said "Yes, sailing is 80% boredom and 20% sheer terror. I'll welcome some terra firma."

Chapter Forty Four

Sailing into Pearl Harbor was nostalgic for both of them. It had been years since they had called Honolulu home. This is where it all began. Where they had met on that blind date, where they had married and lived while working on fishing boats to save money to buy the original Sea Rose. So many happy memories came back and now they would call it home again for awhile until the baby was born. Then they could make their way back to Tortolo where they hoped to spend the rest of their days.

Kent had called their old marina and found that he could birth the Sea Rose II there with no problem. The marina manager was an old ship mate of his and would see to it that he got a good slip. There were restrictions on living aboard so they could only stay on the boat temporarily until they found an apartment. That was okay with Teddi. She found she needed more space at this stage of the game.

They soon found a furnished apartment on the outskirts of Honolulu and with the used pick up truck Kent was able to buy, they started moving needed items and set up housekeeping in the apartment.

It didn't take them long to settle in and they soon felt right at home. Teddi was able to contact her former gynecologist, make an appointment for a check up and make arrangements for delivery of the baby. Everything checked out as normal and the doctor marveled at her great condition. He remarked that the exercise and diet were key factors in keeping her healthy. Her delivery date should be in about 2½ months.

Kent kept himself busy catching up with correspondence to accountants, banks and other business that had backed up while they were gone. He also had to catch up on maintenance on the Sea Rose II. He had the boat hauled out and blocked up ashore so he could clean all the barnacles off of the bottom and apply new bottom paint. He also checked all the standing and running rigging and replaced any that was worn or damaged. He replaced the cutlass bearing on the prop shaft which would make less vibration while motoring. It would take at least a month to put everything in tip top shape for the trip to Tortolo.

In the meantime Teddi busied herself in the apartment and looked up old girl friends who were either pregnant or already had a baby or two, compared notes and made mother talk.

Several months later, on a Sunday morning, when they were getting ready for church, Teddi sighed and said "It's getting very difficult to move around Kent, if this baby isn't born in a week or so I'll need a derrick to stand up."

Kent chuckled "looks to me like we're going to have a big and healthy baby in the very near future my dear."

They got into Kent's little pick up truck and started out to go to 12:00 Mass. As they pulled into the parking lot Teddi breathlessly said "Oh my God Kent, I just wet myself. The back of my dress is all wet. Take me home, quick."

Kent sped out of the parking lot and quickly headed for home. They lived a few blocks from the church so he got her into the apartment and quieted her down in just a few minutes. He immediately picked up the phone and dialed the doctor's service and fortunately got a very fast return call.

He said to the doctor in a semi-panic tone of voice "Doc I think she must have a kidney infection or something. She keeps passing water and has pains in her lower stomach."

The doctor calmly said "Son, her water has broken and she's going to have her baby very soon. You'd best get her to the hospital as soon as possible. I'll meet you there."

Kent walked Teddi out to the truck. She was now experiencing some pretty severe labor pains. He didn't delay getting her to the hospital and by the time they reached emergency she was bending forward and moaning.

A heavy set veteran nurse saw them coming and ran out to the truck with a wheel chair and loaded Teddi into it. As she gently put her in the chair she patted, cooed and calmed this scared expectant mother. As she wheeled her in she didn't have the same gentle way with Kent. She said "All right young man. Why did you wait so long to bring her in. She's practically ready to deliver right now."

"It happened so quickly" said Kent.

They wheeled Teddi to delivery and told Kent to see the admissions clerk to get the necessary admitting data entered and then come to delivery wearing scrubs. He hurriedly did so and by the time he got to delivery he heard a baby crying and as he entered Teddi was holding a chubby little baby girl in her arms. Everyone was smiling so he knew it was all okay.

The doctor said "Congratulations Mr. Allison. You have a fine baby girl and both mother and daughter are doing great. But I will say that if you would have been much later you would have had to deliver the baby yourself."

"Thank you, doc but I'm sure glad I wasn't faced with that. Can I see the baby?"

"Absolutely. We'll let you and Teddi get acquainted with your daughter for a bit, then the nurse will take her and clean her up. I'll check her over and then we'll bring her up to the room."

Teddi and Kent basked in the delight of looking at their beautiful baby girl.

Later when Teddi left recovery and they were settled in her room with the baby sleeping peacefully Kent asked "Have you made a decision on a name for the baby?"

Teddi said "Well you know we discussed names for both a boy or a girl, since we opted not to know ahead of time, so I really hadn't made a final choice. Do you have any preferences?"

"I think I'm going to leave this decision up to you, darling, especially since it's a girl" said Kent.

"But Kent, I want you to help me decide. Just as a thought, my mothers name was Eve and my grandmothers was Rosemarie. I can't decide which I'd like better. Help me."

"I think we should use both. How about Eva Rose?"

"You wonderful man. I love you so much. Eva Rose is beautiful."

The happy little family settled in at their apartment and the adjustment of having a new responsibility set in. Suddenly the day and especially the night revolved around this new addition. Decisions were made according to how it would affect the baby. But both Teddi and Kent adjusted to it very quickly and soon they had a new daily routine and enjoyed this new life to the fullest.

In about a month or so Teddi mentioned baptizing the baby and Kent said that he would call the parish and arrange for it.

She said "Gosh honey, wouldn't it be nice if Father Tom could baptize Eva?"

"It sure would be but he's pretty far away covering his island parish and I don't think we could get him this far away from his flock."

"Then let's go to him" she said "we planned on going back to Tortolo to live."

"Honey, Eva is too far young to make that trip on the Sea Rose. It wouldn't be safe."

"Couldn't we fly back to a port in Indonesia where Captain Roger makes his run and sail to Tortolo with him?"

"Hmmm—that's food for thought. I'm pretty homesick for Tortolo myself. Let me see what could be worked out. I could probably reach Captain Roger on his satellite phone and see what kind of schedule he's got. But I sure would like to have our boat on the island with us. Maybe I could hire a captain and crew to deliver it for us."

It was several weeks later that the Allison family landed at the Jayapura Airport in New Guinea. They had made reservations at a downtown hotel where they would wait the arrival of the Kon Tiki captained by Roger McNulty. A rest here would feel good, after a whirlwind of excitement when they found they could meet Roger here in New Guinea, for transport to Tortolo his next stop.

As a bonus they also found that father Tom McCann was already on the island and would be there until Captain Roger transported him to his next island parish.

A few days later they got a call from Captain Roger telling them that he was in the harbor at Pier 23 and would be getting underway the day after tomorrow. They could board the ship on the morning of departure and would be in Tortolo in about a week.

The sail from New Guinea to Tortolo was idyllic, an episode of charming simplicity. Captain Roger was typical with his Irish blarney and kept everyone upbeat telling his wild tales. It was a happy time and all were looking forward to Tortolo.

As they entered the beautiful, natural harbor quietly, under sail and the shoreline came into view, it was filled with the people of the village. It seemed as if the whole island population stood smiling and waving. Soon the beautiful sounds of Polynesian singing floated out on the gentle breeze.

The ever present canoes were winging their way towards them. Shirtless men with those spade shaped wooden paddles were propelling them through the water. Laughing young girls with flowers in their hair were waving from the middle of the canoes. There was Adam and Marte, frantic with waving and calling "Welcome home! Welcome home!"

As they got closer they saw Arlis, standing on the dock, along side of Ben Fletcher Adams and Teio. "The Sea Rose must be here" excitedly said Teddi. "Yes, there she is, tied up at the main dock with the whole crew on the fantail waving a welcome." Standing at the rail, waving enthusiastically was Matteo, Giuseppe, Antonio and pretty Rosa Maria

Teddi turned and looked into Kent's misty eyes and said "Home at last—home at last. I'm so happy darling." She turned and enthusiastically waved to her island family waiting on shore to welcome them home.

EPILOGUE

"Mommy, mommy will Daddy and Ross make it back for my birthday party?" called Eva Rose as she excitedly ran towards her mother.

"Don't worry honey" answered Teddi "your daddy and your little brother just called in on the radio and the Sea Rose II is just a few hours away. They've only been gone for three days on their little sailing trip and your party isn't until tomorrow."

"I know mom, but I miss my little brother even if he does tease me a little bit."

"He takes that from his daddy who just loved to tease mommy all these years. It's just how they show their love for us girls."

"Did Uncle Adam go with them this time?"

"Yes Eva, daddy is teaching Ross how to sail so he needed Uncle Adam to help him handle the boat. Now go play with the other kids while mommy gets things together for your party. Turning seven is a big step so we want to have a nice party."

Meanwhile........

"Okay Ross, I'll take the wheel while we're coming in to the harbor. Uncle Adam will handle the bow line and I want you to take the stern line but first we have to drop the sails. You can use the winch to furl the foresail like I showed you." instructed Kent.

"Aye Aye Captain Kent" said the giggling, tow-head little five year old boy as he grabbed the winch handle and scooted to the winch.

Adam smiled and gazed at the little guy and said "Skipper I think you've sired a natural born sailor. He's as happy as any one I've ever seen on this boat."

"I think you're right Adam and it probably won't be long before he's giving me orders on how to sail" laughed Kent.

Adam chuckled and said "I know what you mean, I've got a couple of my own that are starting to test me."

"We're a couple of lucky guys Adam."

"Hey look at the dock. I can see our wives and all the kids waiting for us. Yeh, we really are a couple of lucky guys" said Adam with a big smile on his Polynesian face.

The End

Printed in the United States
by Baker & Taylor Publisher Services